LAST SUMMER

Center Point
Large Print

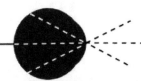

**This Large Print Book carries the
Seal of Approval of N.A.V.H.**

LAST SUMMER

KERRY LONSDALE

CENTER POINT LARGE PRINT
THORNDIKE, MAINE

This Center Point Large Print edition
is published in the year 2019 by arrangement with
Amazon Publishing, www.apub.com.

The text of this Large Print edition is unabridged.
In other aspects, this book may vary
from the original edition.
Printed in the United States of America
on permanent paper.
Set in 16-point Times New Roman type.

ISBN: 978-1-64358-383-9

The Library of Congress has cataloged this record
under Library of Congress Control Number: 2019946708

For Evan, my favorite skier:
may the snow always be plentiful, the air crisp,
and the mountain yours.

LAST SUMMER

PROLOGUE

INTERVIEW TRANSCRIPT EXCERPT

August 18, 2018
Fairmont Hotel, San Francisco, CA
Interviewer: Ella Skye, Senior Features
Writer, *Luxe Avenue* **magazine**
Interviewee: Amira Silvers, Academy Award–
winning Actress

[Continuation of Recording]

Amira: My mother always preached that the more bite marks on your tongue, the happier your marriage.

Ella: What did she mean by that?

Amira: Marital success isn't measured by what you share with your spouse. It's what you don't. Are you married, Ella?

Ella: Yes. For three years.

Amira: What's your husband's name?

Ella: Damien Russell.

Amira: That's right. Isn't he that rich tech entrepreneur who built a company to compete directly with his father's? I thought I read that somewhere.

Ella: I wouldn't exactly put it that way.

Amira: Hmm. Are you happy?

Ella: With Damien? Very much.

Amira: Then take my advice. Hold your tongue. You won't end up like me.

Ella: You recently divorced. It was all over the tabloids but you haven't talked to anyone until now. What happened?

Amira: I learned that my mother was right. Funny how that happens. I said too much to Harry, simple as that.

Ella: Care to elaborate?

[Pause]

Ella: I know this must be difficult for you to talk about, but—

Amira: No, I wouldn't have asked you here if I didn't want to tell you.

Ella: Take your time.

[Pause]

Amira: I was fourteen when my stepfather sold me to pay off his debts to his drug dealer. I spent six months in forced prostitution until the authorities raided the house where they kept me and six other girls locked up.

Ella: Jesus.

Amira: The day I turned eighteen, I left home and never looked back. I legally changed my name and buried my past. I told no one about what I'd gone through until the day I told Harry.

Ella: How long had you been married?

Amira: Five years.

Ella: Why did you tell him?

Amira: Guilt. I hated keeping secrets from him.

Ella: How did Harry react?

Amira: Oh, he was sympathetic until he started to change.

Ella: How so?

Amira: It was subtle at first. He'd tense when
           I'd hug him. Then he stopped initiating
           sex, and eventually the sex just stopped.
           He could barely look at me when he
           served the divorce papers. He claimed
           that when he closed his eyes and kissed
           me, all he could see were the dozens of
           faceless men who had had their hands
           on me.

Ella: What an asshole. [Pause] Sorry, that
           was uncalled for.

Amira: You're right. He's an asshole. And
           shame on me, I still love the fucker. I
           want to forget . . .

[Pause]

Ella: What do you want to forget?

[Pause]

Ella: Are you all right?

Amira: [Crying] Yes . . . I mean, no.

Ella: Do you need a moment? [Pause] No?

All right, then, can you tell me what it is you want to forget?

Amira: Everything. What happened to me and what I told Harry. I want to forget that I love the asshole, and I want to forget him. I know how to do it, too.

Ella: You what?

[Pause]

Amira: Turn that thing off.

[End Recording]

CHAPTER 1

November 2018

"Ella."

A soft murmur comes from somewhere beyond her dreams. Her name.

"Ella."

Another whisper.

Damien.

He says her name again. It draws her from the depths of slumber. She was dreaming. Dreaming about . . . what?

Biting tongues and keeping secrets.

"Ella, sweetheart. Wake up."

Her eyes flutter open. She looks up into her husband's blue-grays, the whites of his eyes bloodshot. Her heart goes out to him. He must be working late nights again. She tries to recall which client is giving him difficulty: the new commercial bank in Atlanta or the social media company based in London touting itself as the Facebook for the iGen? But she doesn't know. Her mind is blurry, a camera lens that can't focus.

Damien leans over her. Dark whiskers dust his jaw. Locks just as dark sweep back from his forehead. He's been running his fingers through the thick mass. He does that when he's stressed.

And worried. He's definitely worried. Why? And why are his jeans rumpled and shirt crinkled? That's not like him. He looks like he hasn't showered in days.

With a quick glance over his shoulder, he shoots her a conspiratorial smile, a flash of straight teeth. He drops a white bakery bag on a food cart. "I got you an omelet, as promised."

When did he promise that?

And where did that food cart come from?

Ella looks past her husband's looming form and her heart stalls. Stark walls surround them in a box-shaped room. Lysol and antiseptic cling to the air. The drone of unfamiliar voices penetrates the closed door. A door she doesn't recognize.

This isn't their bedroom.

Ella inhales harshly through her nose, the chemical smell burning the back of her throat. Her chest rapidly rises and falls as her gaze bounces around the hospital room. How did she get here? Why is she here? And why is Damien acting as if waking her up here isn't surprising? Doesn't he realize where they are?

Damien removes a cardboard take-out container with a Luna's Café sticker from the bag. Luna's is their favorite café around the corner from their Russian Hill flat. They eat there most Saturdays. Ella frowns. What day is it?

Saturday. She's sure of it, because last night was Friday. She cooked Damien dinner.

16

Damien opens the box, bending back the flaps. Steam rises, carrying the scent of cooked onions and bell peppers. Ella's stomach turns over. He positions the food tray over the bed. Ella instinctively recoils, scooting out of the way. Jagged pain tears through her lower abdomen. Her left wrist throbs from putting pressure on it. She gasps, a sharp, audible intake of air.

"Easy now." Damien presses a button on a panel attached to the bed rail. Slowly, the head of the bed rises. Ella stares at her splinted wrist. She slips her other hand under the covers, searching for the source of discomfort as her husband adjusts pillows behind her shoulders. Gauze and tape over her pelvic region meet her wandering fingers.

"What happened to me?"

Damien gives her a tired smile. His fingers lovingly caress her cheek. "Relax." He points at the food in front of her. "Eat up before Nurse Grouchypants catches a whiff and makes me toss it."

She watches the steam diminish as the omelet cools. She turns her face away, sickened by the smell.

Damien pops open his oatmeal. He shovels a spoonful of the ungarnished oats into his mouth. He eats his oatmeal plain, and he's eating ravenously. Ella wonders when he last ate. When did she last eat? Did she even eat the dinner she cooked?

He glances up to find her watching him.

"Aren't you hungry? You've hardly eaten this week."

This week?

Damien nudges the food tray closer to her. "You need your strength to recover."

Recover from what?

"Why am I here?" She kneads the bedsheet.

The spoon pauses midway between the cardboard cup and his mouth. "What?"

"Why am I in the hospital?" She truly doesn't know and tries to recall the past week. Checking into the hospital. Talking to a doctor. Eating the horrible food hospitals are known for. She can sense the memories are there. She reaches for them, stretching. She tries to grasp them, to hold on to something, anything about what landed her in a hospital bed with a splinted wrist and taped-up abdomen. She comes up empty-handed, confused and bewildered.

Damien stares at her like she's asked the most ridiculous question, which she probably did. Ella feels like she should know. She licks her lips. They're chapped. Her throat hurts when she swallows, and she aches everywhere—muscle, bone, and tissue. Everything about her situation feels wrong—her body, this place, Damien carrying on as if her being laid up in a hospital bed is their new normal.

Damien remains speechless, his lips slightly

parted. The skin between his brows creases and his eyes dip down. He drops the plastic spoon in the oatmeal and sets the cup on the table. When he still doesn't say anything, Ella pushes away the food cart and shoves down the sheets. A hospital gown bunches at the juncture of her thighs. She jerks up the hem, exposing her stomach, and gapes. Bigger than she's ever seen it and spongy to the touch, her stomach looks like a partially filled air mattress. A large square gauze pad is taped to her pelvis.

She starts picking at the gauze. She needs to see what's underneath.

"Ella, stop." Damien grasps her wrists and she hisses. "Sorry." He releases her braced wrist but keeps a firm grip on the other, holding her hand away from her.

She struggles. She needs to see what was done to her. "Let go."

"Settle down. You'll pull your staples."

"Staples? What did they do to me?" she cries.

"Are you serious?" Damien asks, his face inches from hers.

"Tell me."

"Don't screw with me like this. It's not fair." He releases her wrist and backs away.

"I swear I can't remember why I'm here. I can't remember anything."

"Bullshit, Ella." He vigorously shakes his head. "I call bullshit."

"Why are you upset with me? I'm not lying."

Damien crosses the room and stares out the window. Sunlight too intense to be early morning brightens the rigid angles of his face. His cheek flexes, his tell that he's disturbed.

Ella draws the sheet up to her breasts. She feels exposed, lost. She doesn't want to be here.

She wants to go home. Better yet, she wants to wake up from this dream.

That must be it. She's still dreaming.

She pokes at the bandage on the back of her hand, where an IV must have been inserted at some point. The area feels tender. Bile rises. The room, the equipment, her injuries. It's all real.

From across the room, Damien warily eyes her. She stares at him in horror. "Say something. I'm freaking out over here."

"You really don't remember?"

Ella slowly shakes her head.

"Do you remember the car accident?"

Her heart plunges into her stomach. "No."

Damien closes in on her. "What about Simon?"

"Who's Simon?"

His face blanches. "Our son," he whispers.

Ella would laugh if she weren't so terrified. They don't have children. Damien doesn't want kids. "That's not funny."

"No, it's true. Simon died. The impact of the airbag tore the placenta. Simon didn't survive."

He cups a hand over his mouth and nose. He stares at Ella, shaking his head. "Impossible."

That she lost her memory? Maybe she hit her head in the accident Damien mentioned. Amnesia makes more sense to her than Damien saying she was pregnant. But her bandaged pelvis and the drastic changes to her midriff prove he's probably telling the truth.

"You forgot Simon. Our baby. Christ, El. You weren't supposed to forget *him*. What about your emergency C-section? Do you remember that? What about last night?"

"What happened last night?"

"Seriously? You don't remember any of it?"

"No. How can I? I don't even remember being pregnant."

Damien's mouth falls open. One second. Two. He snaps it shut. "No. Way." He cuts a hand through the air. "There's no way you could have forgotten that. What the hell, Ella? Tell me you're joking."

"I'm not! I don't remember any goddamn baby! Now tell me what is going on."

Damien swears and stabs a button on the remote beside her. She startles.

"What are you doing?"

"Paging the nurse."

He shoves the food cart out of his way. Long strides take him to the door.

"Where are you going?" Mindful of her

21

injuries, Ella sits up, ready to climb from the bed and follow him. She's disoriented and scared. It takes a lot to frighten her and Damien isn't helping. She doesn't understand his anger. Why is he upset with her? It's not as if she forgot on purpose. She'd expect her husband to be compassionate and understanding. Maybe even a little scared himself.

Damien stops at the door. "Stay put . . . *please*. You'll hurt yourself."

"Not until you tell me where you're going," she demands, swinging a leg over the side of the bed.

He yanks open the room's wide metal door. "I'm getting your doctor. You're freaking *me* out."

CHAPTER 2

Dr. Tate Allington, a neurologist, stands at the end of Ella's bed. Bleached-white hair, a stark contrast to his sun-soaked skin, dusts the back of the wide hands holding a smart tablet. Silver wire-rimmed glasses sit on the end of his weathered nose. As he studies Ella's CT scan from earlier in the week, her mind drifts. She wonders if he spends his afternoons golfing or on the tennis court. Maybe he likes to garden. He did mention his wife's beautiful rose vines. Right after he announced he's one month away from retirement. He wouldn't mind working until he found himself in the morgue downstairs. Medicine is his passion. The brain is his favorite puzzle to unravel. But it's the wife, you know. She wants to travel. He smells like sunscreen, Ella thinks, sniffing the air. The coconut aroma is a pleasant relief from the hospital's sterile environment. And thoughts about the doctor's personal life are less unsettling than her own problems, which seem insurmountable. She can't remember her pregnancy.

She sniffs again, a deep inhale that draws Damien's attention. He tosses her a funny look, then goes back to brooding. Ella folds her hands in her lap and waits for the doctor's diagnosis.

He's just finished explaining that they've met before. He evaluated her on her admission to the hospital. But for Ella's benefit and because of the sudden memory loss, he recounted his findings. After her emergency C-section and due to the nature of the auto accident, Ella had undergone a CT scan. The scan revealed no evidence of trauma. No bruised brain tissue, bleeding, or other signs of damage. Other than her unfortunate miscarriage and a sprained wrist, her injuries are limited to scrapes, bruises, and aches from shattered glass and whiplash. That would explain the stiffness Ella feels in her neck and shoulders.

Ella would have preferred a visit from her ob-gyn, Dr. Lynn Noriega. She and Lynn go way back. They met almost ten years ago in their early twenties at a mutual friend's dinner party. Once Lynn opened her practice, Ella was one of her first patients. She trusted Lynn. She wants to ask Lynn about her pregnancy. Had it been an accident? She can't recall when she and Damien discussed having a baby. The only time they did talk about kids was before they married. Damien was quite clear on his position. No kids. Ella went into their marriage knowing this, so when did everything change?

She doesn't remember, which worries her. So does Damien.

He stands apart, keeping vigil by the window, arms crossed tightly over his chest. He'll glance at her every so often but he won't make eye contact.

Maybe he's frightened and this is how he deals with it. Pulling back and closing himself off. In the four years they've known each other, Ella can't recall ever seeing him afraid or uncertain. He always has a handle on whatever dilemma he's facing. He always has a plan. He's a brilliant strategist at the office and at home. And he's the first to praise her published articles and compliment her dress when he escorts her to the opera season's opening night. He talks her through her writer's block and is ready with an open bottle of champagne whenever she wins a prestigious assignment after going head-to-head with *Luxe Avenue*'s other staff writers.

"What's the last thing you remember?" Dr. Allington asks, bringing Ella's attention back to him.

"Dinner with Damien." She glances at her husband. His attention is on the doctor. "I cooked pork loin," she adds.

She remembers their meal clearly. Damien arrived home from work, tie loosened, with a fitted dress shirt that showed off the muscles in his shoulders and lean hips. From the kitchen, she could hear him walk through his *Honey, I'm home* routine. He hung up his coat on the rack by the door, dropped his biometric briefcase on the floor, and shuffled through the mail Ella had left on the side table. He then joined her in the kitchen. She felt his breath on the back of her neck before his arms wrapped around her waist. It sent an intimate ripple of warmth through her. He kissed her shoulder, rubbing his nose along the curve of her neck. Her skin tightened, tingling in anticipation of what might come next. She's always been so responsive to his touch.

"You smell good." He rested his chin on her shoulder. "Dinner smells good. You're cooking." He sounded amazed.

"I'm trying." She wasn't a fan of cooking. Neither was Damien. But there were three things they did exceptionally well in their kitchen: brew coffee, make screwdrivers, and screw. Since the day they met, they've always eaten out or ordered in. But Ella had grown weary of take-out dinners and remembered she'd wanted to start cooking more often. They had a beautiful gourmet kitchen. Why not use it? Why not be more like a family?

The memory stalls.

Family.

Maybe she wanted to practice cooking since she had a baby on the way. Damien had something urgent to tell her.

We need to talk.

About what?

"When was the dinner?" Dr. Allington asks, looking from her to Damien.

26

Who cares when the dinner was? Isn't what her husband had to tell her more important? She wishes she could remember what it was.

"Last week," Damien answers when she can't. "The evening of Ella's accident."

Dr. Allington tucks his tablet under folded arms. "Are you pregnant in this memory, Ella?"

"I don't know."

"Think back. How do you see yourself?"

Ella focuses inward. She can feel her shoulder blades pressing into Damien's chest. His hands are on her stomach. She looks down, and when she does, the area blurs, much like an image that a photographer has touched up to obscure the subject's identity.

"Are you pregnant?" he asks again, more gently.

"I can't tell. I sense something's there." But she can't see it, and she feels no emotions for what could be there, growing inside her.

Damien shakes his head and turns back to the window. He keeps his back to the room. A dismissal of her or her condition? She wishes she knew.

Dr. Allington needs to leave so that she can have time alone with her husband. It's been chaotic since he paged the nurse and left to get the doctor. That was several hours ago. Damien doesn't believe her. As much as it disheartens her not to have Damien's trust, she didn't believe

27

him either. It took Nurse Jillian showing Ella her medical charts before Ella could accept she'd been pregnant and miscarried.

"Poor dear," the nurse cooed, adjusting Ella's pillows and checking her stats. "I don't blame you for forgetting. After what you've been through and the ruckus yesterday your guest caused, I'd want to forget, too. Margaret—she's the head nurse on this floor, in case you don't remember—she was right to call security. Your husband, though, we couldn't get him to leave until you calmed down. You were crying something fierce. We gave you a sedative and you finally relaxed. That wonderful man of yours talked to you and held your hand through most of the night. I know I shouldn't have been watching, but I couldn't help it. He's a keeper, and so good looking." She winked at Ella and patted her arm. "Dr. Allington will be here shortly." Jillian left the room, leaving Ella even more confused than before.

Damien turns around, hands on hips. "What's your diagnosis, doctor?"

"Selective memory loss, given recent events and judging by the partial memory recollection. You have recent memories that you can't recall in their entirety," he clarifies, addressing Ella. "Losing a baby twenty-one weeks into your term is quite traumatic."

"Twenty-one weeks?" Ella says, incredulous.

For five months she and Damien would have shared the joy of starting a family. It's inconceivable. Them. Parents.

"Will I get my memories back?" she asks the doctor.

"More than likely. Give it time." Dr. Allington pushes his glasses so they sit more securely on his nose. "Our minds can be sneaky. They'll plant false memories when we can't make sense of something and bury others when we can't deal. Your memories are there, but for whatever reason, you can't retrieve them."

"This happened almost a week after my accident. Why now?"

"It's probable your memory loss is motivated."

"She did this on purpose," Damien states.

"Subconsciously, yes. How was she this week? Emotionally speaking."

"Emotional." Damien moves closer to her. "Depressed. Devastated. We both are."

Dr. Allington brings up Ella's records again. "I see Dr. Noriega has you scheduled for release tomorrow. I'm going to recommend that you go home and rest, and then you should see a psychiatrist. In fact"—he waves the stylus at Damien—"you should both go."

Dr. Allington leaves and Damien closes the door behind him. He turns to Ella, taking up the doctor's position at the end of her bed. He stares at her, his expression perplexed.

"You still don't believe me." It hurt more to say the words out loud than it did for Ella to think them. Why wouldn't he trust her to tell the truth?

"I don't know what to think. We discussed—" He stops, flattening his lips with a finger. He then looks at his watch. "I'm going to see if there's any paperwork we need to complete before you're released."

"Damien." Ella reaches for him. "Sit with me. Just for a moment, please." She needs to feel his touch. She wants his reassurance.

Damien takes her hand and kisses her forehead.

"Thank you," she says.

"For what?"

"The kiss. I needed that."

His face softens. He keeps his gaze locked on her mouth and runs his thumb along her lower lip. "Everything will be all right."

Ella hopes so. She has always prided herself on having a sharp memory. *Disconcerting* doesn't begin to describe what she's experiencing inside her mind. To know the memories are there, just elusive, unattainable, floating downstream like a discarded flip-flop. It's horribly unsettling.

CHAPTER 3

Ella stands at Damien's side as he unlocks the door to their condo in Russian Hill, an upscale San Francisco district of steep hills and corner cafés.

The jangle of Damien's keys reminds Ella of the first time they saw their place, two months after they'd met. Damien had proposed the week before. He was thirty-two and she was thirty. They weren't twenty-year-olds interested in late nights at the bars and weekends at concert festivals. They didn't want the pomp and circumstance that accompanied elaborate weddings at the Top of the Mark. Neither of them had parents to please. They knew what they wanted in a relationship and spouse, so why wait to get married?

Kate Wu, their Realtor, had met them on the street outside the building. Balancing on her four-inch Jimmy Choos, she took them up to the tenth floor, opened the condo's front door, and with a grand gesture, stepped aside for Ella and Damien to enter first. Ella fell in love with the space the moment she took in the panoramic view outside the wall-to-wall, floor-to-ceiling windows. It stretched from the Golden Gate to the Bay Bridges, with the Marin Headlands between and city streets below. The weather couldn't have been more perfect, a welcome mat of blue sky and sunlit bay.

Kate trailed them into the flat with the click of her heels on the dark walnut-stained wood flooring. "The entire condo faces the bay. There are four bedrooms and two and a half baths. You can see the Golden Gate from the master, and Sausalito at night is gorgeous," she explained, her arms flapping like she was a flight attendant pointing out the exits as she indicated each room down a wide hallway. "The entire unit has been remodeled and updated."

As Kate ticked off the list of features, Ella wandered into the kitchen. Damien followed, his hand on her lower back. She traced her fingers along the veins of the marble countertop. The kitchen was three times the size of the nook she had in her Cole Valley apartment.

"What do you think?" Damien asked Ella when Kate took a breath.

"Can we afford this?" Ella earned a decent income, and Damien . . . well, she'd had to pick her jaw up from the floor after he disclosed his portfolio. Still, she worried. What if something happened to him? Ella had been able to financially handle the house she and her brother, Andrew, had inherited from their great-aunt Kathy, their dad's aunt and the woman who'd raised him, and later Ella and Andrew, when she'd passed. The mortgage had long been paid off. Once Andrew graduated from high school, they'd sold off the house and used the income for their college tuitions. Andrew even used some of his inheritance to launch his first app.

But this condo on Russian Hill where real estate values were well above five million? It was way out of a journalist's price range.

Damien cupped the back of her neck and pulled her in for a solid kiss on her lips. "Easily."

Kate's phone trilled. She glanced at the screen. "I have to take this call. Look around. I'll be a few." She excused herself and left through the front door. Damien crossed the flat and locked the bolt.

"What are you doing?"

"Buying us some time." He grinned and took Ella's hand, leading them back into the kitchen. She knew exactly what he was up to.

"We're doing this now?" Her gaze darted back to the front door. Despite her nervousness, her blood thrummed with anticipation.

"Only way to tell if we like it here," he said with a wink.

She giggled. "I'm sure there are other ways."

"Where's the fun in that?"

He smiled, sly and sexy. His hands glided up the sides of her thighs, lifting the hem of her skirt over her hips and then lifting her, effortlessly, onto the island. Her skin tightened with goose bumps, and a chill scampered across her body when her bare ass met the cool stone.

He kissed her, wet and openmouthed. He tasted of watermelon and orange from the salad he'd eaten at lunch. His hand kneaded her breast.

"Oh, my god, we're seriously doing this."

Damien chuckled at Ella's husky murmur against his lips, further spiking her arousal. Wasting no time, he pushed fully into her. They both gasped.

"Yes," he groaned into her ear. "We're doing this. Right here, right now." And then he moved, quick, short jerks of his hips.

Sex in someone else's kitchen, with the Realtor just outside the door. A daring move. Their coupling was hot and hurried. Ella grasped his shoulders and held on.

"This is incredible. You're incredible. Perfect," he panted.

They were perfect together. They needed each other, always needed, especially in this way.

Damien bit her ear. "I love this about you, Ella Skye. You'll let me fuck you anywhere."

She grinned saucily. "No, you'll let me fuck you anywhere."

He laughed.

Afterward, spent and winded, he assisted her down and straightened her skirt. He kissed her, lingering and sweet, and brushed aside the hair that had fallen over her face. A tender gesture. "I want this place to be ours," he whispered. "At the end of the day, at the end of a hellish workweek, after we've spent weeks apart traveling, and after we argue. Hell, after everything. I want us to always come back here and find each other."

His words meant everything to her. They also meant more than he was letting on. She searched his face. He was hiding something from her or was afraid to tell her. Worried how she'd respond. She'd sensed this about him from the day they met. That was okay. She wouldn't push him to talk. She trusted he would when he was ready.

They heard Kate rattle the doorknob, then slide the key into the bolt. They shared a secret smile. The scent of them was overpowering. Kate would know what they'd just done. But Ella didn't blush, and she didn't try to hide behind Damien. She wasn't embarrassed. She was in love. And they were going to buy this condo anyway, so what would Kate care?

It had four bedrooms. One for them, one for her office, and maybe, hopefully, two for kids. A boy who looked like Damien and a girl they could name after Grace, a childhood friend she'd lost too early. She visualized their children running down the long hallway, giggling, Damien chasing after them with threats of tickles and raspberry kisses, a big goofy grin on his face. But the visual vanished in an instant. Damien had been clear. He doesn't want kids.

If giving up the thought of having children meant she could be with Damien, she'd do it. She'd already lost so many loved ones. She didn't want to lose one more. Damien was her life. And aside from Andrew, her only family.

The rattling of keys whisks Ella back to the present. Damien holds open the door and she hesitates.

"What's wrong?" he asks.

"I was remembering the first time we saw our house. It's . . . weird. I can recall explicit details from that day—what we did, what I was feeling. What I was thinking—but I can't remember what happened two days ago."

"Dinner the night of the accident is the last thing you remember?" he asks suspiciously. "You swear you don't remember anything else from that night?"

"I swear."

He briefly closes his eyes and nods.

She touches his cheek. The scratch of stubble tickles her palm. His clothes are clean today, but he still hasn't shaved. Her eyes seek his. They dodge hers.

"Damien," she whispers, urging him to look at her. His gaze settles on her mouth. That's as high as it's gone since she woke late morning yesterday. He either looks at her mouth or someplace beyond her shoulders. Maybe he's still in shock from her miscarriage. They must find their way back to each other. She won't let this tragedy tear them apart.

"I want to remember," she says in earnest, then unexpectedly yawns. "Excuse me. The painkillers are kicking in."

"Let's get you inside so you can rest," Damien coaxes. He shuts and bolts the door and tosses his key ring. Various keys to their condo, their flat in London, and his offices; two thumb drives; and the fob to his BMW sedan clatter on the table.

Ella shivers. "Why's it so cold in here?"

"I turned off the heat. I wasn't home much."

"You stayed at the hospital with me the whole time?" The thought of Damien sleeping in the vinyl chair in the corner of her hospital room brought tears to her eyes. No wonder his clothes looked slept in yesterday.

"For the most part. I was at the office last night."

"All night?"

He nods. "I had to catch up on some work."

Understandable. She reaches for his hand. "Thank you for staying with me. I'm sure it hasn't been easy."

He nods, then takes her overnight bag to their bedroom.

Ella adjusts the temperature on the thermostat to a tolerable seventy-two. The furnace rumbles and vents expand, pushing artificially warmed air through the condo.

Putting on the wrap sweater that was hanging on the coatrack, she hugs her chest and crosses the condo's open expanse to the wall of windows overlooking the bay and city below. She draws open the curtains, exposing November's leaden sky. Low clouds hang over the bay, its waters rough and white-capped. Rain streaks the windows, muddling her view. Looking through the glass is like looking into the mirror. The outside world reflects her current mood. Gloomy and disoriented.

Her incision itches and her hand involuntarily rests over the area. She still finds it hard to believe that she'd carried a baby for over five months. Lynn, her OB, referred to Ella's loss as a miscarriage when she removed her staples before she was discharged. "Women miscarry for any number of reasons," she had said. "They happen more often than you'd realize. Think of it as a minor setback in your plans to start a family." There'd been no complications with the pregnancy. She's confident Ella will carry to term next time.

Lynn was only trying to help Ella feel better, to ease her confusion. But Ella knew the truth. She'd asked Damien to look it up on his phone since hers had been damaged in the accident. Ella had carried for twenty-one weeks. It's considered a miscarriage up to twenty weeks. Simon was stillborn.

And that made the tragedy of losing him, then forgetting, that much worse.

"Simon," she whispered.

Damien had suggested to say his name out loud. Maybe thinking of their son as often as possible will help her remember him.

But why bother? She'd only feel the emptiness and worthlessness she'd read women experience. Ella had found the pamphlet discarded on the bedside table at the hospital: *What to Expect in the Emotional Aftermath of a Miscarriage*.

Even the hospital staff couldn't get it right.

Try again, Lynn had encouraged.

Ever since she and her best friend Grace played "house" as kids, Ella's wanted a baby. A part of her thought she could eventually change Damien's mind. At some point, she must have. Damien seems like he was ready to welcome Simon and is devastated they've lost him.

Maybe they can try again.

But first things first. She needs to warm up.

Ella goes to the kitchen and finds her favorite mug, a teacup-shaped ceramic with a hand-painted floral design she'd picked up at Anthropologie. She searches for the stainless steel coffee filter, yanking open cabinet doors. A sharp pain radiates up her forearm and she cries out.

Damien comes up beside her. "What's wrong?"

"I can't find the filter," she says, close to tears. She holds her injured wrist close to her chest.

He opens the dishwasher and pulls out the filter. The one place she didn't look. She gestures for it.

"I got it." He sets the filter atop her mug.

"Thanks," she murmurs, resting her forehead against his deltoid. He tenses under her weight. "Are you okay?" she asks.

"Fine." He drops a scoop of ground coffee into the filter and fills the kettle with water, setting it on the stovetop to boil. He watches it.

"You know what they say about a watched pot," she teases.

"Humph." A short laugh, but he doesn't take his attention off the pot.

"Did I do something to upset you?"

He glances at her. "No, why?"

"Oh . . . I don't know, except we've hardly spoken since I woke up yesterday. You can barely look at me."

"Sorry. I'm just tired." He pats her shoulder in reassurance.

Ella does not feel reassured.

He can't look at her and he's hardly touched her. But she needs to touch him.

She runs a hand down his spine, smoothing the creases in his shirt, relishing the solid plane of his back. She lingers over his tapered waist. It feels like months since they've been intimate. Maybe it has been, for all she knows. All she wants is for him to look at her. To see her and how scared she is.

Once again, his muscles go rigid at her touch. Ella sighs, letting her arm fall. She moves to the other side of the kitchen and watches him wait for the water to boil. She should ask him about the accident. How did it happen? Where? Were other people involved?

Oh, god.

What if she was at fault and injured or, worse, killed someone?

No, the police would have been waiting for her, right?

But she had killed someone. Their son.

Her chest clenches and a heavy sadness falls over her.

"Damien," she says in a thin whisper as hot tears flood her eyes. She waits for him to look her way, and when he does, her face crumples. "I'm sorry. I'm so, so sorry."

He frowns. "For what?"

"I killed our baby." Tears fall.

Damien's expression softens. "No. No, no, no." He crosses the kitchen and gathers her in his arms. "It was an accident." He cups the back of her neck and presses his lips to her forehead. "A horrible accident."

"I wish I remembered." She coils her arms around his waist and tucks her head under his chin and whispers, "I'm scared."

"Me too. But we'll get through this. I promise."

Damien leans his cheek on the top of her head

and draws his arms around her, careful not to hold her too close because of her fresh scar. For a long moment they stand there like that, arms wrapped around each other, gently swaying. She listens to the rain pelt the window. His heart thumps under her ear, and slowly, her limbs grow heavy and the steady rocking lulls Ella toward sleep.

The kettle whistles and Ella startles.

Damien kisses her head, then turns to the stove. He slowly pours the water over the ground coffee in a swirl motion. The grounds bloom like a balloon and the water steadily drips into the mug.

Ella yawns and bundles her sweater tighter. "How'd the accident happen?"

He adds cream to her coffee and gives her the mug. "Some guy in a truck T-boned you at Jones and Filbert. Pushed your Range Rover head-on into a telephone post."

She gasps. She knows that intersection. Drives it almost every day. "Was he heading toward the bay?"

He nods. "He claims his brakes failed. The police are investigating."

That section of Jones Street has one of the steepest grades in the city. With the downhill momentum, he would have slammed into her hard. She mentions this to Damien.

"Witnesses report him running multiple stop signs." Damien tucks an errant cluster of hair behind Ella's ear and cradles her jaw. He looks at her, finally meeting her eyes for the first time. "It wasn't your fault, El."

She nods but finds it hard to believe him. Not because she doesn't trust he's telling her the truth. More because she feels guilty. She's the one who got into the car and drove through the intersection. Why hadn't she seen that truck coming?

"The police will want a statement from me."

"They already took it."

"I guess that's a good thing, since I forgot what happened." She isn't trying to be funny, but the corner of Damien's mouth lifts. She answers with a weak smile.

Damien retreats, putting space between them. He blinks a few times, then looks toward the window. He presses his fingers into the corners of his eyes.

"What is it?" Ella asks.

"I was just thinking about when the hospital called that night. I got there as fast as I could, but you were already in surgery. Placental abruption, that's what the doctor told me. You were bleeding and they couldn't detect Simon's heartbeat. By the time they let me see you—" He stops abruptly and looks around, unfocused. There's a tic in his jaw. "I'm going to shower. You should rest. Davie will be here in a few hours. She's bringing dinner."

And with that, he leaves. It feels like a dismissal, something she'd never expect from him.

The husband who brought her home from the hospital is not acting like the one she knew last week. Or even the man she met and tumbled into love with during their first night together.

Then again, with so many holes in her head, she isn't the same woman either.

CHAPTER 4

Four Years Ago

Ella met Damien Russell on a cool February evening in Las Vegas. She'd recognized him immediately when he walked up to Lobby Bar at the ARIA Resort & Casino, where she and her best friend from college, Davie Mayer, were spending a long-overdue girls' weekend.

There was a magnetic vibe about Damien that summoned attention. She wasn't the only woman captivated by his striking good looks. Heads turned. Eyes trailed him to the bar. Tall and athletic with dark-walnut hair and stormy eyes, Damien was apotheotic. Quite simply, he wasn't the type of man Ella would let sleep on her couch. He belonged in her bed, assuming she got the chance to have him there.

Davie, golden-blonde hair shimmering as she turned to see what caught Ella's attention, groaned suggestively. "Wow. Who's that?"

"Damien Russell. He's the CEO and founder of Phantom Defense Networks, a private cyber-security firm out of San Francisco."

"Oooh. He's hot, and he's local."

"I read an article in *Forbes* last year that he's

some sort of master business strategist. His intellect is off the charts."

"Hot and smart? I call bullshit. Men like him don't exist, unless they're already married. Is he?"

Ella shook her head. "Divorced, I think. But listen to this. He used to work for his dad, Clyde Russell. Have you heard of him? He owns CyberSeal."

"Didn't they recently go public? I think I read something about that in the *Chronicle*."

"Right. Damien was on track to take over the company after his father retired, but he suddenly up and quit five years ago."

Davie plucked an olive from her martini. "Why?"

"No one knows exactly. But he immediately launched his own cybersecurity company. It's speculated that he'd been working on plans while still working for his dad and that he intentionally positioned his firm as a direct competitor."

"Obviously Clyde Russell never retired. Took his company public instead," Davie finished for her, chewing on the olive. "Talk about family drama."

"Seriously."

Damien had graced plenty of magazine covers, his face splashed across the internet since CyberSeal went public, much to Clyde's consternation, Ella was sure. She could visualize him poring over a pile of magazines with his son's image, media coverage that should have been reserved for his company.

But where's the drama in that? Drama sold, and so did Damien's face. Plus, Damien had been silent, which only made the media more frenzied for answers. *What is Damien's opinion of his father taking the company public? Does he plan to do the same with PDN?*

Not a single reporter had yet been able to get his *real* story. What a coup it would be for *Luxe Avenue* if she did.

What she wouldn't give to have one hour alone with him. Tonight.

She and Davie watched Damien settle on to a recently vacated barstool and order a drink.

"I'm going to introduce myself," Ella announced, setting down her unfinished gin and tonic.

Davie smirked. "As yourself or as a journalist?"

"If I could get his story . . . his *real* story . . ."

"You're serious. Now?"

Ella bit into her lower lip and nodded. "Do you mind?"

Davie waved her hand, brushing aside Ella's question. "Oh, my god, not at all. If I had the chance to talk to a guy like that . . ." She shook her head. "There are days when I envy you. The people you meet. *Luxe Avenue* will put your byline on the cover with that one." Davie offhandedly wagged a finger in Damien's direction.

It would be her first cover byline, something she'd been dreaming about since *Luxe Avenue* hired her. That and landing the Senior Features Writer position she'd been vying for. The magazine had a wide female readership. Damien Russell's face on the cover would be a gold mine of issues sold.

Ella grinned and Davie sighed, but she couldn't contain the smile that followed. "I'd love to be a fly on the wall, but guess I'll have to settle for the article. It's late; I'm turning in." She finished her cocktail and stood.

Ella rose and hugged her friend. "I'll make it up to you tomorrow," she promised.

"You can buy me breakfast. I'd say 'good luck' but I don't think you need it."

Ella watched Davie sashay toward the elevators and laughed. "You look gorgeous tonight," she called over the noise of slot machine winnings.

Davie blew her a kiss. Ella sent one back, then turned toward the bar. The patron beside Damien paid his bill and vacated his stool.

Lucky her.

She settled on the warm seat, her arrival going unnoticed. Damien was watching the Warriors game. She, on the other hand, was all too aware of him. His scent, discreet and classy yet modern, was enticing. She would bet his cologne was something from Tom Ford.

Capturing the bartender's attention, she ordered a drink.

"Bourbon on ice." Damien's drink of choice. She'd watched the bartender prepare his cocktail and was pleased when her drink order made Damien finally look her way. He took her in, from her coiffed sandy-brown hair to her Helmut Lang slip dress, with an expression that bordered on disinterest. But she smiled, undeterred, and he flagged the bartender.

"Put her drink on my tab."

"Yes, sir."

Damien's attention returned to the game.

When her drink arrived, Ella lifted her glass. "Thank you," she said to Damien.

Damien raised his. "Of course."

"I'm Ella Skye," she said, setting down her drink and offering her hand.

He shook her hand. "Damien Russell. I suspect you already know that."

Her nose wrinkled. "You do? How?"

"Your drink order. And your name. It sounds familiar."

Ella's face lit up. She couldn't help it. He'd read her work. How else would he know of her?

"Maybe you've read one of my articles. I write for *Luxe Avenue*."

His head tilted back and he smirked. "You're

a reporter." He shook his head and went back to watching the game.

"Ouch. Blacklisted already."

"You're all the same. Yes!" He shook a fist when Curry scored.

"I beg to differ," Ella said, trying not to take offense.

"You all ask the same questions. 'Why'd you leave CyberSeal? Why are you still single?' That's a foul," he blasted the screen when Durant tripped and there was no call.

"Why *are* you single?" she dared, her tone teasing. She stroked a finger along the edge of her cocktail napkin.

He remained focused on the game, nursing his cocktail, and said, " 'It is not a lack of love, but a lack of friendship that makes unhappy marriages.' That's all you'll get out of me. My personal life isn't up for discussion."

Ella arched her back, brows lifting. "Did you just quote Nietzsche to me?"

Damien set down his drink. He turned so that he fully faced her. "Impressive. Not many people know of him."

"Or have studied him. I spent a semester abroad in Germany."

"Where did you study?"

"University of Freiburg. But I graduated from San Francisco State. You got your bachelor's in computer science at Berkeley and master's in business from Stanford," she said, reciting facts from his public bio. "Serious question, though." She tapped the bar beside his elbow.

He smiled, unsure. "What's that?"

"On which side of the stadium do you sit for football games?" His two alma maters were longtime rivals.

He exhaled a long stream of air. The corner of his mouth pulled up in a lopsided grin. "It's a tough call. Depends who I watch the game with."

They shared a smile and Ella sipped her drink. Damien hadn't glanced once at the screen since she cited the philosopher. She took it as a good sign.

"You know, your quote is telling."

"Is it?"

"Your ex-wife hurt you," she said, intentionally being direct. It was a gamble, but he quoted Nietzsche. The political philosophy class where she'd studied the German philosopher had nearly put her to sleep. But Nietzsche's personal life had always stuck with her. Nietzsche had been betrayed twice, in life and postmortem. The woman he loved and proposed to had married his friend, and after his death, his sister, who inherited his estate, misinterpreted his literary work to her advantage and political gain.

Damien's face went blank. "You get right to the point."

She shrugged. "It's the reporter in me. Bad

51

habit. We can talk about your relationship with your dad instead." She stroked her leg, let her Christian Louboutin slip off her heel.

"Or . . ." His chin dipped, his gaze following her hand. "We can talk about why you're in Vegas."

"Girls' weekend."

"Yet here you are. Alone."

"Davie's upstairs."

"And Davie is . . . ?"

"My best friend from college. She went up to our room when I told her I was going to introduce myself to you."

"So I was a target from the beginning." He sounded disappointed.

Ella swirled the stirrer. She tapped the straw on the lip of the glass and set it aside. He was going to lose interest real fast if she didn't come up with something more interesting than the game that had his attention. She needed his trust or else he wouldn't open up to her. Honesty wasn't always the best policy, but honesty gained trust. And this was one instance where honesty would pay off to her advantage. It would land her an interview and, with that, a cover feature.

"I'll be up-front," she started.

"Haven't you been already?"

"True, but . . ." She took a deep breath. "You're seriously good looking, and I'd be dead if I wasn't attracted to you. I'm *really* attracted to you, and I'd like to spend time with you. I'd love the chance to get to know you." Her cheeks warmed from her boldness. She'd never been so direct about her feelings when she'd met a man. It was too revealing. It made her feel vulnerable, exposed. But she wanted this man to know exactly how she felt, that her fascination with him was more than professional. She dared to touch him and traced her finger down the lapel of his sport jacket. The hard muscle underneath flexed and Ella had to force her hand away. She could touch him all night. "But in all seriousness, I also want to interview you."

A discerning laugh escaped him. He shook his head. "Here I thought we were having a good conversation."

"We are. But I bet you'd love to sit down and have another conversation with me, on the record and off."

"You'd bet, huh?" He stroked a finger over his mouth. "We are in Vegas."

"Yes, we are."

He lifted his glass and took a deep drink without taking his eyes off her. He slowly set it down and wiped the corners of his mouth with his thumb and forefinger. "All right."

She blinked. "All right? You'll do it?"

"On two conditions." He showed her two fingers. "We don't talk about my father and you let me buy you another drink."

"Deal." She beamed, already plotting how she'd get him to tell her everything.

Damien bought her another bourbon on ice and told her what had brought him to Vegas. He was the keynote speaker at a network security conference. Ella gushed about KÀ, the Cirque du Soleil show at MGM Grand she and Davie saw that evening. They talked about their favorite restaurants in San Francisco—Ella insisted Fog Harbor Fish House had the best clam chowder, hands down—and where else they'd traveled. Damien owned a flat in London. One cocktail led to another, which led to an elevator ride to his suite after Ella sent a good night text to her friend.

Ella: Don't wait up for me.

Davie: Girl, I want deets in the AM. Have fun.

Her and Damien's conversation in the bar was charged, stoked by a look here and a touch there. He kept a possessive hand on her lower back in the elevator, and the instant he closed the door to his suite, his lips landed on hers. He kissed her, a lingering kiss that quickly became more demanding.

It wasn't the first time Ella had charmed a potential interview subject into sharing secrets in between the sheets, but she wondered if Damien would be the last. There was something about him she was drawn to that she couldn't quite pinpoint. Maybe it was because she felt like he was a kindred soul. She wasn't positive and she didn't have proof. The feeling was more instinctual. But when you'd been abandoned more than once like Ella had, a certain element of loneliness set in. Because she sensed that, Ella didn't just want the scoop on his relationship with his parents or what happened with his ex-wife. She wanted him.

They fucked hard that night and in ways Ella hadn't allowed another man. He pushed her limits, leaving her drunk on arousal. When daylight broke, she sat up in bed, sore and savoring every ache. The thought of leaving him made her a little sad. But she owed Davie breakfast and Ella was never one to overstay her welcome the morning after. She expected they'd exchange phone numbers and the promise of an interview, but Damien grasped her wrist before she climbed out of bed.

"Stay."

Ella hesitated. She looked at him, sleep rumpled and sexy. He could break her heart if she wasn't careful.

"I have a rule," he said in a gravelly voice. "Never fall in love again."

"You fell in love with me after one night?" She winked when his face paled. Then he laughed.

"No, but I wouldn't mind having you as a friend."

"Oh, so you're friend-zoning me."

"God, no," he barked with laughter, giving her

hand a sharp tug. She collapsed on his chest. "Remember my quote?" Ella nodded. He cradled her face and softly kissed her lips. "I think friendship is a good place for us to start."

Ella couldn't have agreed more. Because she was already falling for him.

CHAPTER 5

Ella received the promotion to Senior Features Writer, but she earned it with a profile on Charlize Theron, not a feature on Damien Russell. She never interviewed him. Instead, she fell in love with him and realized his private life didn't belong on the glossy pages of magazines or splashed across media websites. Besides, she'd be his biggest news if there was a new profile on him.

We'd had several wonderful years together before this happened, Ella thinks, her hand gingerly rubbing the tender area around her scar. How does a couple bounce back from a late-term miscarriage, especially when the wife can't remember being pregnant? She doesn't have the answers, but she wants to talk with Damien, about them, the baby, the accident, and what else she can do to retrieve her memories.

She finishes her coffee and goes in search of her husband.

In their room, she listens for the shower but hears only the rain. Obese drops splatter the window, sliding down the glass like tears. She calls for Damien. He doesn't answer.

Did he leave the condo while she was zoning out in the kitchen, lost in memories of when they met? Thank goodness she didn't forget that night. She'd feel more lost than she already does if she forgot her husband, too. It would be like living with a stranger.

Ella returns to the hallway. She finds her home office empty, but the guest-room door is ajar. She eases the door wider and stops up short. Her fingers touch her parted lips. In place of the queen bed and dresser is a half-finished nursery. Paint cans and tools sit on a plastic tarp in one corner. A cherrywood crib in another, the mattress still encased in plastic. Two adjoining walls are painted in a buttery yellow, and on one wall, a name has been stenciled: Simon.

Ella weaves, slammed by a wall of dizziness. She grasps the doorjamb, steadying herself. The pregnancy, the accident, the loss of Simon. It hasn't felt more real to her than in this moment. The nursery waiting to be filled with love and laughter, to smell of talcum powder and diaper rash cream, will remain empty.

Her throat burns around a knot lodged just below her voice box. Tears bead and she swipes them away with the backs of her hands, sniffling as she desperately wishes she could remember what it felt like to carry her son. Did she talk to him? She wonders if she read aloud or sang to him. Did she play him music?

A rustle of fabric draws her attention to the corner of the room. Damien sits on an antique rocker, gripping a stuffed blue bunny. He stares stonily at Ella, eyes glistening.

"Damien." His name is a breathy whisper, heavy with sadness.

He kneads the bunny's ear.

She comes into the room and kneels at Damien's feet, her movements stiff and cautious. She rests her hands on his knees. "Talk to me."

He pinches off tears collecting in the corners of his eyes and roughly clears his throat. "It's just hitting me there won't be a baby."

Tears well in her eyes. "I'm so sorry."

"I never thought . . . I didn't realize you'd forget every—" He swallows hard.

"Forget every what?" she prompts when he doesn't finish. "Forget *everything?*" Is that what he meant to say? As if she had a choice in the matter. Like that's even possible.

With a long, tired sigh, he stands, dropping the bunny on the chair.

"I'll be in the shower." He touches her shoulder and leaves the room.

Ella watches him go, her mouth agape. He'd walked out on her. Again. Earlier, he'd said the accident wasn't her fault, but he sure isn't acting like it. Obviously, he's grieving, yet he's doing so alone.

Why?

She lost Simon, too. Just because she can't

remember him doesn't mean she isn't capable of feeling for him. Ella lost her parents at six, her best friend Grace at fifteen, and her great-aunt Kathy at eighteen. If anyone knows how to grieve, she does. She loves Damien too much to let him do so alone. And she especially isn't going to let him bottle up his pain. She did that more than once, and it's its own worst sort of hell. Exorcising grief takes that much more of an effort the longer it's contained.

Rising to her feet, Ella leaves the nursery and enters the master bedroom to find Damien toweling off from a shower. He pulls on sweatpants and a white T-shirt. With a glance in Ella's direction, he folds back the bedcovers. She goes to him and holds his smooth jaw so that he must look at her. He smells of shaving cream and soap, his skin damp to the touch.

"I'm sorry." The apology doesn't seem enough. It won't return their son. It won't help her remember. And it won't take away her husband's pain. But saying the words makes her feel better. Maybe they'll soften him, too.

Damien gently holds her hand and plants a kiss on the inside of her good wrist. "Don't beat yourself up. It's not your fault."

"You think the memory loss is," she challenges.

He looks down at the bed. "Take a nap with me. I didn't get any sleep last night."

"Why did you have to work all night?"

"Had some things to take care of. I was worried about you, too. Made it hard to sleep."

"Okay. But please don't shut me out. I want to be here for you."

He wraps his arms around her, holds her to his chest, right where she wants to be. "You are." He kisses her forehead. "Get into bed. You need to rest."

Ella crawls under the covers. Damien slides in behind and spoons her. She yawns, murmuring, "I love you."

Damien doesn't reply. He kisses her shoulder. Too exhausted to read into it, Ella slips into the darkness of sleep.

The lobby buzzer wakes Ella. She glances at the bedside clock. Teal numbers glow 7:00 p.m. and she blinks in surprise. She slept for three hours. Muted light drapes the room in charcoal grays. The rain has let up, allowing the familiar sounds of the city to reach her. Taxicab drivers punch their horns in irritation and police sirens blare. There's the occasional sound of people shouting and the shrill brakes of a cable car traveling down Hyde. Off in the distance, the foghorn. Light reflects off low-lying clouds, and below, the city sparkles. Clean and wet, the street filth washed away for at least the night.

Ella slowly eases from bed, stiff from sleep and still aching from her injuries. The large contusions on her left shoulder and ribs have deepened to a Halloween purple. She finds Damien in the great room. He's dressed in dark wash jeans and a fitted black T-shirt, his feet bare. She watches him for a moment, wondering how he feels after his rest, as he scans Pandora stations on the iPad they have linked to their Sonos speaker system. Then she comes up behind him, wraps her arms around his waist, and presses a kiss to his spine. He startles but quickly recovers and pulls her into his side.

"How'd you sleep?" he asks.

"Good, thanks. Who rang?"

"Davie. She's on her way up."

"That's right."

"She's brought lasagna."

"Mmm." Surprisingly, food sounds good. Then again, it's Davie's lasagna, made from her Italian mom's recipe. Mama Mayer's lasagna would make anyone salivate.

Damien settles on Imagine Dragons and adjusts the volume to background music level.

Ella rubs her eyes. "Those meds knocked me out."

"I can send Davie home if you're not up for company."

A part of her wants Davie to leave dinner at their doorstep so that she and Damien have more time to talk. She still has so many questions. But she's hungry, and she misses her friend. And if memory serves her correctly in this instance, it's been a while since she's seen her.

"No, I'm good," she says. "I want to see her and her food. I'm starving. I'm going to freshen up."

In the master bath, Ella strips off her clothes and puts on the plastic cover the hospital provided her to keep her wrist brace dry. Lynn covered her C-section scar with paper tape-like Steri-Strips. Ella's not supposed to mess with them. They'll fall off on their own. But they can get wet. She's just not supposed to scrub the area.

Stepping into the steaming shower, she avoids her reflection in the mirror and soaps her body quickly, but she can't avoid how much bigger she is. Heavy breasts, soft belly, and fuller hips. All this new weight and no baby to show for it.

She slams off the water.

After her shower, she carefully towels off and pats dry the Steri-Strips. Getting dressed, she slips into an oversize button-down blouse and stretchy, high-waisted black yoga pants. The only loose and comfortable articles she could find that aren't maternity clothes, clothes she doesn't remember.

Damien and Davie are at the dry bar when Ella joins them. Damien has mixed Davie a Manhattan and poured himself a Macallan over ice. When Davie sees Ella, she bursts out crying. She sets down her drink and rushes to

Ella's side, hugging her as though she hasn't seen her in years. But Ella catches the floral scent of Davie's CHANEL Chance perfume and she remembers. They went shopping at Bloomingdale's last week. Davie needed shoes for a function at SFMOMA. One of her publicity clients was exhibiting.

"Oh, Ella," Davie says, teary-eyed. "Your baby." She sobs, overcome with emotion, and gives Ella another lung-crushing hug. "I'm sorry."

"It's okay," Ella says, even though it's not. She's the one who's sorry. She's the one who messed everything up by getting into the car after . . .

After what? She has the vague sense she and Damien had been arguing.

About what?

Davie releases her grip and holds Ella at arm's length. "It's not okay. It's horrible. I can't imagine what you're going through. You forgot your baby."

"Damien told you about my amnesia?" She looks at her husband. He's staring into his drink, looking like he's working through a particularly complex coding issue.

"Yes, while you showered. Do you remember shopping with me last week?" Ella nods. "What about seeing *Hamilton* last month?"

"Yes. Loved that musical."

"Me too. But you don't remember anything about the accident?"

Ella shakes her head. "Or my pregnancy." She doesn't remember decorating the nursery or wearing maternity clothes. Ella felt like she was snooping through a stranger's closet while looking for clothes after her shower. Her wardrobe of designer jeans and dresses had been pushed aside for blousy, A-line stretchy shirts and pants with elastic waistbands.

"How unusual," Davie murmurs.

"That I can remember buying a size large *Hamilton* shirt but not the reason why?" She wore a size small. Used to, anyway.

"Well, yes, but more that you lost your memory, rather, fragments of your memories—"

"That's a good description," Ella replies.

"It is, isn't it? I'd drink to that if I had my glass with me." She looks back at the dry bar. "I meant that your memory loss happened five days after the accident."

"I know. It's unusual."

"Did the doctor say why?"

"He thinks losing the baby was too much for me to handle."

"Did something happen at the hospital to bring it on?" Davie whispers. She glances at Damien. He has moved into the kitchen and is popping the lasagna into the oven.

Does he know something? Ella wonders.

Damien returns to the dry bar and mixes himself another cocktail.

"I have no idea," Ella answers, turning back to her friend. "If something did happen, I blocked it out."

The lobby buzzer sounds.

"Who's here?" Ella asks Damien, who hands Davie a tissue on his way to the door. She takes it graciously and dabs her eyes.

"Andrew. He called while you were in the shower."

"How is that annoying little brother of yours?" Davie asks.

"Still annoying, I'm sure."

When Andrew comes in, dressed in baggy jeans and a faded red hoodie, he shakes Damien's hand. He then sees Ella and his face falls. In two long strides, he is at her side and grabs her up in a tight embrace. Ella makes a noise of distress when she feels a burn in her abdomen. He quickly lets go.

"Yikes, sis." He grimaces when Ella gently massages the area around her scar.

"I'm fine."

"Really? 'Cause Damien told me about your head. Damn."

"With any luck, I'll recover. My doctor said my chances are good."

Nodding as though he's trying to understand, Andrew bites his lip. Andrew, the one who's always so lighthearted, looks like he is going to cry. She hasn't seen him cry since their parents died. They both cried a lot that year.

Ella clasps his hands. "Trust me, everything will be fine."

"If you say so, sis."

"I know so." She'll make sure of it.

They sit for a dinner of lasagna, garlic bread, and roasted vegetables, and despite the dark cloud of the week's events, talk is lively. Damien has always shone at dinner parties and he keeps the conversation light, asking Andrew about his latest project, Come Over Rover, an app that connects dogs in the neighborhood for canine playdates.

"I have two interested investors," Andrew announces.

"Fantastic! I knew there would be." Ella gives her brother a fist bump. His latest app wasn't his first venture. Andrew's been designing and selling off apps since he was nineteen. He'll do the same when he gets bored with Rover. Poor doggy.

Damien cuts into his lasagna. "I guess that means my human resources department shouldn't expect a call from you."

"You know Andrew abhors the eight-to-six grind," Davie says. She nods when Damien offers to pour her more Cabernet. "Andrew's just saving you from the hassle of firing him."

"It's true, honey. He's never going to come

work with you," Ella agrees. "He spends mornings at the gym, afternoons at the coffee shops, and evenings at the bar," she ticks off, then corrects herself. "My mistake. He spends his evenings at the Blue Light."

"I watch the Niners there. Doesn't everyone?"

Three heads shake.

"Sorry, Damien, my brother only works nights and in his pajamas."

"I don't wear pajamas."

Davie leans forward, resting her chin on her palm, intrigued. "Really?" She likes to egg him on. Harmless flirting because, frankly, she finds him a bit of a tool.

"Shorts! I wear gym shorts. And a shirt, except when it's hot." He throws his bread down. It bounces off his plate. "What is this? Andrew roast night?"

He sounds annoyed but he's grinning. Ella knows it doesn't take much to get her brother riled.

"I was thinking about your app the other day. TinderPooch, right?" Damien asks in all seriousness.

"Come Over Rover," Andrew grumbles.

"You should program a feature where a dog barks to find a match. Once for yes, twice for no. Or you could train them to swipe."

Ella and Davie burst with laughter.

"Ow," Ella whines, grabbing her waist. Everything hurts, but she can't stop. Damien's too damn funny when he gets on a roll.

"You're in rare form tonight, Russell." Andrew stuffs a forkful of lasagna into his mouth. "Normally, I'd be quick with a retort full of awesomeness, but given the shitty week you've had, I'll refrain."

Damien's face darkens.

"Andrew," Ella reprimands.

He looks at her. "What?"

Damien's jaw ticks. He puts down his fork and pushes away from the table. "If you'll excuse me."

They watch him head down the hallway until they hear the door to his office close.

"What's his deal?" Andrew asks.

Davie shoots him a dirty look. "He just lost a baby. Give him a break. He's having a hard time."

"Crap." Andrew cups his hands over his mouth and nose. "My bad," he says into his hands. His gaze darts to Ella. "I wasn't thinking. And come on, he was picking on me first."

"Oh, my god, seriously? How old are you?"

"Thirty-two."

"That was a rhetorical question, you dimwit." Ella gives him a playful punch in the shoulder. She's quiet for a moment, then says, "It's not you. He's upset I can't remember Simon."

"Sure he is. But obviously you'd remember if you could. And it's going to come back, it just takes time," Davie says. She comes over and bends down to wrap Ella in a hug.

Davie's sweet perfume and warm skin comfort Ella and she feels her tears coming on. "I should go see how he's doing."

Davie rubs her back. "No, you should cry. Come with me." Davie straightens and holds out her hand. "Excuse us, Andrew."

Andrew gets up from the table. "I'll go find him and apologize, I guess."

Ella follows Davie down the hall to her office, right next to Damien's. She can hear Andrew's and Damien's muffled voices through the wall and wonders what they're talking about. Her brother isn't exactly famous for his apologies.

"I'm okay," she tells Davie after she closes the door. She plucks a tissue from the box on her desk, dabs her eyes, and wipes her nose. "I think Damien thinks I'm lying."

"About what?" Davie asks, sinking into the chair across from Ella's desk.

"My selective memory loss."

"He does? Did he say something?"

"Not really. It's more a feeling than anything."

"Forget a moment about what you think and what you think he thinks." She waves her hands in front of her, confused. "Why would you fake something like this? There's no point."

"Exactly."

"Don't be so hard on yourself. You guys will

figure it out and deal when you're ready. The memories will come back. Give it time." Davie folds her legs under herself. "You know, I visited you in the hospital."

"When?" Ella asks, sitting on the edge of her desk.

"Umm. Let's see. Five days ago."

"How was I?"

"Miserable. So was Damien. You were both in shock."

"Makes sense." Ella looks at her bare toes, the pink polish chipped and dull.

"Your pregnancy wasn't planned," Davie says softly.

"What?"

"I wasn't sure how much you remember. I thought you'd want to know."

Ella's heart races. "Damien *did* want Simon, right?"

"Yes, he was ecstatic."

"Good." Ella sighs, relieved.

"But . . . it took him a while to come around. That's what you told me."

Ella chews her lower lip, her mind tracing back to Damien's reaction to her memory loss. "You weren't supposed to forget *him*," he'd exclaimed. Why would he say something like that?

"Did I say anything at the hospital, anything strange?"

Davie frowns. "Like what?"

Ella shakes her head, unsure how to make sense of what Damien said and how to phrase it for Davie without it coming across as bizarre. Damien could have simply been shocked and the words came out of his mouth all wrong.

"What do you know about my accident?" she asks instead.

"Only what Damien told me." Davie reiterates the same story Damien gave Ella that afternoon.

"Nothing else?"

Davie shakes her head. "I take it you don't remember the accident."

"No." But she has the impression she and Damien argued beforehand. She asks Davie about it.

"If you did, you didn't tell me."

Ella hears laughter outside her door and the music on the Sonos speaker in her office abruptly stops.

"Game night is on," Andrew shouts for them to hear. Davie groans and sags in the chair. Ella, though, is relieved Damien's mood has shifted.

"Come on. It'll be fun." Ella could use an insane night of Cards Against Humanity. She slides off her desk and pats Davie's knee.

"Fine," she grunts, getting up. "As long as it's not 'Exploding Kitties' again. I refuse to give your little bro another belly rub."

"You weren't supposed to give him a literal

belly rub. And it's Exploding *Kittens,* by the way."

"Whatever. His fault for lying about the rules."

"Maybe he'll purr this time if you're lucky."

"Fuck you."

CHAPTER 6

Ella wakes the following morning with the vague memory of Damien kissing her goodbye.

"I'll try to be home early," he murmured. But the softness of his tone belied his worry. He'd read an email from his vice president of sales before bed. They'd lost Imperial Properties, a nationwide commercial real estate company. Ella didn't want him to go in to work. She'd rather spend the day in bed in his arms. The painkillers make her so sleepy. But after seven days off, he needed to make an appearance at the office and meet with his sales staff. He had to find out what went down with Imperial. Damien left before the sun was up with a promise. He'd pick up dinner at Bob's Steak and Chop House. Ella loves their steaks.

Ella boils water and fixes her coffee, skipping breakfast. Her appetite seems to have taken another hiatus. Coffee in hand, she makes her way to her office, still wearing her wrinkled sleep shirt and ratty terry cloth robe. She's ready to dive into work, grateful for the distraction. She's also grateful Damien kept the door to the nursery closed. Easier to imagine the room as the guest room it was before. Empty for a very different reason than it really is: no houseguests rather than no baby.

She settles into her chair with a groan and sets down her mug beside a white iPhone box. A large silver bow is taped on top with a note from Damien.

All set up and fully charged!

Couldn't find the same case so I got several.

They're in the Apple bag on your credenza.

Love, D.

Ella swings her chair around and peeks inside the bag. Her throat swells with emotion. The past week had to have been hell for Damien. One of the worst in his life. Yet he still had the forethought to replace her damaged phone. God, she loves this man.

One of the cases looks similar to the one she had before, an owl pattern. She unpacks the case and the phone and powers on the device. Everything she had on her previous phone since her last backup loads, old emails and hundreds of new ones. Her voice mailbox is full—plenty of calls came in during the past week she'll have to go through. Damien even synced to her cloud account. All her settings are the same.

Tears well. She swallows roughly, then laughs

at herself for crying over a stupid phone. But it's a phone from her husband, who'd labored over it while she'd been laid up. That man.

She sends him her first text. Thank you.

He doesn't reply, but she didn't expect him to, not right away, considering how busy he must be today.

Time for her to get busy, too.

Launching her laptop she opens Outlook and sags in her chair. Seven hundred fifty-eight unread emails. That'll keep her busy for a while, but rather than culling through them, she opens the most recent message from her editor, Rebecca. Rebecca, whose tasteful bouquet of white lilacs and garden roses Damien had brought home from the hospital sits on her credenza. Her editor can be tough, but she's always been Ella's biggest cheerleader, and for good reason. Ella's one of *Luxe Avenue*'s most dependable staff writers. She's never missed a deadline, and memory loss or not, she doesn't intend to break that record.

Rebecca's email arrived earlier that morning.

Rest up and call me when you're ready.
Rebecca xo

Ella calls her.

"I said when you're ready, not when you get out of the hospital," Rebecca answers after the second ring.

"I'm fine," Ella insists.

"I have it on good authority from your husband that your doctor put you on a two-week hiatus. Call me then or later. Take more time off if you need it. I've got assignments in the pipeline and I want you in top form when you get back." Rebecca speaks a million miles a minute as usual and arguing with her when she's like this is pointless. Ella sinks further into her chair with a long sigh.

"And Ella." Rebecca's tone softens. "Damien told me everything. I'm sorry about the baby."

"Thank you," Ella says, sitting upright. She wonders exactly what Damien mentioned. Does Rebecca know about her memory loss?

"Did he say anything else?" she asks.

"Not much. We didn't talk long, and he hasn't called since the day after your accident."

Good. Rebecca doesn't know about the amnesia and Ella wants to keep it that way. No need to give her editor reason to doubt her capabilities or redirect those assignments in the pipeline to someone else.

Unfortunately, that also means Rebecca can't tell her anything more about the accident or what led up to it than what she's already heard from Davie. Come to think of it, she'd be surprised if either of them knew anything. If she and Damien were fighting, he wouldn't share those details. He's too private and he's yet to share them with her.

"Listen, why don't you walk me through your calendar," Rebecca suggests. "I can reassign whatever you're working on and we can postpone everything else. Your job for the next two weeks is to get better. Everyone here is so devastated for you, including Paul."

"How is Chief?" Ella asks. Their editor in chief rarely cracks a smile.

"The same. Every deadline is too long and every article is too short. He sends his best, by the way."

For the next ten minutes, Ella takes Rebecca through her calendar. When they finish, Ella hangs up and dives into her laptop, clicking on documents and bookmarks, reading emails. She searches, peruses, and digs, looking for anything that can trigger her memories. There has to be something that explains why she's blocked them out. But she finds nothing.

Andrew arrives around one with lunch. As kind as it is of him to check on her and bring food, she wants to be left alone so that she can try to unravel this puzzle. What happened to her? She buzzes him up and unbolts the door but goes back to her office, intent on remaining focused.

She hears him come in, and a few seconds later, he's standing in her doorway, SF Giants cap on his head. He removes his blue-mirrored aviator sunglasses and whistles.

"What country did you piss off? Looks like a ballistic missile blew up your office."

A patchwork of manila folders covers the floor. A career-length pile of papers and article clippings clutters her desk. Ella still hasn't dressed or combed her hair.

"I think I'm going crazy."

Andrew smirks. "That's not news." He comes into the room and flops onto the chair across from Ella. Kicking up his heels, he plants his DayGlo-green Nikes on Ella's desk. "What's going on?"

"I lost a baby I can't remember," she clips, sarcastic.

"Whoa! Easy on the DoorDash delivery guy." Andrew looks around. "Anything I can do to help?"

She shakes her head. "I was hoping to find something that would help me remember. I'm also curious if there are any assignments I've forgotten." She gestures at the mess on the floor, then lets her arms flop against her sides, hopeless. "Why do you think I forgot?"

"Uh . . . you're in shock?" He snags a stress ball from her desk and squeezes it. "Have you called the psychiatrist yet?"

"Therapy's not going to bring Simon back." She's not antitherapy, but after her parents' deaths and then Grace's, everyone's solution was "get therapy."

Been there, done that.

Though she did promise Damien she'd go. In fact, they're supposed to go together. Doctor's orders.

"I'll call her later," Ella responds. She scoops up the folders.

"Attagirl." He smiles at her and then his tone changes. "I'm worried about you."

"I know," Ella says, then gives him a hint of a smile, whispering, "Thank you."

She drops the files on her desk, then bends over to retrieve more. She straightens quickly, and blood rushes from her head to her stomach. She weaves, overcome by a sinking sensation deep in her belly, and grips the desk for balance.

Andrew's on his feet in a flash. He grasps her arms to steady her. "Hey there, you okay?"

Ella pushes the hair from her eyes. It takes a moment for her head to stop spinning and her stomach to settle.

Her brother eyes her. "When was the last time you ate?"

"Last night . . ."

"That explains the attitude." He grins. "Good thing I brought lunch."

They park themselves on the barstools at the kitchen island. Andrew passes her a white cardboard carton and paper-wrapped chopsticks, not bothering with plates and forks. "Veggie chow mein."

"My fave." Ella opens the carton and digs in.

Andrew snaps apart his chopsticks and rubs them together to remove the splinters. "Everything okay with you and Damien?"

"Aside from my head case and losing the baby? I think so. Why?"

"I didn't want to say anything last night with Damien around. But you seemed agitated the last time I saw you at the hospital."

"How do you mean?" She eyes him curiously.

"You were crying. Damien looked like he wanted to punch the wall. You kept going off about some sort of promise. You wanted Damien to do something for you."

She frowns at him. "Do you know what it was?"

"No idea. You guys didn't tell me."

"Did you ask?"

"And give your husband something to hit, like my face?" he says, holding up his chopsticks and carton of broccoli beef in defense. "Not a chance."

"Damien wouldn't hurt you." He might be ruthless in the boardroom, but Ella has never seen him get violent.

Andrew seems doubtful. "You don't remember the look on his face."

Okay, Damien could be intimidating. She'll give him that.

"When was this?" she asks.

"Wednesday night."

The night before her memory loss. The night of the commotion Nurse Jillian talked about. What happened that night?

Not only that, what happened right before the accident? Where had she been driving to? Why'd she leave right after dinner? Did she even eat the pork loin she'd cooked that night?

"Did I say anything else at the hospital?" she asks, curious.

"Like what?"

"I think Damien and I were arguing before my accident. I'm not positive. It's just a feeling."

"You didn't mention anything to me. Have you asked Damien?"

Ella shakes her head. She chews a noodle, contemplating. She'll ask him tonight.

"So you and Damien are good?"

"Yeah." She hopes they are.

That evening Ella showers, and after, as she towels off, she catches her reflection in the full-length mirror. This time, she doesn't avoid her image. She drops the towel and takes a good, hard three-sixty-degree look, from her full breasts to her wider waistline and distended, hollow abdomen. She gingerly touches the paper sutures taped over her fresh scar. Lynn said the redness and bruising around the area is normal and that the incision line will still be purple up to six months after the C-section.

Eventually it'll start fading to a pale pink. "Hardly noticeable and below your bikini line," she reassured.

Turning, Ella looks at her calves and backside. She's lost muscle tone. She probably traded laps from the Marina Green to the Golden Gate Bridge for prenatal yoga sessions. Definitely not at the intensity she's conditioned for. Used to be, anyway, she thinks with a grimace.

Turning back around, she cups a hand over her scar. "I'm sorry," she whispers to the life that is no longer there.

A fleeting memory, more of a feeling, touches her mind. The sensation of butterfly wings, the faint press of something against the inside of her abdomen wall. She starts to cry, turning away from the mirror and straight into Damien.

"Sorry," he says, his voice gruff.

"How long have you been standing there?" She'd been so focused that she didn't hear him come in. Embarrassed, Ella picks up the towel and wraps it around her torso. She doesn't want him to see her body like this. Misshapen and unfamiliar to her own eyes. She hardly recognizes herself.

"Ella." Damien edges toward her, corrals her in his arms. "You don't need to cover up. You'll always be beautiful to me."

The familiar scent of him and the comfort of his arms—it's all too much. She buries her face in his chest and falls apart. Damien, thankfully, just holds her.

After some time, Ella lifts her head. Her husband offers her a washcloth. She wipes her face. She hasn't cried like that since . . . Well, she can't recall since when. Damien's dress shirt is drenched. Tears glisten on the inside corners of his eyes. He thumbs them off.

"It must be the hormones," she excuses.

"It must be a lot of things." Damien kisses her hair, pulls her into his chest again, and holds her even tighter. Like he's afraid to let go, afraid to lose her.

Leaning back, he looks down at her and gently pushes damp hair away from her sticky face. "You good?"

Ella nods. "For now."

"Join me for dinner?"

She nods again.

He kisses her softly on the lips. "Get dressed. I'll meet you out there."

Damien has set the dining table and dimmed the lights. Outside the wall of windows, the Golden Gate Bridge and, across the bay, Sausalito glitter against the darkness of night.

Damien uncorks a bottle of Cabernet Sauvignon. "Wine?"

"Small glass," she says. She is still taking painkillers and doesn't need to get loopy. She sits down to a plate of prime rib and blanched string beans. "Smells delicious."

Damien joins her, dropping his napkin on his lap.

"How was work?" she asks. Such a normal question when everything is far from normal.

He looks at her and his mouth parts like he wants to say something. He hesitates.

Something's wrong. "What is it?"

He sets down his utensils. "I have to fly to London in a couple of days."

"Wait. What?"

"I don't want to go."

"Then don't." Why would he leave now? They lost a baby. She's losing her mind. And they haven't discussed either.

He loosens his tie and takes it off. Tosses it over the empty chair beside him. "We lost Royal Gateway."

A credit card processing company. One of PDN's larger UK clients.

"That's your second client in a week," Ella says, worried. Damien sure must be.

He cuts into his meat with force. "I meet with the CEO in a few days. I have to try and salvage the account."

"You suspect something."

"Two clients in a week after several years of perfect retention. That's not coincidence."

"You have to go," she says, understanding. Business has called her away with little to no notice. An assignment comes in and Ella can find herself on a plane within several hours of

Rebecca's call. But she and Damien always came back to each other.

Damien lifts her hand and kisses the inside of her good wrist. Their eyes meet. "Will you be all right without me?"

"I'll be fine." She needs to be, for him. She doesn't want to add to his worry any more than necessary.

His eyes brighten with an idea. "Come with me."

She thinks of the flat in London. Walks along the Thames. Pies and mash. Exploring the shops at Camden Passage. It's all so tempting. She shakes her head. "I'll only be in the way. You'll worry about me when you should be focused on your business."

Damien nods, looking a little relieved. Staying home is the right choice.

"I'll still worry about you, whether you're with me or not."

"I know. That's why I'm okay with you going. We'll wait until you get back to see the therapist."

Damien's withdrawal is immediate. He releases her hand and cuts into his steak, jabbing a bite into his mouth. She hears the fork scrape against his teeth.

"I can tell you don't want to go. What's wrong?"

His face shutters. "It's a waste of time. Talking won't bring Simon back."

His words echo the thoughts she had earlier but hearing him speak them out loud hurts. She decides to hold off asking him about that night in the hospital. There's something about his demeanor that stops her. It'll only push him away. Years spent interviewing reluctant politicians and tight-lipped actors who relish their privacy have taught her well. Patience. Besides, Damien prefers to mull things over, take his time to process. He'll talk, eventually. He always does.

Ella looks at her plate, appetite gone. She takes a steady breath.

"Hey." Damien reaches for her hand again. "I tried therapy once."

"With Anna?" she guesses.

He solemnly nods.

His first wife. A marriage straight out of college that ended in a divorce five years later.

He squeezes her hand. "I love you. But this is hard for me."

"Losing Simon or me losing my memory of him?"

"Both, if I'm being honest. Can you be patient with me?" His voice catches on the last word.

She stands and Damien scoots back his chair. She crawls onto his lap. His arms snake around her. She cradles his jaw. "Yes, I can. But Davie said something last night that's been bothering me."

"What's that?"

"Is it true that my pregnancy was an accident?"

Damien's eyes close. He drops his forehead on Ella's shoulder.

Ella's fingers sift through his hair. "Damien?"

He nods, the movement almost imperceptible.

Ella presses her face into Damien's hair and lets his admission sink in. Simon was a mistake.

"Why didn't I get an abortion? You didn't want children."

"But you did," he says, lifting his head. His eyes meet hers. His fingertips caress her cheek. "You were scared when you first told me, but you couldn't hide your happiness. I couldn't take that away from you."

"But you didn't want Simon."

"I did. I loved him. And now I'm going to miss every milestone that I'll never get to experience with him. God, El." He presses his lips to her forehead, keeps them there.

"I'm so sorry to put you through this," she says through tears.

"No. God, no, Ella. This isn't your fault. I've already told you that. We're in this together. I'm right here with you. We're a team."

A team. Then why does she feel so alone?

It's the memory loss, she reasons. She's confused.

"I love you," she says, hugging him tighter.

"I love you, too. So much. I don't know what

I'd have done had I lost you, too. You're the most important person in my life. The only family I care about. You're my world, Ella. I only want you to be happy. I'll do anything to ensure your happiness."

"I know." She kisses him softly.

Later, Damien turns in early with her, his body curved around hers. Ella quickly falls asleep, and when she wakes, he's already gone.

Damn meds, she thinks, disappointed she slept through his goodbye kiss. But he left a note, as he's been known to do. This one comes with a bakery bag from Luna's.

E.

I picked up a muffin for you on my run.

Take it easy today. Rest.

Don't lose faith in me.

I love you.

D.

Don't lose faith in him. Of course she won't. What an odd thing for him to write.

CHAPTER 7

Four Years Ago

Three weeks into her relationship with Damien, they went for a morning run in Golden Gate Park. It was late spring in San Francisco, when the days are shrouded in gray and the light is softer as the fog sits on the city like an unwanted houseguest. They ran past a team of middle school boys playing soccer. An errant ball cut across the field and bounced off Ella's ankle. She stumbled, but Damien grasped her arm, preventing her fall.

"I've got you."

"Thanks," she panted, short of breath. "That wouldn't have been pretty." Ella laughed off her embarrassment.

Damien eased their pace until she fell back into her runner's zone. She watched two opposing players chase after the ball and smiled at the parents on the sidelines bundled up in parkas and fueling up on lattes in metal thermoses. Someday that might be her and Damien, their Saturdays filled with soccer games and family movie nights. She'd started falling for him the night they met and, even though she hadn't told him yet, was now hopelessly in love. She could already picture a future filled with their children's laughter, summer vacations in Hawaii, and winter breaks playing in the Tahoe snow. Damien would make a wonderful father. He's patient and affectionate while at the same time authoritative and encouraging. Their kids would be well rounded and good natured. If they were anything like their father, they'd excel at almost everything they did.

"Any interest in kids?" Damien asked, jogging beside her.

Ella felt a certain thrill their minds were on the same track, but the sideline referee chose that moment to blow his whistle as they ran past him. The shrill noise pierced Ella's ear and she shook her head.

Damien smiled. "Me neither."

"You neither what?"

"Kids."

What?

Ella stopped abruptly. Damien looked back over his shoulder, surprised she wasn't beside him, and jogged back to her. "You okay?"

She squinted at him. Had she heard him correctly?

"You don't want kids?" she asked, incredulous.

"No, not really."

"Why not?" Waiting to have kids is one thing, but to consciously decide not to have them? That's an entirely different story with an ending Ella didn't see coming.

Damien shrugged. He wiped his face with his shirt, looking uneasy at the way she stared at him dumbfounded.

"What?" he said after a moment.

"That's a pretty definitive decision, Damien. One you've obviously put some thought into. I'd really like to understand why."

He tapped the toe of his shoe against a park bench leg. "Anna wanted kids."

Damien had told Ella that he divorced Anna over irreconcilable differences. With this new tidbit of information, she'd bet their marriage ended over kids. Anna wanted them. Damien didn't. He'd break it off with Ella if she told him the truth about what she really wanted. Their relationship would end before it truly started.

"I don't see kids in my future," he said. Such a simple statement, yet so powerful. A dream killer.

Hands on hips, Ella turned away from him and watched her plans of motherhood disappear downfield with the ball. She was in love with Damien, no doubt about it. But was she willing to give up children to be with him? She didn't even know yet if he loved her back.

"Ella?"

She turned back around. Damien looked unsettled, almost heartbroken, and it made Ella nervous and a little sad. "If you really want kids, maybe it's best that we . . ." He swallowed roughly. "I love you, Ella. I don't want to lose you, but at the same time, I don't want to be that guy who keeps you from getting what you want. You'd never be happy with me. You'd leave—"

Ella didn't let him finish. She closed the distance between them and looked up into his face, her heart racing. "You love me?"

He smiled broadly. "Yeah. Yeah, I do. So much," he whispered vehemently.

She beamed. Grasping his shoulders, she stood on her toes and kissed him. "I love you, too."

He flashed another smile, but it quickly faded. "But . . . kids?"

Ella knew that if she was honest with him, right here and now, what she'd tell him would destroy everything that had been and still was budding between them. Ella might not have his disinterest in kids, but what she did have was time. Maybe, one day, once he saw how great their life could be together, she could convince him to change his mind.

She smiled lovingly. "It's *you* I want, Damien." More than anything. More than kids, she silently reaffirmed, hoping to convince herself that was truly how she felt.

CHAPTER 8

March 2019

Ella smacks the alarm squawking 5:00 a.m. and rolls out of bed. After a visit to the bathroom, she brushes her teeth and slips into her running attire, grabbing up her Nikes.

Damien waits for her at the front door. "Morning, sweetheart." He kisses her solidly on the mouth with a groan that sends a delicious ripple through her. "Let's skip the run and go back to bed."

"Uh-uh." She pushes him away. "Run first." They didn't make it out the door yesterday. Ever since Lynn released her for full activity, including bedroom aerobics, Damien hasn't kept his hands off her. That was two months ago. The sex has been great. Okay, it's been mind blowing. But she feels like it's become an excuse not to talk, which they haven't done much of in four months, not the kind of talking they should be doing. Either he's still too raw about the accident or he's too busy with work. Whichever, Ella feels like she's been left hanging. Her memories haven't returned. Looking at photos of her pregnant self and staying immersed with familiar people in familiar places as Dr.

Allington had suggested when she was released from the hospital hasn't helped at all. She doesn't know anything more today about what led up to the accident and what happened at the hospital afterward than she did last November. Only Damien knows what made her leave their condo that night and get into her car, and he's not talking.

He also doesn't want to try for another baby.

At her eight-week post-op appointment, Lynn asked if Ella wanted to go back on birth control. Ella had been excited to discuss with Damien the prospect of getting pregnant again. But he was adamant. No way. He wasn't ready. How could she think about another baby when the loss of Simon still gutted him? What if something happened to the baby again? Or worse, what if he lost her instead? Did she have any idea what that did to him, seeing her bruised and battered in the hospital bed?

Lynn had also asked her about the psychiatrist. Had she been?

"Once," Ella answered. Alone.

The session hadn't helped. Ella spent an hour expressing her frustrations about Damien and her sadness over losing Simon, but she couldn't answer most questions the therapist posed. Why did they decide to have a baby when her husband was clear he didn't want a child? What changed his mind? Where was she going when she got into the accident? Had they been arguing, and if so, about what?

"On and on the questions went. I couldn't answer a single one," Ella explained. "I tried to get Damien to come to a follow-up session, but between his work schedule and his excuses?" She shrugged, tugged up the paper examination gown that had slipped off her shoulder. "I gave up. I stopped asking him to come and I didn't go back."

Lynn touched her arm. "I've seen husbands take several years before they can talk about it, let alone try for another kid again. It's difficult for them to watch their wives lose a child."

Ella nodded. She wanted to be sympathetic to Damien's feelings, but she was the one who carried Simon. She'd do it again given the chance. Looking at her hands in her lap, she picked at a loose hangnail. "Did I tell you Simon was an accident? I think I forgot to take a pill."

"No. I didn't know. But there are other options besides the pill." Lynn rolled her stool to the end of the exam table and motioned for Ella to scoot her rear to the edge and lie back. She peeked around Ella's raised knees. "Options you don't have to remember to take each day."

"Can I think about it?"

Lynn smiled. "Take all the time you need."

Damien unbolts the front door, bringing Ella

back to the task at hand. She laces up her shoes. Damien is scrolling through his email. He frowns.

"Everything all right?" she asks. Four clients have left PDN since January, in addition to Royal Gateway. Damien had said his trip to London last November was a waste. He wasn't able to convince them to stay. He's found the losses to be more than frustrating. They're personal. Because each business has moved to CyberSeal, his father's company.

"Not sure." The lines between his brows deepen as he reads the memo, swearing as he closes his email and launches his music app. He drops one of his ear pods in Ella's hand so that they can listen together. "I'll deal with it later. Ready?"

"Yeah." She plugs the pod in her ear and Damien brings up their Tuesday playlist, a mix of U2, Gang of Youths, and other alternative rock music that gets them fired up.

They run a seven-mile route through the city streets, making their way to the Embarcadero, where they follow the wharf. The air is damp but the sky clears as the sun breaks over the city skyline and spills its golden light.

As they run, Ella plots her day. She has to drive to Sacramento to interview the governor over lunch, and on her way back, she hopes to finally nail down the double interview with Emily Blunt and John Krasinski about their latest project. With any luck, she'll be back in the city by dinner with Damien, maybe even surprise him at the office with Thai takeout. He's been wound tight, working late hours and traveling almost nonstop trying to retain his clients.

They reach the final stretch on their route and head back up the hill toward home. Damien changes the playlist and Eminem blasts her ear.

"Really?" She rips out the pod, knowing it'll immediately stop the music.

But Damien doesn't stop. He picks up speed and Ella has to work to keep up with him. She hollers his name, but he doesn't answer. He doesn't slow down. The concrete between them expands and the music cuts out, her pod losing the connection with Damien's phone. He's a block ahead and Ella eases to a saner pace, letting him work off whatever's steaming in his head. Besides, the last hill home is a killer.

By the time she rounds the corner to their building, Ella's calves burn and her side cramps. Damien's waiting outside, pacing the sidewalk to cool off.

"Lost you back there," he says when he sees her.

"The hell, Damien?" She gasps, hands on knees, catching her breath. "What's wrong with you?"

He has the audacity to look confused. Ella shakes her head, disappointed, and glances at her watch. It's getting late and she needs to shower and get on the road. There isn't time to get into it with him. There never seems to be enough time.

Ella fires him a dirty look, shoves open the building's glass doors, and stomps through the lobby.

Damien follows her inside. She stabs the elevator button.

"Ella?" he asks, cautious.

Screw it. She's so over him not opening up.

She turns on him. Even drenched in sweat and smelling like a gym locker, she finds him breathtakingly gorgeous. She could jump him in the lobby and not have a care in the world who walked by. Except right now she's pissed.

"You ditched me. What's up with you? Is this just about work or is something else going on?"

"You know there's a lot going down." His tone has softened. She doubts he'll admit it, but he must realize his speed burst up the hill was a dick move.

"Then talk to me about it. Don't shut me out. Or run off with my music. Eminem sucks, by the way."

The corner of his mouth twitches.

The elevator doors slide open and they step inside. Damien presses the button for their floor. "Can we talk about this later?" he suggests, staring at the panel of buttons.

"Let me guess. You're not ready."

"No. I have to get to work and you have to drive to Sacramento."

"Do you realize it's been four months?" His brow furrows and Ella gets into his space. The elevator isn't small, but she makes sure he can't look anywhere but at her.

"Four months, two weeks, and three days. That's how long it's been since we lost Simon. And we still haven't talked about it. We haven't talked about *him*."

He rakes a hand through his damp hair. "No memories yet?"

"You know they haven't come back. Not talking about it doesn't help me. Or us," she snaps. "I think you've had enough time to process. Don't put off your grief. It only makes it worse."

Damien grinds his jaw. She doesn't care. She's feeling punchy and her patience is at an end. She wants her memories back, and he's the only one who can help her.

The elevator dings and the doors open. Ella leads the way into their apartment. She doesn't stop until they're in the master bathroom. She toes off her shoes and kicks them out of the way. Damien peels off his shirt. He watches her strip and turn on the shower, but he doesn't say anything. Ella tests the water temperature, and he's still silent. He removes his shoes and tugs down his shorts. He stands there with his cut abs and the indents on the sides of his glutes, and she wants to forget about being pissed and have hot sweaty sex with him on top of the double vanity.

But a quickie won't resolve her frustration with him. Why won't he talk with her? What's his deal? Why is he biting his tongue?

Biting his tongue.

Ella doesn't have the chance to dwell on where she's recently heard that phrase before because Damien says her name when she steps into the shower and under the spray. Turning, she meets his gaze. It locks with hers.

"I'm sorry," he says in a heartfelt manner.

She sighs, gives him one last look of frustration, then holds out her hand.

Damien doesn't hesitate. In three short strides, he's in the shower and she's in his arms. Then he's kissing her, thoroughly, and their hands travel everywhere.

She lets him work out his stress on her. He takes her hard against the tile, then again on the bed, their skin slick and wet, their hair dripping. He drives into her with the same ferocity he had during their run. This time, he doesn't leave her behind.

When their heart rates steady and breathing evens, Damien rolls off her. He drapes an arm over his eyes.

"Damien," Ella says. "What's going on with you?"

He sighs.

"I want to help, but you have to talk to me."

"Ben emailed me." PDN's legal counselor.

Damien rolls to his side to face her. He absently touches Ella's hair, wraps a section around his finger.

"I had his team look into our client retention issues."

"What did he find out?"

"One of my employees sold our client list to CyberSeal."

"Oh, my god. That's illegal. Why would he do that?"

"You know how my dad has wanted to buy me out?"

"Yeah, and you've always said no." Ella pauses for a moment, piecing it together. "He's trying to put you out of business."

"We don't have proof he's directly involved, not yet. But yeah, it's not like this is a surprise. He's had it in for me since before I started my company." Damien drags a hand down his face. He looks and sounds tired.

Ella's never understood how a father could act toward his only son the way Clyde does with Damien. But then, Damien hasn't told her much about their relationship other than things got rocky when Damien's marriage to Anna eroded.

Damien glances at the clock over her shoulder. "I have to get into the office. Ben wants to meet."

Ella looks at the clock and swears. "I gotta get going, too."

Damien gives her hair a gentle tug. "Sorry about the run."

Ella playfully scowls at him. "Forgiven. Don't do it again."

"Promise." He kisses her.

An hour later, Ella's packing up her laptop and the voice recorder she uses for interviews when Rebecca calls.

"Have you left yet?" she asks.

"Almost out the door," Ella says, sliding her laptop into its case.

"Don't bother. I've reassigned to Jordan Talbot. She's already on her way there."

The hell? Ella goes rigid.

Jordan is a recent recruit. Rebecca lured her over from *Town & Country*. She has field experience, but she's still green in Ella's book. She reminds Ella of herself when she first started at *Luxe Avenue*.

"Why did you do that?" Ella asks, her tone measured, trying to quell her anger and panic. Did Rebecca hear about her memory loss? Does she think she's unfit for the assignment? Ella thinks back over the assignments she's had since early December. She can't pinpoint where, or if, she made a mistake that would jeopardize her position or her seniority when it came to the divvying up of assignments.

"Nathan Donovan called."

"Who?"

"You heard me. The Nathan Donovan exclusive is back on and he assured me that he's one hundred percent on board. As long as you write it."

Air leaves Ella's lungs in a rush. She slowly sits in her chair. She stares blankly out the window.

"This assignment's priority over your others. You spent so much time working on it before. Won't it be nice to see this gem in print? Hold on a sec, I've got his contact info. He wasn't sure if you still had it. Ah, here it is." Rebecca rattles off his info and Ella scrambles for a piece of paper. Can't find one. She grabs an old issue of *Luxe Avenue* from the corner of her desk and quickly scribbles Nathan's phone number and address. Truckee. Just over a three-hour drive from San Francisco, assuming the weather and roads are clear.

"He wants you to meet him at his house this time, not on some godforsaken mountain trail. I don't know how you did it, backpacking in the wilderness for five days with no running water. You're a braver woman than me, but that's why you're my best."

Ella's hand trembles. She drops the pen.

"He'll only talk to you, so don't botch this like you did last time. I'm not going to let you convince me to kill this article. Call Nathan right away. He wants to start the interview tomorrow."

Start the interview? That meant this would be a major feature. The interview would be involved, tedious. Ella broke up those assignments into several blocks over the course of a few days. Sometimes they lasted a week, depending on the subject's schedule.

"All right. I'll call first thing." She forces out the confirmation.

"Don't worry about the governor. He's in good hands with Jordan. I think it's time to toss the gal into the pool, see how she swims. Check in with me in a couple of days, let me know how it's going. Meanwhile, I'll reassign your other projects so that you can prep for tomorrow. Paul wants to run the Donovan piece in May's issue."

"Sure."

Rebecca ends the call and Ella gently, slowly, sets down her phone.

Who the hell is Nathan Donovan?

CHAPTER 9

Ella unpacks her laptop and searches *Nathan Donovan*. Pages upon pages load, and within minutes, she has his basic stats. Nathan Donovan, celebrity adventurer and star of the hit Nat Geo Wild series *Off the Grid!* Thirty-seven, separated, and father to one son, who tragically died almost a year and a half ago, right before *Off the Grid!* was canceled midseason.

Ella clicks the Images link and a mosaic of photos, from professional headshots to stills of his survival television series and blurry paparazzi photos, fills the screen. With his dark-brown hair, ice-blue eyes, and a physique carved from military training and the grueling survivalist stunts he showcased on his series, Nathan Donovan isn't hard on the eyes. He also looks like her husband. Damien's doppelgänger. Minus the military training and celebrity status, of course. Damien loves a good, long run and bench-pressing weights, but Nathan's an adrenaline junkie and thrives in the outdoors.

Wow, she thinks. It's uncanny how much they resemble each other.

Ella feels uneasy. Nathan is well known. She should have at least heard of him and his television series. She should definitely remember meeting and interviewing him.

But she has nothing. Not a single memory. Not even a faint recollection of a phone call or email, let alone an in-person interview that she apparently conducted on some godforsaken mountain trail, as Rebecca described it.

She's blocked him from her memory. Just like Simon.

Ella's gaze drifts to the office door. Across the hall is Simon's nursery. The door is still closed. She hasn't ventured into that room since early December. She did for a month, every day. She'd stand in the middle of the room, hoping the scent of the new furniture or sound of the musical mobile above the crib would jog her memory. They didn't, so she gave up on trying to remember.

Well, she's not giving up any longer. If she did, in fact, interview Nathan Donovan, she'd have files. There would be emails and a log of phone calls. Documents of research notes and uploaded recordings of the interview. But she doesn't recall his name or seeing a file with her interview notes when she looked through her computer four months ago when she'd hoped to find a document or an email that would help trigger her memories. She'd looked through so many files last November. Maybe she forgot. Frantic, she searches again. She clicks folders and skims through her bookmarks. She looks through emails, sent, trash, and draft folders. She opens her trash bin. Over and over she plugs in variations of Nathan's name. Not a single document, saved web page, or transcribed voice recording pops up.

Her phone. There has to be something. A call out or in. Certainly, she would have at least called him to confirm their interview time and location. Her log downloaded from her cloud account when Damien set up her phone.

Ella scans her calls and contacts, but she can't find a match with the number Rebecca gave her. The phone's location services are on but the history comes up empty, too, so she can't tell where she might have traveled.

It's almost as though the interview never happened.

Ella finishes her search and realizes she's shaking. Nauseous, she drops her head in her hands and takes several deep breaths to calm her queasy stomach. She's losing her mind.

Ella can't ask Rebecca about it. She might slip about her memory loss and then her editor would question whether she can pull off the Donovan interview. Nathan would retract the exclusive. Then Paul will fire her. Or worse, assign her to writing fluff pieces on Hollywood divorces and fashion faux pas.

Ella has to be the one to tell Nathan, she

reasons. He's going to find out anyhow when he realizes she has to redo the interview because she doesn't have any notes or recordings from the original. Best to tell him face-to-face. Less of a chance of him kicking her off his mountain once she's already made the trek. Either way, she fully intends to convince him to do it over. She can be very persuasive when she needs to be.

In the meantime, she needs to dig up as much information as possible about him and their original time together. Who would know?

Damien.

She calls him but is sent directly to voice mail. She hangs up without leaving a message and calls Davie.

"Ella Bella. Calling about lunch tomorrow?" she answers.

"Hey, yeah, about that. We need to reschedule. I received a new assignment and need to drive to Truckee tomorrow. What do you know about Nathan Donovan?"

"Other than the man is a god and I'm disappointed your article never ran?"

So there was an article.

"Do you know when I met with him?" she asks.

"You don't remember?"

"Uh-uh. I don't remember anything about him."

"At all? Wow." The word comes out long, spoken with incredulity. "And you're interviewing him again?"

"Yes, he called my editor this morning."

"Geez, Ella. What are you going to do? It'll be like you're meeting him all over again."

"Tell him the truth, I guess. I don't have another choice. It's an exclusive and he'll only talk to me."

"Well, for the sake of preserving your job and serving up the juicy bits us females have been dying to hear about him, I hope he doesn't mind rehashing his life story with you. You spent *a lot* of time with him."

"How much time?" Ella asks unsteadily.

"Ten days, I think."

"Ten?" Rebecca said five.

"You left right after you and Damien got back from the Maldives."

She remembers that trip. The mornings sunbathing on their private deck, afternoons snorkeling in turquoise waters, and evenings dining on succulent yellowtail kingfish. The hours spent nestled in Damien's arms or pressed underneath him. The long conversations about love and life and careers and their future, spoken in soft whispers and loud laughter under a blanket of stars or the glow of the sun. They'd been celebrating their third anniversary.

"Last June then, right?"

"Mm-hmm."

"Do you know why the article didn't run?"

"Uh-uh. You didn't tell me. But you never tell

me anything. Code of ethics, dear. I can't get anything out of you beyond what you print in your articles."

Biting into her lower lip, Ella logs into her cellular account. What if, for some reason, she deleted the calls and his contact info from her phone? Seems logical since everything else about the interview is missing. Sure enough, several lines down on her June billing statement, she finds it. One outgoing call to Nathan Donovan's number.

"How long do you think you'll be gone?" Davie asks.

"Not sure, but I've got to go." She closes the statement and logs out. "I have a full day of research ahead."

"Anything I can do to help?" she asks.

"No, but I'll let you know if something comes up."

"Okay. Oh, hey," Davie says before Ella disconnects. "My client has an art show next week. I think you'd like his work. Interested in coming?"

"Sure," Ella agrees, a little distracted as she opens various browser windows.

"Great. I'll put your name on the list."

Ella thanks Davie and ends the call. She dives into research, immersing herself in Nathan's life. She reads every article she can dredge up and binge-watches *Off the Grid!* He's masterfully skilled, athletic, agile, and borderline psychotic when it comes to the feats he designed to challenge his celebrity guests. And he's hot, with a smile to die for and an infectious laugh that Ella is far from immune to. No wonder Rebecca thinks the Nathan Donovan exclusive is a coup for *Luxe Avenue*. With *Off the Grid!*'s 65 percent female viewership, Nathan's face on the cover could be their bestselling issue in years.

But who is he for real?

What little material there is on him since the series was canceled is speculation. According to his publicist, Nathan was devastated at the loss of his son, Carson. He then, unexpectedly, canceled his series. Since then, he's been somewhat of a recluse.

How did Carson die and why did Nathan cancel *Off the Grid!* without notice?

Curious. Ella can't find a single bit of info on either topic.

It's after 9:00 p.m. when Damien gets home. Ella meets him at the door. She hangs up his suit coat and helps loosen his tie, eager to ask him what he knows about Nathan Donovan.

"I made a plate for you. I'll warm it up," she says after they kiss.

"Thanks. I'm starving." Damien removes his tie and follows Ella into the kitchen. "How was Sacramento?"

Ella puts Damien's dinner into the microwave and sets the cook time. "I didn't go. Rebecca called with a new assignment. I spent the day researching."

"That's a shame. I was looking forward to hearing about your lunch with the governor." Tossing his flash drive–laden key chain onto the counter, he sets down his briefcase, pressing his thumbs on the biometric reader. The case pops open.

"Me too. But Rebecca assigned an exclusive. It's with Nathan Donovan."

"Really?" he says, his tone mild.

If Ella hadn't been looking at Damien's hands when she said Nathan's name, she would have missed the slight hesitation as he removed his laptop.

Ella frowns. What's with the pause? Is it because of Nathan?

"I thought you killed the article," Damien says.

"It's back on. Nathan called Rebecca this morning."

"He did?" Damien removes files from his case and stacks them on the laptop. Ella catches a glimpse of one file label. ReAlign Software Inc. One of PDN's UK clients.

"Damien." She pauses until he looks at her. "I don't remember him."

His eyes darken. "Like you don't remember Simon?"

Ella nods. "Exactly like that."

The microwave dings. She removes the plate, grabs up the utensils, and sets them on the table. Steam rises from the reheated fettuccine with pesto sauce. A toasted pine nut aroma fills the kitchen. Damien doesn't join her at the table.

"Do you want wine?" she asks.

"When do you meet Donovan?"

"He wants to start the interview tomorrow." She pours herself a glass of Cabernet Sauvignon and holds up an empty glass for Damien.

He shakes his head, then his brow wrinkles.

"What is it?"

"There's been a development. I leave for London tomorrow to meet with our UK legal team. Why don't you ditch the interview and come with me? We'll catch a show."

"A show? Damien, I don't remember anything about Nathan Donovan. He didn't exist to me until Rebecca called about him this morning. I spent a week or so with this guy and I don't remember any of it. Thanks for the invite, but no, I can't go to London, not now. I need to meet with Nathan and find out what's going on with me."

"What if I asked you not to take the assignment?"

She balks. "Why would you do that?"

"Answer the question, Ella."

"No! This is my job we're talking about. I don't

tell you what companies to pitch." She flings her arm at the client files. Damien just stands there. "What is it about this guy that bothers you?"

Damien puts his files and laptop back in the case. Tosses his keys on top. A flash of red catches her attention. The drives on the ring. Two of them. Those are new. Postmiscarriage new, that is. She doesn't have the chance to think of asking about them, let alone ask. Damien slams the case closed.

Keys.

"What if Nathan's the key to fix my head?"

"Why him?"

Ella sets down the wine bottle a little too hard. "Nothing I've done has triggered my memories, no thanks to you. Why not give this Nathan guy a try? What've I got to lose?" The assignment probably. Ella inwardly cringes. Hopefully Nathan will be understanding. She also hopes he'll be more forthcoming than her husband. God, what's with him? She really doesn't understand why he's being so difficult.

Damien rubs some of the tension out of his face, then sighs. "You're right. Go. It's your job," he says.

Damn right it is, she wants to snap. But she grinds her teeth, willing herself to calm down.

"What do you know about my interview with him last summer?"

"Not much."

Ella sighs, frustrated. "I want to remember Simon," she says, wishing Damien would finally talk to her, really talk to her about all they've been through.

He slides his hands into his pant pockets. He looks at his shoes, nodding, thinking to himself. "Do me a favor," he says after a moment. "Think before you go. Ask yourself if you *really* want to remember."

She frowns. "Of course I want to. Why wouldn't I?"

He shrugs. His expression looks pained, uncertain. There's a reason he's been holding back. But for the first time in months, his reluctance gives her pause. What if whatever it is he's hiding from her—and she's sure there's something—is powerful enough to destroy their marriage?

Is she willing to lose him just to remember a baby they never planned to have?

She considers what might have happened before the accident and her gut feeling only grows stronger. They'd been arguing moments before. About what?

Or more to the point, considering his reaction to Nathan, about whom?

CHAPTER 10

Three and a Half Years Ago

Four months after they married, Ella spent one Sunday afternoon with Damien on the couch watching the Bills decimate the 49ers. On the third play into the second quarter, Kaepernick got sacked, again, and Damien kicked the coffee table, shouting at the flat screen. His beer toppled, spoiling the nachos Ella had just prepared.

"Damien!" Ella blotted the table with the few napkins before beer spilled on the area rug.

"He holds the ball too long in the pocket," Damien fumed, oblivious of the mess he made.

"You ruined the nachos." Ella got a towel from the kitchen and wiped the table dry.

"Sorry, hon." He patted her thigh, watching the replay.

Ella tossed the wadded, wet napkins on the food and took the platter into the kitchen. She dumped the nachos into the trash and dropped the platter in the sink. The earthenware cracked in two.

"Shit." That had been Aunt Kathy's.

"Everything all right?" Damien called from the great room.

"Fine," she snapped.

She picked up the pieces from the sink and blinked back tears. It had been the only dishware she'd kept of her aunt's. Maybe she could superglue the pieces together.

Later, she thought. She wasn't in the mood now. She wasn't in the mood for football either.

"I'm going to write," she announced.

"Don't you want to watch the game with me?"

The Niners were losing. They sucked this season. And her mood, for reasons she couldn't pinpoint, was foul.

"No. I have a deadline tomorrow. Watch without me. Let me know if they score." Doubtful they would.

Ella set aside the broken platter and retreated to her office. But she didn't wake up her laptop. She just sat at her desk and stared blankly at the black screen, feeling irritable and edgy. Everything Damien did today set her off. He'd sneeze and she mothered him to cover his mouth. He blew his nose and she snapped at him to wash his hands before he touched her. He'd wanted to give her a kiss. Then he had to go and ruin their nachos. If he hadn't, she wouldn't have broken Aunt Kathy's platter, the one Aunt Kathy used to serve dinner when they had company. The same one her aunt had served homemade mac and cheese on the last time Ella had had her best friend Grace spend the night.

Grace.

Ella jiggled her mouse, waking up her laptop, and looked at the date. October fourteenth. The day Grace had died.

No wonder she was in a funk.

Tears welled and Ella let them fall. She dropped her head in her arms and cried.

A short time later, Damien knocked on the door trim. "Ella?"

She lifted her head off the desk and wiped her face with her sweater sleeves.

Damien's expression transitioned from curiosity to concern. "What's wrong?" He came into the room and knelt beside her, spinning her chair so that she faced him.

Ella plucked a tissue from the box on her desk. She dabbed her eyes and blew her nose. "It's Grace."

He frowned. "Who's Grace?"

"My friend. She died." She sniffled.

"God, Ella. I'm so sorry. When? How?" He grasped one of her hands. "Are you okay?"

She shook her head, waving her free hand. "Oh, no, she died a long time ago. I'm just sad." Ella tossed the tissue in the trash and exhaled a long sigh. "She died on the fourteenth. I didn't realize the date until I just saw it."

"She sounds like someone who was very important to you." Damien's thumb absently stroked Ella's hand. "Who was she?" Damien knew so much about Ella, but she'd never told him about Grace. She never told anyone about Grace. The memories hurt too much.

"My best friend. We met when Andrew and I moved in with Aunt Kathy in Los Altos after our parents died. She was our next-door neighbor. We were both six and instant besties. She died our sophomore year. She was only fifteen."

Damien inhaled sharply. "So young. I'm sorry you lost her, Ella."

"Me too." Ella sniffed and Damien waited a beat before he asked, "Do you want to tell me about her?"

Ella shrugged.

"What's something the two of you did together?"

"Oh, I don't know. All sorts of things. Typical girl stuff, like makeup and dress up. We played house a lot when we were younger. She also liked to write. We joined the newspaper club together in high school. Umm, what else? Her dad always took us to Ghirardelli Square for ice cream sundaes. Sundaes on Sunday, he liked to say. That always made us laugh. We had fun."

Damien squeezed her hand. "How did she die?" he asked softly.

Ella felt her mood shift, growing more sullen. Guilt crept in, casting shadows over her memories.

"Grace had problems," she began. "I mean, we

all had problems, but hers got worse after her parents divorced."

Ella explained to Damien that after Grace's parents divorced, Grace, who'd been close with her father, had fallen into a depression when he moved across the country. Her parents thought Grace should stay in Los Altos with her mom. Her school was there, Ella was there, and everything else that was familiar. The less upheaval Grace endured, the better. Or so her parents had thought.

Grace had difficulty coping with the changes in her family dynamics. First there were the dark shadows under Grace's eyes that never faded. She blamed late nights up studying. Ella suspected Grace suffered from insomnia and her classes had nothing to do with those late nights. Grace wasn't studying either. Her grades were sliding.

Next came the cuts on her best friend's arm. Ella called her out about it when she noticed one day during class transition. Grace's sleeve had bunched at the elbow while she juggled a load of textbooks. On the soft, white flesh inside her left forearm, Ella spied four angry, red welts, each an inch long.

She gasped at the sight of them and grasped her friend's wrist. "What did you do?"

Grace's eyes dodged left then right as she pushed down her sleeve. She shushed Ella.

Ella wasn't having any of that nonsense. She

pulled her friend into the handicapped stall in the girls' bathroom. "Show me," she ordered.

"It's nothing. Let's go. We're going to be late for class."

Ella blocked her way. "Not until you show me your arm."

"Shush, keep your voice down. Others will hear."

Bella Fields and her princess posse had walked into the bathroom, squawking like chickens with their gossip. Through the crack in the bathroom stall, Ella peeked at them lined up before the mirror, applying thick coats of foundation and voluminous mascara to their already made-up faces.

Ella turned back to her friend. At her prodding, Grace reluctantly revealed her arms. Ella hissed, getting a closer look. The cuts weren't deep, and they'd already scabbed over. But the surrounding skin was pink and raised.

"The other one." Ella gestured for Grace's right arm.

"It's just the left," Grace murmured, embarrassed.

"Why?" Ella was scared for her friend.

"My therapist says I blame myself for my shitty life."

"Your life isn't shitty. It's just . . . different than it used to be. Before you know it, it'll be your new normal and just as awesome."

"My new normal sucks."

The bell rang.

"We have to go." Grace, eyes glazed dark and stormy, unlocked the stall door. Ella wanted to see the sun shine in her eyes again.

"Spend the night at my house," she suggested. "I'll get Aunt Kathy to whip us up her mac and cheese you love so much, then we'll binge-watch *Friends*. I've TiVo'd the whole season."

A tiny smile peeked through Grace's gloomy expression. "Sounds like fun."

"It will be." Ella hugged her friend.

Grace arrived around five. They gorged on mac and cheese and ice cream, then settled down on the couch to watch *Friends*. Around ten o'clock, long after Aunt Kathy had gone to bed, Ella's boyfriend, Mike Tate, showed up. Ella was going to send him away but Grace had followed her to the front door.

"It's okay. He can come in."

"Are you sure?" Ella asked. She didn't want to take time away from Grace. Tonight was girls' night.

Grace nodded. "I'm kind of tired. Think I'll go to bed. Okay if I take a bath first?"

"Totally." Ella led Grace upstairs. She got a towel for her friend and gave her one of her bath bombs, warm vanilla sugar. She even lit her favorite candle, avocado coconut. "I'll be up shortly, but relax. Take your time." She hugged her friend, then joined Mike on the couch.

As the bathwater ran upstairs, Ella made out with Mike. Eventually, she started to drift off to sleep, and Mike, kissing her good night, let himself out the front door. Ella woke up at 2:00 a.m. and, feeling guilty, dragged her weary body upstairs to her room, where Grace had crashed hours earlier. Ella was such a shitty friend to leave Grace alone on their girls' night. She couldn't believe she passed out on the couch. She should have sent Mike home. She was going to see him tomorrow anyways. They had plans to go see a movie.

But when Ella got to her room, Grace wasn't asleep in Ella's bed. She wasn't in the room either.

Soft light oozed from the crack under the closed bathroom door. Ella knocked softly, thinking Grace had woken and gone to the bathroom. But Grace didn't answer.

Ella tried the knob. It was locked. She called for Grace again, and when her friend still didn't answer, Ella unlocked the door with a bobby pin she found on her dresser. Ella cracked open the door and stopped short, unable to process what she was seeing.

In the bathtub lay Grace, beautiful, innocent Grace. Fully clothed and soaking in water that looked the color of wine. Ella remembered thinking that the shade wasn't the color of the bath bomb. It was too dark. Had her friend traded out the warm vanilla sugar for the Japanese cherry blossom? But then Ella saw the long, vertical slits that marred Grace's pristine forearms, and the steak knife from the kitchen. Grace's face, pale and serene, angled toward the door. And her eyes. Ella would never forget her eyes. They stared emptily at a point somewhere beyond Ella.

"Oh, my god," Damien said, bringing Ella back to him and her office. He leaned across her and yanked free a tissue. He dabbed Ella's face. "It wasn't your fault, Ella. I hope these tears aren't because you blame yourself."

"I don't, other than wishing I'd sent Mike away. Maybe then Grace wouldn't have gone through with it."

"Maybe not, but she probably would have another time. It's tragic, but it's not your fault."

"I know it's not. It's Stan's. Grace's father," she added when Damien frowned.

"What does he have to do with it?"

"He had an affair early in his marriage to Grace's mom. He never told her, but I guess it festered, and he finally confessed ten years after the fact. If he hadn't, her parents never would have divorced, and Grace would still be alive. His honesty killed my best friend."

Damien's mouth pressed flat. Ella knew he was trying to reason through what she'd said. He'd look for flaws, then challenge her. But he only exhaled roughly and stood. "Grab your coat."

"Where are we going?" she asked, taking the hand he offered.

"You'll see."

"What about the game?"

"Not important. You are."

Damien took her to Ghirardelli Square, where he ordered a hot fudge sundae to share. He told her jokes and tried to spoon-feed her ice cream, only to smear fudge on her nose. She laughed, and she cried, and it felt good.

"Thanks. I needed this," she said when they'd finished.

"You're welcome."

"It's Sunday," she said with a sad smile. "Sundaes on Sunday. You always know how to make me happy."

"I try." He smiled and she kissed him.

"I'm happy with you."

"Good. That's all I want. And your love. That would be cool to have, too." The corner of his mouth lifted into a lopsided grin.

"You've got it. All of it."

CHAPTER 11

Late the following day after she received Rebecca's call about the Nathan Donovan assignment, Ella arrives at his house, a large A-frame off a private, narrow road on the outskirts of Truckee, a vibrant Lake Tahoe ski community that is part old Wild West and part filthy-rich winter playground populated with Silicon Valley multimillionaires and extreme athletes. Beyond Nathan's house is a view that would be the envy of anyone who loved the mountains. A horizon of snowcapped granite giants sleep majestically in the waning sunlight.

Ella cuts the engine and pushes her arms into the sleeves of her olive-green quilted coat. She unfolds from the car and inhales deeply. Crisp, cold mountain air burns her nostrils and fills her lungs. A breeze rustles through the trees. Aspen leaves dance and pine needles whistle. She rubs her hands together, and bundling her coat tight around her, she shakes off the nervous energy. Nathan knows things about her that she doesn't. It's disconcerting. A feeling she's not accustomed to when going into an interview. Again, she hopes he'll be more forthcoming than Damien. She wants to get over the interview and on with her life.

She approaches the house, mounts the porch steps, and rings the doorbell. She waits. And then waits. A minute or so later, she rings again, following it up with a knock on the solid wood door. From somewhere deep in the belly of the house, dogs bark.

Is he home?

She looks around. One of the three garage doors is open. Parked inside is a black Chevy truck. Maybe he's out back.

Ella follows the deck around the house to the back and stops short, startled. The view is breathtaking, unexpected. So is the man leaning against the railing. She should have anticipated him, but seeing him lounging there, staring off over the canyon below, uncaring that he's expecting a guest and not greeting her at the door, is unnerving. He drinks from a steaming mug, either unaware she's there or choosing to ignore her.

A board creaks under her boot. He jerks his head in her direction. Recognition sparks in his eyes. Caught off guard, Ella rocks back a step but quickly chastises herself. She may not know him, but he knows her. She solidly plants her feet and smiles.

Nathan smiles back, his teeth bright against a jaw dusted with a week's worth of growth. He straightens to his full height. He's taller than she anticipated, and her gaze drops to the heavy boots he wears, the soles an inch or so thick.

His mountain man outfit of jeans and a flannel shirt, unbuttoned over a graphic navy T-shirt with the Heavenly Ski Resort logo, tells Ella he's acclimated to the cooler climate. He's not wearing a coat and she's shivering in hers.

"Hi, Ella." His voice rolls over her, deeper and richer than the one she heard over the phone or in his *Off the Grid!* episodes.

Unsure if she should wave at him or hug him, Ella approaches and thrusts out her hand. "Nathan Donovan? Ella Skye. I know we've met but—"

She stalls when his gaze falls to her hand, then slowly rises to lock on to her face. He frowns, and a short laugh erupts from him. It tells her exactly how ridiculous her greeting seems to him. So formal.

"But," she presses on, "there's something you should know. I had an accident last November and suffered some memory loss."

"This is a joke, right?" The corner of his mouth twitches. There's a glint in his eyes. He eases in on her, head angled to the side, looking at her curiously, and for a split second she thinks he's going to kiss her. She also thinks he believes she's messing with him.

With a pounding heart, she holds up her hands. "I'm afraid it's not. I'm also afraid we have to start from scratch. I don't remember much from our time together before."

"You're serious." He frowns. "How much is much?"

She glances at the trees beyond the deck and back. "Anything."

His eyes go wide. "Anything?" He chokes out the word.

"But," she rushes to explain, "I promise our time together won't be wasted. It won't take nearly as long as it did last time, I'm sure of it. You know me, and I bet you're comfortable talking with me, that's why you asked for me specifically. You want to tell me your story, and we both want to share it with your audience and *Luxe Avenue*'s readers. I'll do it justice, I promise."

His laughter is gone. His nostrils flare, and a muscle throbs in his cheek as he clamps his jaw. He looks away from her, taking in the snowcapped mountains. Shadows elongate with the setting sun. She notices his white-knuckle grip on the handle of his mug when he turns back and glares at her.

"This won't work."

She blinks. "What won't work?"

"The interview."

"Why not?"

"Sorry you drove all the way up here. There's a hotel in town if you don't want to drive back tonight."

He puts down the mug and abruptly walks off.

What the hell?

Okay, she anticipated she'd have to do some negotiating, but the cold shoulder he gave her? She didn't foresee that.

Her fault. She barely gave the guy a chance to say hello before she blurted everything. Nerves kept her yapping.

Nice going, Skye. Rookie move.

But reluctant subjects aren't foreign territory. She's handled them before and Nathan isn't any different. Patience and some word finesse, that's all it should take. She's got to appeal to him on a level he'll understand.

Ella follows Nathan toward the front of the house. She calls his name. "Wait up."

He turns around, walking backward, hands up to ward her off. "I told you. I changed my mind. We're not doing this."

"Why not?" she pushes. "You called us. You asked for me. You insisted I meet you here."

"We spent two weeks together last time. I don't have time to start over." He bounds down the steps. Long, determined strides take him toward the open garage. Gravel crunches under his boots.

Two weeks? She thought they'd spent ten days together. Where did those extra days come from? What did they do?

"Give me five days," she negotiates, falling into step beside him. "That's all I need."

"I leave for Alaska in three."

131

"I'll go with."

He laughs. "Nope. Not happening."

"Why not? Tell me where you're staying and I'll make the arrangements. Give me two hours a day, three max. That's all I ask. Outside of that, you won't even notice I'm there."

"I'd notice. And I'm heli-skiing. Your weight alone mandates that I make plan adjustments."

"I don't expect to go skiing with you," she says, trying not to bristle over his weight comment. Obviously, it has something to do with the helicopter. She isn't carrying any extra weight since she last saw Nathan. In fact, she might weigh less. Exercise shed the pregnancy weight. Stress and anxiety over the memory loss dropped a few more pounds.

"I'll wait at the lodge until you're done," she proposes, far from ready to give up.

He laughs again. "You, wait? Doubtful. Look, El"—he stops and turns to her—"this interview isn't going to happen. I told you everything already. Do you really expect me to relive it?"

Ella's face falls. "I'm sorry. If you'd just—"

"I won't go through this again. I shouldn't have read that email from Rebecca's assistant and called her."

"Is this because of my amnesia?"

"I thought—" He cuts off, looks at the sky.

"You thought what?"

"It's getting dark. You should leave." Long

legs carry him across the front yard to where the house meets the adjoining garage.

"You wouldn't have insisted I do the interview if we didn't already have a connection," she calls after him. "You wouldn't have reached out to Rebecca and offered the exclusive—again, I might add—if you didn't have something to say."

"Good night, Ella. Go home," he shoots back over his shoulder, not breaking his stride.

"I lost my son, too."

Nathan stops.

"I was five months pregnant when an Escalade T-boned my Range Rover. The impact pushed my car into a telephone pole and ruptured the placenta. I survived, fortunately, but my baby was dead by the time I arrived at the hospital. I had an emergency C-section. That's the story I've been told. I also had to read about it in the police report and my medical records. Do you know why?"

Nathan slowly turns around.

"Five days after my accident I lost my memory. Not all of it, just some, like the parts about the car accident and my pregnancy. And you. I can't remember you. Why is that?"

"I don't know," he says quietly, walking back to her.

"Do you know what I want most?" she asks, tapping her chest. "I want to mourn the loss of my baby, but I can't remember him. I can't remember what it feels like to have him growing inside me. Do you know what happens when you can't remember having something? You don't miss it. I haven't been able to grieve, not the way I should. Not the way I want to. And god, the guilt. I can't begin to describe the guilt." She pauses, remembering she's the one who got into the car. She's the one who didn't pay attention when she crossed the intersection. Tears surface, burning her eyes and throat.

"El." Nathan takes a step forward, reaches for her.

She holds up a hand to ward him off. She didn't mean to share this much with him, but once she started talking, she couldn't stop. She's been wanting to talk for months, but Damien hasn't been willing. And goddamn it, she just wants to talk it out. To, once and for all, grieve.

Ella wipes her tears with her jacket sleeve. "I know my miscarriage can't compare on any level to what you've been through."

"Don't discount your own experience," Nathan says.

Ella nods, looking at her boots.

"Ella? Look at me."

She does, and she notices he, too, looks ready to cry. He's not immune to her story. He opens his mouth, ready to say something, but Ella stops him.

"Please, let me finish. Miscarrying at twenty-one weeks is awful. But losing a nine-year-old child? Someone you've read bedtime stories to and made peanut butter and jelly sandwiches for, kissed good night and held his hand? I can't imagine that."

Nathan's lips press into a tight line.

"I know you've been grieving, Nathan, and I know about the guilt. You believe you could have done things differently and he'd still be alive. Because that's how I feel every single day."

He shifts, takes a step back.

"I bet you haven't talked to anyone about Carson except me. You live up here like a recluse and avoid the public like the plague. Has anyone visited you? Do you allow anyone to visit?"

"That's not your concern."

"Isn't it, though? *You* invited me here. *You* wanted to see me. *You* want me to write about you."

"I wanted you to come because I wanted to finish what we started, not start over."

Ella unconsciously steps back. This isn't just about an interview. There's so much more going on in this conversation that isn't registering with her. What exactly happened between them?

She'll speculate on that later. Right now, she needs to nail down Nathan's commitment and get his help in return.

"What's wrong with starting over?" She takes a step forward. Then another. "You called for me and I'm here. Talk to me. About you, Carson, whatever you want. Because if you don't, your son's death will eat at you until there's nothing but an empty shell." It's been happening to Damien. It almost happened to her after her parents, after Grace. "Maybe talking and spending time together will help me remember the first interview. Maybe it'll help me get my other memories back, too. So what do you say? Let's help each other."

Nathan doesn't answer. His expression is unreadable.

Ella looks at the sky. It's almost dark and the wind has picked up. It's up to him now. She prays he's game to take another chance on her.

When he doesn't say anything right away, Ella purses her lips and slowly nods. Okay, she tried. Hopefully Paul won't fire her.

"I'm staying at the Ponderosa Lodge in Truckee," she says. "I won't check out until noon. Sleep on my offer. Call me in the morning if you change your mind." She watches him for a moment, then turns to walk to her car.

"All right, I'll do it."

"You will?" She turns back to him and grins, her smile broad and bright. "You won't regret it, I promise." She opens the passenger side door and reaches for the bag with her voice recorder and notes.

"One condition." He holds up a finger, stopping

her. "You're not coming to Alaska. We'll cover everything in two days, starting tomorrow morning."

"Why not now?" Two days wouldn't be enough time to finish the feature or to get to the bottom of her amnesia.

"I'm not in the mood. Meet me here at eight in the morning." He turns and retreats into the garage.

Ella raises her hands in exasperation, tempted to run after him. But he's already in the garage and tinkering with god knows what, so reluctantly she shuts the passenger door. She doesn't like that he's making her wait until tomorrow, but at least he changed his mind.

Ella folds into the driver's seat and shuts the door. Tomorrow she'll worry about negotiating more time with him. Meanwhile, her mind reels back over their conversation, picking it apart as she tugs off her gloves and pushes the ignition button. Turning the car around, she thinks about the man she just met. The man who apparently knows her better than she initially thought.

He said they spent two weeks together. Why had Damien and Rebecca told her otherwise?

He called her El. Only Damien does that, and she isn't sure how that makes her feel.

His eyes teared up when she told him about her accident. Her story hit a chord. Ella could have sworn he wanted to hold her, offer comfort.

"Who are you, Nathan Donovan?"

And what role does he play in her memory loss?

Glancing in the rearview mirror, her skin prickles as an eerie sensation, something akin to déjà vu, falls over her. Nathan stands in the middle of the driveway, arms at his sides, watching her.

Ella picks up dinner and checks into the lodge. It's after 7:30 p.m. when she settles in. She wants to call Damien, but his flight doesn't land in Heathrow until after 2:00 a.m. her time. She texts instead, requesting that he call her when he gets to their flat. She wants his confirmation about the time she spent with Nathan last summer. Fourteen days on one assignment is a long time. One would think she was working on a biography, not a ten-thousand-word article.

Her conversation with Nathan left her bewildered and his familiarity with her uneasy. The sooner she can finish the interview and question Nathan about last summer, the sooner she can join Damien in London. He doesn't expect to be home for a couple of weeks, what with the investigation, so she promised this morning she'd meet him there after her assignment.

She already misses her husband, the deep timbre of his voice and the warmth of his body.

She misses the way he was before her accident. The little things he'd do to show that he loved her. The phone call in the middle of the afternoon because he wanted to hear her voice, make her laugh as he told her a silly story about something that happened at work. The coffee mug and stainless steel filter he'd leave on the counter for her pour-over coffee after he left for the day on those mornings she slept in. The bunches of daisies he'd buy on a whim as he passed the floral cart on his walk home at the end of the day. Or the way he'd look at her when they went out, as though he couldn't believe she was there with him. Or that she stayed, as he asked of her that first morning together and other mornings since.

Of course she'd stayed that first time. She was already falling in love with him. And she's so in love with him right now, despite their tragedy and lack of communication.

They'll get through this. She knows they will. Their love is strong. They are a team.

Setting aside her phone, Ella boots up her laptop and pores over the notes she wrote yesterday about Nathan, reorganizing. They have a lot of ground to cover tomorrow from his youth to his marriage to Stephanie. For the more involved lifestyle pieces, Ella likes to understand how her subjects tick, and to do that, she has to delve into their childhood.

CHAPTER 12

Ella wakes at 6:00 a.m. more tired than she felt before going to bed. The altitude does that to her. It always takes a day or two to acclimate.

She yawns and stretches, then gets out of bed. After a quick shower and a stop at the café across from the lodge, where she picks up a coffee and breakfast sandwich, chugging a Red Bull along with, Ella arrives at Nathan's promptly at 8:00 a.m. Pulling to a stop in his drive, she cuts the engine. Two large dogs charge the car. Rising up on their hind legs, they peek in her window and, seeing Ella, start barking. Madly.

Ella's heart lodges in her throat. She eases down the window a few inches and yells, "Sit!"

Her command doesn't do squat. If anything, it aggravates them. Spittle foams at their mouths.

Lovely. She's the red shirt ensign in a *Star Trek* episode. An extra in *Cujo*. She's going to die.

Scanning the yard, she searches for their owner. Where *is* Nathan?

She goes to dial his number only to notice the lack of bars on her phone. No cell service. Wonderful.

A whistle pierces her ear. Furry heads rotate on shoulders and large, triangular ears angle forward. To Ella's relief, Nathan's first line of defense lopes back to the house, stopping at Nathan's feet, where he stands on the porch watching Ella. A big, shit-eating grin lights up his face. Ella's face, on the other hand, is white, completely void of blood, which pools in her feet.

Scowling, she gets out of the car and slams the door. "Don't even try scaring me off. I'm not leaving."

"I didn't expect you would."

The dogs whine at Nathan's feet. Tails wagging, their eyes lock on her.

Her pulse beats in her throat. She keeps her hand on the door handle, ready to dive back into the car if they charge her again. "Do you have them under control?"

"Yep."

"Then what's their problem?" Those dogs need to calm down.

"They're excited to see you. It's been a while."

She presses back against her car. "I've met your dogs?"

"You love my dogs. Come inside." He waves her over. "I have coffee ready."

Taking a deep breath, she grabs her things from the car and approaches the dogs. She lets them sniff her hand. They look up at her with dopey eyes and toothy smiles. She pats their heads and scratches behind their ears, and that's it. They're done with her. She's old news. Following their noses, they wander off the porch, sniffing a trail on the ground.

"What breed are they?"

"Malamute. The big one over there is Fred and the other guy is Bing."

"Let me guess, you like big band music."

He takes offense. "I like the classics, you know that."

"I don't remember. Sorry," she says, and she means it. The next couple of days will be a trial for them both.

Nathan drags his hands over his jaw. "No, I'm sorry. I assume you remember stuff, and . . ."

"And what?" she prompts when his voice stalls.

He lets his arms fall. "It's not going to be easy talking about this again."

"You mean talking about your son?"

He nods. "I didn't expect to rehash everything. I figured we'd pick up where we left off. Wrap things up. Be patient with me?"

"One condition," she offers, repeating his words from yesterday. "You're patient with me. Pretend we just met."

"That's two conditions."

She rolls her eyes. "Okay. Two conditions."

"I can live with that."

She shares his smile and he opens the front door, inviting her inside. Fred and Bing follow.

"For the record," he says when she crosses the threshold, "I do like big band music. And

Elvis, and the Beatles, Rolling Stones, Hendrix, Steppenwolf, the Doors. In case you want to make me a playlist or something."

Ella smiles. He's funny, though his humor is a tad dry. Letting his dogs loose on her hadn't been coincidence or an accident.

She takes in Nathan's house. High above, an open beam ceiling angles upward. The living, dining, and kitchen areas, decorated in natural materials and neutral tones, share one space on the main level. Stairs lead up to an open loft that faces the canyon and next mountainous rise. She can see a desk and computer monitor and feels a little comfort that she's not completely off the grid. She bets he has Wi-Fi. She'll have to ask him for the password. Another set of stairs leads down to what Ella assumes are the bedrooms.

The house is well crafted, the design impressive. But the most stunning aspect is the view outside the A-shaped patchwork of windows that bookend a stone fireplace, the flue yawning skyward through the ceiling.

Beyond the windows, a crystal-blue, cloudless sky bathes snow-drenched mountains. White firs and Jeffrey pines freckle the landscape. Being late March, the snowpack has melted in spots, exposing dirt and granite underneath, but for the most part, the mountains are still a winter wonderland.

"Your home is beautiful," Ella says, joining Nathan in the kitchen area.

"Thanks," he says, working an espresso machine.

"That's a fancy coffee maker for a guy who prefers cooking over campfires."

His brow lifts. "You do remember something about me."

"No such luck. I read it in *Outside*."

"Here I thought my charismatic personality brought it all back to you." Ella's lip quirks and Nathan smiles. "As for the coffee"—he turns a dial and steamed milk pours into a mug—"I take it seriously." He nods in the direction of the table. "Have a seat."

Ella drops her bag on the table, removes her laptop and voice recorder, and sits. Nathan brings over a steaming mug. He didn't ask Ella how she takes her coffee when she has a fancy option, but one sip of the vanilla latte tells her it's perfect. Exactly as she would have requested.

Because he knows her.

"Thank you," Ella murmurs. She clears her throat, calling on her willpower to keep her hands from trembling. She doesn't want Nathan to see her nerves. But he probably already senses her unease. He's a guy who relies on his instincts for survival, and he's had a lifetime to hone his. He detects nuances others don't pick up. And from the way he's studying her, he's picking up on something.

Ella pushes out a breath and gives him a reassuring smile. But he doesn't join her at the table. He leans back against the counter, ankles crossed and left hand tucked into his pants' front pocket. He drinks his coffee and continues to watch her.

"So . . . how do you want to do this?" she asks. "Sit here or over there?" She gestures at the L-shaped leather couch. It's deep, sturdy, and well worn. A perfect fit within the home's aesthetics.

"Outside," he says.

"Outside?" Ella glances out the windows behind her. It's cold out there. Is he crazy?

"I thought we'd go for a hike."

In the snow? He's certifiably insane.

Of course his dogs don't share Ella's sentiment, clearly knowing the word *hike* the way a city dog would know the word *walk*. Sitting by the front door, they whine, excited, tails thumping, front paws prancing. Bing picks up his water pack and gives it a good shake. Another water pack, Fred's, rests against a compact backpack. Nathan has everything set and ready to go.

"There's snow." Ella states the obvious.

"Yeah," he remarks like it's no big deal. "The trail's relatively flat and the snow's worn down. We'll be fine. The dogs and I hiked it the other day."

She stares at him. "You're serious about this?"

"Completely."

"I—I'm not dressed to hike," she sputters. Any other day and under any other circumstance, she'd be game for an adventure. But up here, she's isolated with a man she has a shared history with. What if she ticked him off last summer and he plans to push her off a cliff?

Don't be ridiculous, El.

She imagines Damien laughing at her, shaking his head. He'd then kiss her and reassure her she has nothing to worry about. People know she's here. Nathan wouldn't do something stupid, not when she's the one he invited up here to help him. He wants an article in *Luxe Avenue* specifically, not *Outside,* a more logical choice given his audience. Ella intends to find out why.

Nathan eyes her attire: turtleneck sweater, skinny jeans, and calf-high leather boots. "Hold on a second." He crosses the expansive room and goes downstairs.

Ella looks at the dogs. "Is he always like this?" Going places and doing things? She doubts she can convince him to sit still for the length of time she anticipates for their chats.

Fred lets out a yelp. Bing shimmies closer to the door so that his side is plastered to the wood like Velcro. His jaw clamps on to his water pack.

"Guess that's a yes."

Ella packs up her laptop and slips the recorder

into her pocket. Today's interview will be conducted on the go.

Nathan returns. He sets a pile of folded clothes and a jacket on the table in front of her. Drops a pair of hiking boots at her feet. Ella peeks at the size on the hiking pants and her stomach turns over. She doesn't have to look at the number inside the boots to know they're an eight-and-a-half. She can just tell. She also knows Nathan's wife is petite. These items don't belong to Stephanie Donovan.

Her heart knocks against her chest. Her hands grow clammy.

"It isn't coincidence that these are my size, is it?" she asks, keeping her tone steady.

"Nope. They're yours."

CHAPTER 13

"Mine?"

Ella sits there and stares dumbly at the clothes. She doesn't recognize them. She doesn't remember purchasing or wearing them. The feeling is similar to what she felt several months back when she boxed her maternity clothes and put them in storage. It's as though they belong to someone else.

"You took them backpacking and then left them with me," Nathan says, nodding toward the clothes and boots. "You wanted to keep them here, just in case."

Just in case of what? Ella lifts the pants to look at the long-sleeved white hiking shirt underneath. Not only did they hike together, but they clearly shopped for this outfit. How comfortable had they been with each other?

"Come on, we're wasting daylight." Nathan claps loudly. The sound echoes off the high walls. "Ready, boys?"

Fred and Bing bark enthusiastically.

"You can change in the bathroom. It's over . . . there." He points past the staircase and takes a second glance at her. "Hey, you okay?"

She looks at him, then presses her abdomen to settle her nerves. Nathan's gaze drops to her hand. He swears.

"I'm sorry. I wasn't thinking." Concern softens his features. He gestures at her midriff. "Can you hike?"

She frowns. "What?"

"It's an easy hike. Slight incline. Shouldn't be too strenuous considering you . . . um. Your . . ." He draws a line across his pelvis.

She realizes she's holding her hand directly over her scar. "Oh." She's been running up to eight miles four days a week for almost two months. She's conditioned, but of course Nathan doesn't know that. She lets her hand slide away. "I'll be fine."

"Then what's wrong?"

"The clothes. They caught me by surprise. I don't remember them or your house."

He nods. "We'll take it slow. You aren't acclimated. The dogs and I usually make it there and back in just under three hours. There's a spot I want to show you. We can talk there and have lunch before we head back."

Ella picks up the clothes and boots. Looks like they're going for a hike. "I'll be right back."

"Take your time. I have to get the dogs ready."

In the bathroom, Ella quickly changes. She wants to call Damien, check in with him. He said before she left that he didn't know much about the interview, which is understandable. Ella wouldn't have gone into specifics about what she and Nathan discussed. Everything's confidential until it goes to print. But what about everything else they did together? Would Damien know for how long they hiked and where? What about what she and Nathan did after? Ella can't imagine she'd spent the entire fourteen days on the trail. She's all for being adventurous, but two weeks without a shower and a good meal is extreme even for her.

Ella pulls out her phone, then remembers she doesn't have cell service. Without Nathan's Wi-Fi password, she can't even use FaceTime audio. She looks at the time and does a quick calculation. It's early evening in London. Has Damien tried to reach her since she left the hotel?

She knows he's upset she took the assignment. Over coffee yesterday morning, Damien admitted he was finally ready to talk, just come to London with him. Ella wants to talk with him, desperately so, but it upsets her that it took an assignment from *Luxe Avenue* to make it happen. Almost as if he'd been backed into a corner and had no choice.

Whatever motivated him, whether the interview with Nathan or Damien finally working through his issues with a vigorous workout, Ella had no choice but to meet with Nathan. Only he knows exactly what happened between them when they were on the trail. Ella also has to consider her job. Rebecca's counting on her, and Paul is breathing down Rebecca's neck. She had to come to Truckee.

Nathan is inspecting his daypack when Ella joins him by the front door. He's packed food, water, and emergency supplies.

"Never hike in an isolated area without a compass, SAT radio, medical kit, and a flashlight with a fresh set of batteries," he instructs her like he would one of his celebrity guests on *Off the Grid!* "I also pack foil rescue blankets. You wouldn't believe how easy it is to get lost up here. Something can go wrong like that"—he snaps his fingers—"and no one would know."

"You aren't going to off me or something, are you?" She laughs nervously, slipping on her gloves.

He zips up a pocket and shoulders the pack. "Don't worry. You're in capable hands."

Strong, wide hands with a dusting of dark hair, she notices. Hands that can do any number of things. She quickly glances away, self-conscious of her reaction. Yeah, he's hot, but to get hot and bothered from just looking at his hands?

Not cool, Skye.

Nathan opens the door. Fred and Bing, water packs strapped to their backs, bound outside and round the house. Habit tells them the direction they're headed.

The trail, a slim path that winds through the trees, starts at the edge of Nathan's property and steadily climbs in elevation. The dogs run ahead, pausing every so often to sniff a rock or tree trunk. They walk for over an hour, Ella behind Nathan, their conversation minimal. The narrow trail makes carrying on a conversation difficult, to Ella's frustration, since they can't walk side by side. She tries not to think about how they're wasting valuable time.

Nathan keeps up a manageable pace, hands gripping the daypack's shoulder straps. He wears a wool beanie pulled over his ears. Dark hair, longer than the cropped cut he had on TV, curls up from underneath the cap's edge. He glances at the sky and inhales deeply through his nose. He visibly relaxes with each breath.

"You're in your element up here."

"I can't stand being indoors when the sky's this blue."

"Which has me wondering. Why *Luxe Avenue*? Isn't *Outside* a more suitable audience for you?"

He glances at her over his shoulder. "Déjà vu."

"What?"

"You asked the same question last time."

She steps over a fallen branch, the needles brown and brittle. "Every question I ask will probably be the same. Remember, patience."

"I know. Trying." He whistles for the dogs. They've put some distance between them, antsy to run and most likely used to Nathan hiking faster. They lope back in their direction.

The sun rises higher, burns brighter. Light reflects off the snow. Ella feels the cool heat on her cheeks. It stings like dry ice.

"Do you have sunscreen?" she asks.

He stops midstride and Ella bumps into his back with a grunt. "Sorry about that." He grins and she smiles back.

"Sunscreen's in the small pocket." He points over his shoulder.

Ella fishes out a sunscreen stick. She rubs it around her face and offers it to Nathan. He drags the wax stick across his brow and down his nose, capping the tube and handing it back to Ella.

"Women made up over sixty percent of *Off the Grid!*'s audience," Nathan comments as Ella zips up the pack.

"Are you expecting to reach the same audience through *Luxe Avenue*? What about the men? Thirty-five percent is a large chunk to ignore."

"I don't care about the men. Frankly, I couldn't care less about the female audience." Nathan resumes walking. "*Luxe Avenue* is Stephanie's favorite. She reads it religiously, cover to cover. Always has."

"You're hoping your wife reads the article. Why?" Ella asks when another thought occurs to her from her research. Nathan and Stephanie have been separated since before Carson's death. She jogs to catch up. "Hey, Nathan, when was the last time you spoke with her?"

Nathan stops abruptly. Ella steps off to the side to avoid running into him again and bumps into a tree instead. "Oomph." She rubs her shoulder.

Nathan points off to the right. "Look."

She does. Through the trees, the mountainside drops into the wide topaz-blue sky. Above them, jet streams crisscross the flat blue atmosphere like a tic-tac-toe game. All around them, tree bark creaks, expanding in the sun. A bird of prey swoops and dives like a Cirque du Soleil acrobat. "Wow."

"It's incredible." He grins broadly. "Never gets old."

"I can imagine."

"The view's even better where we stop for lunch. That's what I want to show you. We should be there within the hour."

"How long have you lived here?"

"I bought the place several years back as a vacation retreat. Moved here permanently when Steph left." He reaches for a water bottle. "Drink?"

"Yes, thanks." She drinks some, then Nathan takes his share, sliding the canister back into the pack's side pocket.

"What were you like as a kid?" she asks when they resume their hike, choosing to wait until later to delve into his reasons for using *Luxe*. "Were you always like that guy we see on *Off the Grid!*?"

"How would you describe that guy?"

"An adrenaline junkie. Lives life at maximum speed. He doesn't fear death."

"Wrong. He fears not living. Look around." He gestures at the surrounding scenery. They're walking amid a pine forest blanketed in snow. "Does this look like life at maximum speed?"

It looks like a guy hiding. Hibernating from the public, which isn't living. But she doesn't tell him what she thinks. She wants to keep him talking to the point where he feels comfortable doing so. It'll be easier when she delves into the more difficult topic of his son. By then he should feel at ease with her. Again, she assumes. So she starts with a more neutral subject, his parents. Besides, she wants to understand who he was as a kid. What shaped Nathan into the man he is now? Someone willing to perform extreme feats in front of a camera and have them broadcast worldwide.

"Tell me about your parents. I read that your dad was an army captain," she begins.

"He was. He's the reason I served in the Special Forces a few years after college. As a kid, we moved around a lot. I get attached to land easier than people. Anytime we moved, I could count on Mother Nature being there."

Poetic words for a rough-around-the-edges man.

Ella studies him. His strong shoulders and

masculine hands. Workman's hands. His long legs and rugged good looks, which, she admits, she isn't immune to. His presence is compelling, and from what she saw of his survival series, he relishes being the center of attention. Like Damien, Nathan is partial to control. He must have derived those traits from his military father.

"What was it like growing up with them?" She read that his father, George Donovan, passed away five years previous. Massive heart attack. His mother, Rae, retired to San Diego.

"They did their best to make every home we moved to feel like a castle, even if it was military housing the size of a shoebox. Anytime Dad got leave, he and my mom would pull my sister, Heather, and me from school. We'd pile into Dad's Wagoneer. No destination or care in the world. We'd just go."

"That's spontaneous. Your mom didn't mind?" Ella thinks of her parents. Aside from day trips to the beach or museums, they never went on a *real* vacation, the kind where you pack a suitcase and travel somewhere for an extended stay. There was never enough money. She also can't picture her mother roughing it outdoors. From what Ella recalls of her limited memory of her, her mother liked her fingernails polished and heels high.

Aunt Kathy did take her and Andrew to Disneyland a few times, but then her aunt got too sick to travel. Ella feels like she missed out on that part of childhood. It's one of the reasons she loves traveling with Damien and for her job. Aside from her semester in Germany, she never had the opportunity to go places until she graduated from college and started her career.

Should she be fortunate enough to have kids again with Damien, she'll take every opportunity she can to show their child the world.

"My mom was just as adventurous as my dad. Sometimes more so," Nathan explains. "My grandparents homeschooled her. They raised her in a lakeside cabin in Alabama without electricity or running water."

"She sounds hard-core."

"She is. She was the one who took us camping when my dad couldn't get away. One time she pulled off the highway onto a dirt road. We bumped along for what had to be a mile or so before she parked the car and announced that this was where we were going to spend the night."

"In the middle of nowhere?"

"In the middle of nowhere," Nathan echoes. "Heather and I grabbed the gear and my mom hiked us several hundred yards through the woods until she found a spot to set up camp. The night was warm, the sky gorgeous. We didn't bother with tents and slept beside the campfire. It was perfect until I woke up at two a.m. with a shotgun in my face. I about shit my pants."

"Whoa." Her eyes bug out. "What did you do?"

"Nothing, not right away. I was too scared to move. This guy was huge, with a full beard. He nudged my mom's foot and woke up her and Heather. He ordered us to douse the fire and pack up. Then he followed us to the car and waited until we left."

"You're lucky that's all he did."

"No kidding." He laughs at the memory. "I think half the places she found for us to camp out were on private property. That's the only time we got caught, though."

"Your mother's a daring woman. She met your dad at Tulane?" She recalls his Wikipedia page.

"Yep." He holds back an errant branch so that Ella can pass without the needles scratching her face.

"How would you describe their relationship?"

"Perfect."

"Come on." She shoots his back a dubious look. Nobody's relationship is perfect. "For real?"

"In their case, yes. My parents were as hot and cold as the next couple. But they were a perfect match for each other, which is why they worked." His tone echoes of nostalgia and a trace of disappointment. He envied his parents.

"Were you looking for something similar with Stephanie?"

The trail widens and Nathan falls into step beside Ella. He sighs. "Steph found being married to me 'taxing.' Her description, not mine."

"So you stressed her out?" Ella asks, trying to understand.

"Yep."

Ella can see that. She'd worry, too, if Damien jumped out of planes on a regular basis. "Is that why she left you?"

He stops and slips off his pack, sets it on the ground. Rubbing the scruff on his jaw with both hands, he takes an unsteady breath.

"Everything all right?" she asks, concerned, only to realize her question about Steph leaving him was tactless. With any other celebrity, she'd ask without thinking twice. She couldn't care less how she phrased the question as long as it got the answer she needed. But Nathan has clearly been wounded by the separation, so much so that he thinks the only way he can appeal to his wife is through a magazine article.

Nice going, Skye.

She reminds herself to be more sensitive.

"Yeah, I'm fine," he replies, then gestures at the view, which seems endless. From their vantage point, she can see granite peaks reaching for the blue heavens.

"Is this what you wanted to show me?"

He takes a beat, then looks down at her, his eyes intense. "I've been wanting to show you this since the day we met."

CHAPTER 14

I've been wanting to show you this since the day we met.

He murmured the words, but they'd been spoken with an air of wonder, as if he couldn't believe she's there with him.

You only said something like that, in that way, when the person meant something to you.

Nathan nudges her. "You've got that spooked look. Relax, Skye. It's not a big deal."

But her being here seems like a big deal to him. Her heart beats a little faster as he looks at her. Then he turns and calls over the dogs. They obediently sit at his feet, panting, tongues lolling.

"There're snacks in my pack. Help yourself," he tells her.

At the mention of food, her stomach grumbles. She feels light-headed. She can't tell if it's from hunger, the altitude, Nathan's comment, or her interpretation of its meaning. Maybe a little bit of all four.

She searches his daypack, finding a bag of trail mix and a couple of apples. She takes them out and settles on a flat granite boulder while Nathan sets up the dogs with their water. He's downplaying the comment, Ella thinks. This is one of his favorite spots to think, he told her earlier as they hiked. She can see why, with a view like this, so broad and blue that when she squints her eyes, she can imagine she sees the curvature of the earth. She doubts Nathan's brought anyone else here. So who is she to him?

A gust of wind pushes up from the canyon below, raising goose bumps across Ella's arms. She worked up a sweat during their hike and had removed her jacket, tying it around her waist. She puts it back on.

"Cold?" Nathan asks, settling beside her.

"I'll be fine now." She zips up the jacket and gives him an apple. "Thanks for the snacks."

"You doing okay? The hike wasn't too much?" His gaze roams over her.

She shakes her head. "It wasn't too bad." She's used to the pounding of pavement and steep inclines of Russian Hill, which should have prepared her for this. But she's feeling a little nauseous, probably from the cold and the altitude. It should pass since they're resting, but she'll be sore in the morning.

"This spot is lovely."

"Yeah. I come here about twice a week, and only in the past month since the snowpack started melting. It's impassable most of the winter." He removes his knit cap and scratches his head. "I think better when I'm moving."

He finishes his apple and bags the core. Ella adds hers to the trash when she's done and pulls out her voice recorder from her jacket's deep side pocket. Time to get the official interview started. Time's a wastin'.

"Nathan," she begins.

"Hold up. Before you start recording, is it true what you said?" he asks. "That you don't remember our time together last summer?"

She nods. "It's not just that I don't remember the interview. I didn't know of you until my editor called. I had to Google you."

Nathan whistles. "What a trip. Any idea why?"

"I was hoping you could help me."

"In what way?" He tosses a handful of trail mix into his mouth.

"Did something happen between us?" she asks, knowing her question is loaded. But she wants to know it all, everything she's beginning to suspect. What did they talk about on the mountain? Did they argue? Were they involved? Is that why she convinced Rebecca to kill the exclusive?

Nathan slowly shakes his head, his eyes on her. "I can't think of anything that would cause you to forget me."

Ella helps herself to the dried fruit and nuts. "What did we do on the previous assignment?"

Nathan pulls his legs into his chest and rests his forearms on his knees. "You mentioned yesterday you lost your notes."

"Everything. Research, recordings of our

conversations. Phone logs and voice mails. I have no idea how."

"What do you think happened?"

"I deleted them? That's the only explanation I've been able to draw."

"And what else?"

She looks askance at him. "What do you mean?"

"Are you sure it was just me you deleted?"

"No, I'm not."

"I might not be the only assignment you've forgotten, or person."

Her heart sinks. "You're not. I forgot my son."

Nathan reaches over and tugs off pieces of hair stuck to her lips, blown around by the wind. "I'm sorry. About your son," he says quietly.

Ella cups her mouth and glances away. She swallows, pushing down the knot expanding in her throat. "Thanks," she whispers.

"How's Damien handling this?"

She clears her throat, surprised for a moment that he knows of Damien, but of course he does. She wears a wedding band. He'd know she's married. She would have mentioned him. "We haven't really talked about it."

"Denial?" he asks, and Ella shrugs a shoulder. "You can talk to me, if you want. You did before."

Ella blinks at him. "What did we talk about?"

"Damien. Your parents."

"I told you about my parents?" she says in a

small voice. She rarely talks to anyone about her parents. She and Andrew hardly speak of them.

"What did I say about them?" she asks Nathan.

"You told me they died in a car accident when you were six and that you blamed your mother."

Ella feels the world falling from under her. She weaves. How could she have ever shared such personal information with an interviewee?

"Hey, hey." Nathan grips her shoulder. "Here, drink this." He hands her his metal water canister.

She guzzles a quarter, then wipes her mouth with the back of her hand.

Ella did blame her mom, but she can't fathom why she would have told Nathan. Aside from Damien, the only other person she admitted that to was Aunt Kathy. A few weeks after her parents' death and after the neighbors had helped Aunt Kathy clear out her parents' apartment and moved their belongings to Aunt Kathy's garage, Ella came across her mom's Lladró collection of porcelain figurines, gifts from Ella's grandparents her mom had received every year for her birthday. There were only eighteen figurines, even though her mom was twenty-four when she died. The figurines stopped when Ella's mom married her dad. Her mom was devastated that her own parents wouldn't accept Ella's dad into their family, but she still treasured her collection.

They'd been displayed in the antique curio

cabinet in their tiny apartment. But after her parents' death and after their belongings had been packed away, Ella despised everything that had belonged to her parents because she hated them for leaving her. And she especially hated anything her mom loved.

One evening Aunt Kathy was cooking dinner, and Ella, missing her parents, sneaked into the garage and snooped through their boxed items. But when she came across her mom's Lladrós, a rage Ella had never felt before consumed her. Blistering hot anger poured down her face in the form of heavy tears. She picked up one figurine after another and hurled them against the wall.

The sound of shattering porcelain brought Kathy to the garage just in time for her to witness the last figurine, an angel with white wings, explode into miniscule fragments. Porcelain dust sprinkled the garage like new-fallen snow.

"Ella Skye, what do you think you're doing?" Kathy had shouted.

Ella couldn't answer. Anger spent, a deep sadness filled her. She'd just destroyed her mom's prized collection.

Her mom would have smacked her with a spatula and sent her to bed without dinner. But her aunt Kathy only sank to her knees and pulled Ella against her ample chest in a tight bear hug.

Aunt Kathy smelled of apple fritters and warm bread. She'd been baking nonstop since Ella and Andrew moved in. Ella knew she baked the treats to keep her and Andrew happy. But right then, Ella just wanted to keep crying. She'd been holding in her tears for too long.

"There, there." Aunt Kathy patted her back. "Tell me, Ella. Why did you break your mommy's statues?"

"Be . . . be . . . because," she stuttered. Ella swiped off tears and, wiping her hands on her shirt, tried again. "Because . . . I don't know." She shrugged a little bony shoulder.

Aunt Kathy pursed her lips. "I think you do know but are afraid to tell me."

Ella looked at her dirty sneakers. They used to be white. Now they were gray. She twisted her shirt in her hands.

Aunt Kathy tucked a finger under Ella's chin and lifted her face. "You can tell me. But you must be honest. Honesty is the best policy."

Ella wasn't so sure about that. She'd overheard her parents' last conversation. It was what her mother had said that devastated her father, so much that he not only got them killed but almost killed Ella and her brother.

So yes, Nathan's right. Ella does blame her mom.

Burning pressure forms behind Ella's eyes. She blinks rapidly. "I haven't talked about them in a long time." From what she can recall, she hasn't spoken about them since she told Damien during their first year of marriage. The fact she'd told Nathan can mean only one thing. They'd grown very close last summer.

"I know. You mentioned that to me, too. For what it's worth," he adds, offering her a handful of trail mix, "you aren't to blame."

Ella frowns. "I don't blame myself. My mom was clearly at fault."

"I'm not talking about your parents."

"What then?"

His gaze dips to her midriff and back up to her face. Clarity swoops in like the hawk riding the air currents above them. Yes, she does blame herself for the accident she had last November. Nathan doesn't have the right to convince her otherwise. He doesn't know everything.

Neither does she.

Ella grimaces. Time to redirect the conversation. She doesn't want to talk about her problems anymore. She wants to talk about him. Or them. Yes, that's a good starting point.

She brushes nut dust from her hands and motions to the recorder. "Mind if we get started?"

"Sure."

"On the record," she begins. "What *did* we do last summer? My editor told me you took me backpacking."

Nathan opens his mouth, then promptly shuts it.

"I did," he acknowledges when Ella circles

her hand, eager to get the interview rolling. "We met up June seventh. It was eight months after Carson's death and my head was still in a bad place. I'd been hiking a section of the PCT, the Pacific Crest Trail. You can access it near here. I guess you could say I had an epiphany of sorts. I needed to tell someone my side of the story. I called *Luxe Avenue*, offered the exclusive, and they sent you. Why are you looking at me like that?"

"Like what?"

"Like you don't believe me." He smiles, amused.

"I believe you. I mean, my editor did say we went backpacking. I like hiking. Day hikes, like what we're doing." She thumbs back at the trail. "I can't picture myself on a multiday excursion."

"You were desperate for the story." He tipped back the water canister and took a swig, smiling around the rim.

"We hiked for what, five days?"

"Something like that. Next question?"

Ella wants to ask what they did the other nine days. But when he glances at his watch she remembers she's pressed for time.

"All right. Back to your parents."

For the next few hours they talk, delving further into his relationship with his father. When he asks, she shares stories about her childhood, surprised she feels so comfortable with him. She talks about growing up with Andrew and her time spent with Grace. She doesn't know if she's repeating what she told him last summer, but Nathan doesn't say anything. He listens intently. He empathizes. Ella finds the more that she talks, the more she wants to share.

At some point, Nathan unwraps sandwiches, roast beef and mustard on rye, and they eat lunch. Around two o'clock, he looks at the sky and suggests they head back.

He shoves off the rock and starts packing up their trash. Sensing movement, Fred and Bing yawn and stretch, downward dog–style. Tails swishing, they approach Nathan. He scratches their muzzles and hooks on their dog packs. Recharged and ready to hit the trail, the dogs pace.

Pushing off the granite surface, Ella stands and groans. Her muscles follow suit, complaining.

Her thighs burn. Lunging forward, she warms up her muscles for the return hike.

Nathan comments on her stretching. "How are the legs?"

"Stiff. I think I was a little overconfident when I agreed to this."

"You were hungry for the story," he teases.

"Always."

Arms raised, she leans right, stretching her side. Scarred ligaments in her lower abs spasm. She hisses through the discomfort.

Nathan looks at her sharply. "You're hurt."

"Just sore. Do you have aspirin in that treasure bag?" She nods at the daypack. He continues to stare at her, his gaze more inward than focused on her.

"Nathan?"

He blinks, rubs his eyes, and drags a hand down his face. "Aspirin. Yeah, I do." He drops the pack on the ground and rummages through the pockets.

"Are you okay?"

"Fine." Nathan roughly unzips another pocket and pulls out the medical kit, his motions abrupt. He seems angry, and Ella thinks he probably regrets showing her his spot. The location is secluded, personal to him. He spends a great deal of time reflecting here. Next time he visits, he'll think of her and her complaints about her aches and pains.

Popping the aspirin cap, he drops two tablets in her hand.

"You seem upset. Did I do something?" she asks.

He doesn't answer, only puts away the medical kit.

"The hike wasn't my idea." She downs the aspirin with water.

"Drink more," he orders. "You need to stay hydrated."

"Aye, aye, Captain." She salutes him with

the water bottle and drinks until Nathan seems satisfied. Still kneeling, he looks at the ridge across the valley. He doesn't move, even when Ella finishes the water and holds out the container for him to put it away.

"Knock, knock." She mock knocks the air in his line of vision. "Anyone home?"

He hangs his head and swears, scratches at the scruff on his jaw. He then zips and shoulders the pack, standing. He looks down at her with remorse. "I owe you an apology."

She frowns. "For what?"

"I wasn't thinking. I shouldn't have brought you out here, not this far. You aren't acclimated." He yanks on his knit cap and pulls it over the top of his ears. "I'm a professional. I expected too much of you. I shouldn't have pushed you to go this far."

If he could kick himself in the rear, Ella is sure he would. He looks miserable.

"For the record, you didn't push me. I could have said no. You didn't force me to come out here."

"I didn't give you much of an option."

"True. But a good part of my job is getting to watch the people I interview in action. There isn't much to watch when we're sitting across from each other at a table. You made our day more interesting. I'm a little light-headed and sore. No biggie. I can manage."

"Still, it just proves . . ." He stops and glances away. He looks at his watch. "We need to head back. It's getting late." He starts walking. The dogs scamper ahead, leading the way. Ella doesn't budge.

"Hey, Donovan!" she calls after him. "Proves what?"

He swings around, walking backward. "That my head isn't in the game." Turning back, he continues on.

"Is that why you quit *Off the Grid!*?" she hollers.

"Get moving, Skye. The sun doesn't stay up for anyone. You don't want to be walking this trail as it gets dark."

No, she doesn't. The unmarked path and white landscape make it too easy to get lost in the diminishing light.

She jogs after Nathan and the dogs through protesting muscles, falling into step behind them. Soon the aspirin kicks in and she feels looser. They don't talk much on the way back. Nathan seems to be in a funk so she lets him stew and keeps her attention on the ground. A twisted ankle would ruin their day. She'd be stuck out here, cold and alone, while Nathan ran back to his house to call for help. Or worse, he'd have to carry her. How humiliating.

Pressing fingers to her windburned cheeks, she glances at the sky. Clouds drift slowly overhead.

The toe of her boot catches on a root. Stumbling, she bumps into a boulder. *Ouch.* She rubs her arm.

"Ella," Nathan snaps. Suddenly in front of her, he waves a hand in her face. "Pay attention."

She blinks, glancing up at him, her movements slow and lethargic.

He says a few choice words, then pats his pockets until he finds a smashed protein bar. He tears off the wrapper.

"Eat this. You need fuel." He waits until she finishes. "Better?"

A rush of sugar hits her system. "Much, thank you." She didn't finish her sandwich earlier. She'd been too distracted asking questions and listening to Nathan.

"The altitude messes with you. Why didn't you tell me you felt dizzy?"

She shakes her head, holding on to the tree for balance. "Not dizzy. Not anymore. Just tired and shaky."

"Doesn't matter. Think you can walk now or do you need to rest more?"

"No, I'm good. Let's go."

They resume walking. The sun sets earlier at their elevation, and soon the bright orb is hiding behind trees until it disappears, dousing the sky in pinks and lavenders. It's almost 5:00 p.m. when they make it back to Nathan's, and by the time the trail opens onto his property, Ella wants nothing more than to enjoy a hot bath and to pee in a toilet. How in the world did she backpack five days straight?

"All right if I use your bathroom before I leave?" she asks.

The shadow of a frown touches his forehead. "Don't go." He steps close to her so that she has to tilt her head back to look at him. "I mean, you shouldn't drive just yet. Rest. Have dinner with me."

Ella glances at her car and back. Her stomach growls. She's hungry, and if she stays, they can put in another couple of hours toward the interview.

"Sure, I'll stay."

CHAPTER 15

Nathan moves about the kitchen prepping a dinner of steak, potatoes, and asparagus. He changed into worn jeans and a green flannel shirt. A shock of hair, rich like damp wood, drapes his forehead as he bends over the steaks, seasoning the rib eyes. He hums along to the music playing in the background, the Doors' "Light My Fire," seemingly lost in his own world and obviously used to living alone. Ella doubts he entertains much company up here.

Ella studies him from her chair at the table, piecing together the man she spent hours binge-watching the other day compared to the man she went hiking with. This man with her today is more reserved and cautious than the icy rudeness she was met with yesterday. And right now, he seems relaxed, comfortable in his own skin. All three versions are a far cry from his television persona, the man she expected to meet. On-screen he was confident. He attacked each episode's challenge with precision, guiding his guests with skill and finesse. It was never lost on him that the snap of a rope while rappelling down a cliff face or slip of the foot on loose pebbles on a trail no wider than the width of his boot above a steep ravine could send him and his guest careening to their deaths. As intense as he'd be one moment, he'd crack a joke the next. His brilliant smile would light up the screen.

Today, though, he's a shadow of the man he used to be. The Nathan leading them along a trail that followed the mountain ridge seemed to doubt his own abilities. He'd been hard on himself, second-guessing his assumption she'd been ready for the hike.

Ella powers up her laptop, plugs in the Wi-Fi password Nathan gave her, and furiously types notes from the day's discussion. She also uploads the voice recordings and backs everything up to the cloud. She's not going to risk losing or misplacing her notes again.

Nathan carries a platter of steaks and asparagus to the sliding glass door. "I'll be outside if you need me."

"I'll get that," she says, pushing up from the table and opening the door for him. A rush of crisp air trades places with him when he goes outside. She shivers and rubs her upper arms. Shutting the door behind him, she remains there, watching.

Nathan sets the platter on a table and lifts the grill cover. Smoke billows, carried off by the wind. He preps the grate, scrubbing off burned bits from the previous time he used the grill. He puts on the steaks and closes the lid, then just stands there in the cold and wind, arms folded tight over his chest. He gazes off toward the woods. What's he looking at? What's he thinking about?

Wind sweeps up from the valley, hitting the house. Windows creak and wood groans, absorbing the impact. Nathan's shirt billows and hair ruffles.

Isn't he cold?

Ella shivers again despite the fact that the heater is on.

Masochist.

The word floats into Ella's mind, and she's quickly drawing her own conclusions about him. Nathan seeks out pain. He wants to feel its sharp edges. He wants to live and breathe his losses. But if he continues to wallow in them, he'll spend the rest of his life holed up here on the mountain. Forgotten.

Ella needs to write his exclusive before that happens. His fans could lose him. She could lose him.

Whoa.

She steps back from the door as though the glass burned.

Where did that thought come from?

Thin air. It's just the altitude, messing with her mind, she reasons.

She returns to her notes, dictating them since she speaks faster than she can type.

A short time later, Ella wraps up her thoughts. "It's my opinion that Nathan—"

The door slides open with a blast of cold air. Nathan comes inside smelling of smoke, pine, and grilled meat. He shuts the door. Ella turns off the voice recorder.

"Don't stop on my account." Nathan sets down the steaks and covers the platter with tinfoil. He joins her at the table, sitting across from her. He leans forward, weight on his forearms. "What's your opinion of me?" He nods at the recorder, urging her to continue. A dare.

She arches a brow and presses the record button. "I think Nathan idealized the life he had with his parents. He attempted to re-create that life with his wife, Stephanie, but he always fell short."

Nathan frowns. His chin presses into his neck. "That's a little harsh."

"The truth can be harsh."

"Your opinion of me is harsh."

"I didn't draw the same conclusion before?"

His frown deepens. "No." He glances away. "I don't know. You didn't dictate in front of me. You'd wander off."

"Well, maybe I thought the same thing and didn't tell you. Or maybe I did and that's why you pulled the exclusive," Ella says, going on a hunch. "You didn't like what you heard."

He folds his arms over his chest. "That's not why I pulled it."

Ella's eyes widen. It was him, not her.

Rebecca said she wasn't going to let Ella kill the article again, but for the life of her, Ella can't imagine why she would have killed it in the first place unless she had a good reason.

Unless Nathan had been the reason. He must have convinced her. Why?

"Why'd you pull it, Nathan? What happened?"

His gaze lifts and meets hers. "You're angry."

"No, frustrated. Okay, maybe a little irritated. I thought I'd killed the article, but it was you. Why?" she asks forcefully.

He nods at the recorder in her hand. "Hold that thing any tighter and you'll break it."

She looks at the recorder and wills her grip to soften. "Sorry."

She pushes out a breath and pretends to read her notes. She's frustrated she can't remember anything from before and she's taking it out on Nathan. The fact she's so physically attracted to him doesn't help either. It makes her wonder if she felt the same before. Did she act on those feelings? If so, does Damien know? It would explain why he was so adamant about her ditching the interview. But wouldn't he have been more insistent? Wouldn't he have told her she had an affair?

No, Ella reasons. Nothing happened between her and Nathan. She wouldn't have done that to Damien.

She takes a calming breath and sets down the recorder. "I'm sorry," she repeats.

"Apology accepted. Please, continue. I want to hear this."

"All right." Ella looks sideways at him, gathering her thoughts, her hands clammy. Nathan waits, watching her, which makes her more nervous. There's the genuine possibility he'll kill the article again once he's heard what she plans to dictate. She wipes her hands on her thighs and speaks into the recorder. She keeps her gaze on the notes in front of her so that she can concentrate.

"When a person is placed on a pedestal, which I believe Nathan did with his wife and compared her to the two most important people in his life at the time, his parents, Stephanie had no place to go but down. I don't think she could keep up with Nathan's expectations of her."

"I never expected anything from her."

"You wanted your marriage with her to be what your parents had," she refutes.

"Sure."

"She wasn't wired like them or you. You started to resent her for not being like your mom."

"I loved Steph and my parents. I didn't idealize them. I admired them." His tone is defensive.

"You romanticized them. You did with me this afternoon, anyway. I can't think of one flaw you told me."

"They had plenty of flaws. Mom hated housework and she was horrible at math. Worst tutor on the planet. Dad drank too much, ate like crap, and watched too much TV."

"Flaws, yes, but superficial. Stephanie's from New York, right? She'd never been off Manhattan for any length of time longer than a few weeks until you met her at a dinner party." Ella's glad she read up on Stephanie, too. She was a friend of Nathan's publicist, and Nathan had confessed in one interview that he knew the moment he met Stephanie that she was it for him. They married and then moved to Colorado, where they lived in the Rockies, about an hour from the nearest town.

"You can't take a city girl and drop her in the middle of the woods and expect her to thrive on her own. You traveled a lot, and you left her alone in the mountains. She was lonely. She couldn't hack the solitude you crave. She wanted to move back to New York and you wouldn't go with her." Ella had read all that in the *New York Post*. The article ran around the time his separation from Stephanie went public.

"So there you were, married to a woman you would give the world to, and she despised the one thing you were passionate about. Your pursuit of the rush. Adrenaline is a powerful drug. I know. I got a taste of it when I ran marathons in my early twenties. Stephanie grew to despise you. Instead of adjusting your ways or meeting her halfway, you just kept working. As for your son—"

"What about my son?" Nathan asks sharply.

Ella knows she's pushing him. Carson's a sensitive topic, but she wants his reaction. That's when she'll get to the truth of the man he really is. She also wants him to share with her what Damien hasn't. His grief.

"I'm sure he wanted your attention. What would he do to get—"

"Enough," Nathan says in a guttural voice.

She stops talking. Silence lingers between them. His hands are fists. Underneath the table, his leg jiggles. His gaze darts to the recorder.

"Is that thing still on?"

Ella looks at the device in her hand. Digital numbers climb. "Yes, why? You don't want to hear what I have to say? Because I have a theory. You asked me up here so that I can write an article about your simple life. A life that doesn't involve taking risks or living on an adrenaline high. You want to show Stephanie that you can be the man she needs. You think that if she reads my article and sees you here, like this, she'll come back. Did I get that right?"

Nathan doesn't blink. Ella opens her mouth to continue, but before she can, Nathan snatches the recorder from her hand, turns it off, and slams it on the table.

Ella stares stupidly at her empty hand.

"No more questions."

"Isn't that why I'm here?"

"I didn't invite you to interview me. I invited you to dinner."

He's the one who encouraged her to continue her dictation, but she's not going to mention that now. His eyes remain locked on hers, and with a sigh, she puts away the voice recorder. Nathan exhales.

"Thank you," he says, standing. "Now let's eat. I don't want to reheat our steaks."

CHAPTER 16

"May I ask a personal question?" Nathan says.

They'd eaten dinner and moved to the kitchen. Ella loads the utensils Nathan rinsed into the dishwasher. He didn't want her help cleaning, but she insisted. It was the least she could do after the meal he'd cooked. She'd been famished from their hike. She polished off her rib eye and they consumed a French Burgundy. She probably shouldn't have drunk that second glass and not just because she has to drive back to the hotel on a narrow, curvy road in the dark. Rather, she finds herself wanting to linger longer than professionally necessary.

"Sure." Ella drops the utensils into the dishwasher basket, mindful the fork tines face down.

"It's about Damien. What's his take on your memory loss?"

"I think he resents me," she blurts before she can stop herself. She lets out a shaky laugh. It's not lost on her that her answer is the same connection she drew between Nathan and Stephanie.

Nathan's brows fold. "He told you this?"

"I sense it." Damien wouldn't be so unkind. "It's the way he watches me. I feel like he's trying to figure out what I'm going to do next. He gets—" She stops midsentence and flashes him a smile when she realizes what she was about to do. What she is doing. To distract herself from saying more, she realigns the glasses in the top rack. The last thing she should be doing while on assignment is complaining about her husband. To another man, no less. One she finds very attractive.

But if she's being honest, for the past few months she's felt like a piece of coding Damien's trying to insert in a software upgrade. How will she respond? Will she crash the whole system? Ruin his program?

Nathan watches her, patient.

"I'm not sad and hurt like him," she offers up. "Hard to be when I can't remember what I should be sad about. He thinks I got off easy."

"What do you mean?"

"I think he believes I blocked my memories on purpose."

Nathan looks intrigued. "Can someone do that?"

"Subconsciously, yes. I read up on it after all this, trying to figure out what's going on. The mind will block memories, or parts of memories, even alter memories when the person can't deal with tragedy. My understanding is that the more I talk about it and immerse myself in familiar surroundings and with familiar people, my memories should come back. The thing is, nothing about my being pregnant is familiar—my maternity clothes, the nursery I apparently painted, my medical reports from my routine checkups and the accident, even the bills we had to pay. They didn't feel like mine."

"That must have been tough. I remember that about Carson. Paying the hospital bills and seeing his name printed there on the top. Knowing he's gone and I'll never see him again. There were all sorts of things I still had to do on his behalf. The worst was boxing up his clothes and favorite toys." He pushes out a breath. Ella briefly touches his arm.

"I thought that would be difficult for me, too, but it wasn't," she says, taking the platter he rinsed and fitting it into the lower rack. "Reading those reports didn't feel any different than researching an assignment. Same with paying the bills. It was like they were for a distant relative. I mean, I cared, but the emotional attachment I should have with Simon just isn't there.

"Anyways." She waves a hand, getting them back to Nathan's original question. "Damien barely talks about the accident or my miscarriage, so that doesn't help me either. Sometimes I think he wants to pretend it never happened."

Nathan makes a contemplative noise, a tremor deep in his throat.

"What?"

"I didn't say anything." He hands her a dish and she loads it into the washer.

"You made a weird noise in the back of your throat."

He sighs and tosses the sponge into the sink, turning to her. "You've done what he wants to do. Forget."

Davie had told her something similar. She should be fortunate. Why does she want to remember something that would only bring heartache? Maybe Damien's right. Does she really want her memories back?

Yes, because she believes there's a specific reason she's forgotten, something she's not supposed to remember. Damien's complaint in the hospital keeps coming back to her.

You weren't supposed to forget Simon.

Damien knows something. And he's not talking. Rather, he wasn't willing to talk until she told him about the Nathan Donovan assignment.

"Do you wish you could forget so that it doesn't hurt so much?" she asks.

"No. But there are nights I can't sleep, and I wish . . ." His voice trails off.

"You wish it never happened and that you can forget it ever did," she supplies.

"Is that so terrible? To make myself believe I never had a son just so I can get through the day? Or have a decent night's sleep? I sound like an asshole."

"No, you don't. You sound human. The pain never goes away, Nathan. You have to function, so you learn to live with it or you bury it. Who knows, maybe everyone's right. Maybe I should count my blessings and be grateful I can't remember. I've lost people close to me and getting over their deaths wasn't easy. I'm not sure I ever really have, actually."

"You're thinking about Grace."

"What exactly did I tell you about her?" she asks, still surprised she'd been so open with him last summer. She isn't sure how she feels about that. Uneasy? Yes. Concerned? Definitely. Because that would mean Nathan meant something to her.

Nathan's thumb lightly brushes the back of her hand where she grasps the edge of the counter. The gentle touch zings through her, making her all too aware of his nearness—the height of him and the breadth of his shoulders, the scent of fruit on his breath from the wine, and the faint smell of smoke from the barbecue clinging to the fibers of his shirt. She swallows roughly and forces herself to look up at him, not at her hand, where she can feel the rough, calloused skin on his fingertip. Probably from chopping wood. How cliché, she thinks. But there's a huge pile stacked against the house. Someone had to chop it.

"You told me you lost her in high school and that you blame her father, but you also blame yourself. You didn't tell me why, only that she committed suicide at your house."

Ella pulls away her hand. Whoa! She'd told him all that? With a quick glance at the oven clock, she rubs the area where he touched. "It's late. I should go."

"You're welcome to stay here if you don't want to drive in the dark."

"Thanks, but I'm good." She smiles stiffly, moving to the dining table.

"I scared you off. I told you too much." He follows her out of the kitchen.

"No, it's late." But yes, he did scare her. She's scared of how much she opened up to him. How easily she could grow to care for him. Again, it would seem.

He nods solemnly and backs away, giving her space. "I'll walk you out."

Ella packs up her belongings. She changed back into her turtleneck and skinny jeans earlier and left the hiking clothes folded on top of the boots in the bathroom. They don't feel like her clothes and it doesn't seem right to take them with her.

"What you said about Stephanie earlier," Nathan says when she shoulders her bag. He starts walking with her toward the door. "You were right. I wanted a marriage like my parents'. I knew the moment I met her we didn't have anything in common. But I wanted her to see the world the way I did. A big adventure. She was a city girl who'd never worn a pair of trail shoes before we met. I thought I could teach her to love the outdoors."

"She resisted."

"She did, and I resented her for that. Couldn't she at least have tried?"

Ella senses the question is rhetorical and doesn't comment. Maybe Stephanie did try, and he didn't see it because he wasn't there with her. She follows him into the cold night air.

They reach her car. "Same time tomorrow?" she asks, tossing her bag into the back seat.

"Eight a.m."

"All right, see you in the morning," she says, covering a yawn as she settles into the driver's seat and starts up the car. "Good night, Donovan."

"See you tomorrow, Skye." He shuts the door and taps on the window. She eases it down. "Dress warm."

"Why? What are you planning?" Please not another long hike. While the scenery was gorgeous and the mountain air invigorating, they wasted several hours hiking. Yeah, they talked, and she dictated notes later from memory. But they covered too much literal ground rather than interview ground.

He grins. "Not telling. Drive safe." He claps the roof of the car and backs away, giving her room to turn around.

"Make sure you leave enough time for our interview," she yells out the window as she drives off. He's only giving her one more day.

At the hotel, Ella wants nothing more than to soak in a hot bath and collapse on the bed. But she has work to do—more notes to dictate from today and questions to outline for tomorrow. She also wants to check in with Damien. She'd silenced her phone so that it wouldn't distract her when she dictated, and later, when they ate.

Launching her phone, she notices notifications fill her screen. A voice mail from Davie, a text from Andrew—he secured funding for Come Over Rover. *Boom!* With a gazillion exclamation points. He follows up his text with another. Five bomb emojis. He wants her to tell Damien there is a market for "TinderPooch."

She rolls her eyes. He can text Damien himself.

Speaking of her husband, there's a missed call from him and three text messages.

> Long day ahead. Everything's going to shit.
>
> Sorry.
>
> Talk tonight? I'll fill you in.

That must have been the missed call.

She looks at the time on her phone. Nine thirty p.m., six thirty a.m. in London. He's up, probably already at the office. She calls him and her call goes to voice mail.

She leaves a message. "Hey, sorry I missed you. Call me when you have the chance. I'll be up for a little longer. Love you."

But he doesn't return her call, not while she wraps up her notes and takes a bath. By the time she turns off the lights and settles into bed, he still hasn't called, so she tries to reach him again only to land in voice mail. This time she hangs up without leaving a message.

Everything's going to shit.

She knows he's talking about work, but she can't help thinking it might have to do with them. Lying on her back with the covers pulled to her chest, Ella stares into the pitch-dark room. She tries not to dwell on the fact she and Nathan barely discussed their previous time together or that spending an entire day with him didn't unblock her memories. But it did enlighten her.

Until the other night, Damien had never asked her to turn down an assignment. He'd never requested her to cancel or reschedule an interview. Neither has she where his work is concerned.

Rolling to her side, she clicks on the bedside lamp. Warm light bathes the room. Digging through her purse, Ella finds her wallet. Tucked in the pocket is the last note she received from Damien. Since the day they married, he always left her notes. There was no rhyme or reason to them other than to let her know he loves her and that she's always on his mind. The notes don't show up often, and there isn't a pattern as to when they'll appear. They show up with a new phone or a muffin he picked up for her on his run home. He'll stick them on her mirror. *Good morning, beautiful.* And once, she found a folded scrap of paper with a pressed daisy inside the pocket of her coat. *Missed running with you this morning. This reminded me of you.* Ella had been out late the previous night on assignment and wanted to sleep in. Along the route Damien took was a Victorian home in Pacific Heights. Ella always remarked on the daisy bush in the home's raised planter. It was full and flowering, the yellow daisies like small rays of sunshine.

A week after Ella returned home from the hospital, she came across an envelope stuffed with notes from Damien. She found the envelope tucked in the back of her lingerie drawer. Damien had given her the notes throughout her pregnancy. Reading through them had been difficult and not because she didn't recall them. Rather, Damien's excitement and awe over Simon's arrival was palpable. So was his love for her and their baby. It broke her heart reading them, and it made her question whether she really knew her husband.

The man who wrote those notes about Simon was not the man she'd married. The man who didn't want children.

Ella unfolds the note in her hand, the most recent one from her husband. A lime-green sticky note he left on the steering wheel of the Range Rover he purchased for her in December after she'd totaled her other one. The note is one word. Simple yet powerful and so full of meaning. *Stay.* It's what he asked of her the morning after they met. The first time she had stayed. She hadn't even had to think about it. But this time . . .

She presses the note to her forehead, closes her eyes, and whispers, "I'm sorry."

Because Nathan isn't a new indie artist fresh on the music scene, someone she can easily reschedule or call another day. Damien flat out doesn't want her spending time with Nathan. And when told she can't do something, Ella typically does the opposite. Because she's curious. It's in her nature.

After the looks Nathan sent her way and her own physical reaction toward him, it doesn't take a college degree to add one plus one.

She and Nathan have history. History Damien is well aware of and not sharing with her.

Ditch the interview and come with me, Damien said.

What does he know?

CHAPTER 17

The following morning, Ella wakes to the ghost of a man's lips on her neck, the shadow of his hands on her ribs. The rough ends of his fingers gliding between her breasts, dipping into the concave of her belly, fluttering over her hips. The heat of him moving inside her. It doesn't feel like a dream. More like a memory where everything is three-dimensional, from the texture of his skin to the sound of his breathing. To the taste of him.

As for the man, he isn't Damien.

Ella's eyes snap open.

The time glows in red numbers from the nightstand clock: 7:05 a.m. Her body glows from the remnants of her dream, aching in a different way from the night before. Inappropriate thoughts of Nathan fill her mind. She blocks them, forces her thoughts to her husband. She glances at her phone with disappointment. Damien never called. She quickly sends off a text—Call me. I'm up.— and rises from the bed.

After a shower and a quick stop at the café— still no text or call from Damien and still no answer when she tries calling him again—Ella arrives at Nathan's at 8:10 a.m. She's ten minutes late and he's raring to go. He's stowing a cooler in the rear cab of his Chevy Silverado when

Ella pulls up alongside. Hitched to his truck is a trailer. Parked on the trailer is a two-seater snowmobile.

Oh, hell no.

Ella's adventurous. But she's on deadline. How does he expect her to conduct his interview when they're flying over snowbanks? There's also a part of her that feels like she'd be betraying Damien. They were supposed to go snowmobiling in Vail their first year together. She'd awoken the morning after Thanksgiving in a funk so Damien canceled. Instead, he spent the day with her reading beside the fire after she'd promised they'd go snowmobiling next time. There had yet to be a next time. They haven't been back to Vail since.

Nathan's grinning as Ella eases down her window.

"Morning," he says.

She eyes the trailer. "You aren't serious."

"I'm one hundred percent serious when it comes to snowmobiling."

He wears gray snow pants and sturdy boots. He claps his hands together, his body visibly vibrating with excitement.

"Normal people start their days with caffeine," she complains. Nathan starts his with adrenaline. So much for her conclusion that he's living a risk-free life.

"Go park. We're packed and ready to roll."

She narrows her gaze. "You promised me an interview today, Donovan."

"You'll get your answers, Skye."

"About us, too," she presses, the memory-dream lurking in her mind. "I want to know everything."

He drags his knit cap off his head and, ruffling his hair, glances at his boots.

"Sure, yeah, you'll get those, too," he says, looking straight at her, and Ella inhales sharply as realization hits her. She now knows why Damien didn't want her to come and why Nathan acted so familiar with her when she arrived. Nathan's expression says it all. That dream she had this morning? It wasn't a dream. It was a memory. She and Nathan were involved.

Damn you, Damien, for not telling me.

She should turn around right now, call Rebecca from the road. Insist that she reassign the interview to Jordan or cancel altogether. To hell with her job. Her marriage is more important.

But Nathan . . . She wants to know what happened last summer and what it has to do with her memory loss. The two must be connected. She also wants to know why Nathan hasn't just come out and told her. He's as aggravating as Damien, keeping things from her.

She has no choice but to see this through.

Ella eases up the window and parks her car. When she gets out, Fred and Bing bark and howl from inside the house. They paw the front window.

"You aren't bringing the dogs?"

"Not this trip." He opens the passenger door and pats the leather seat. "Hop up."

She heaves herself into the cab with a grunt.

Nathan touches her arm. "How're you feeling today?"

"A little sore, but I'll be fine."

Concern etches deep grooves in his brow. "Sorry if I pushed you too hard."

"You didn't. I'm in shape, just not used to the elevation, I guess. You live in a beautiful area."

He lifts his head. A slight smile plays on his lips. "Thanks. I love it up here."

Ella breathes in and smiles. "I forgot how much I love the smell of pine. It reminds me of Christmas when I was a little girl. My aunt Kathy would take Andrew and me to the tree farms in the Santa Cruz Mountains. She was old and we were young, and we'd have to ask some other family's dad to cut our tree and put it in the back of her car. When she got too sick to even decorate the tree, Andrew and I would walk to the corner tree lot and carry one back home. Aunt Kathy would sit in her chair and tell us exactly where she wanted us to hang the ornaments. I don't think I've been to a tree farm since I was eleven." She frowns, looking down at her hands folded over the leather gloves in her lap. She smiles slightly on an abbreviated exhale and shakes her head, bemused. "I have no idea why I just told you that."

"It's a good memory."

"It is." Her smile broadens. "I love the mountains, but I'll let you in on a secret."

"Oh, yeah?"

"I'm not a fan of the cold. I make up excuses to get out of the city during fog season."

He laughs. "You'll get used to it."

"Well, your blood is thicker than mine." She points at his snow pants. "Will I be okay wearing jeans?"

"I have shells for you in the back seat. You can wear them over your jeans."

"My size?" she asks with reservation, wondering what other belongings he has of hers.

"No, they're mine. We won't be hiking today so you don't have to worry about them falling around your ankles." The skin around his eyes crinkles. He grasps the seat belt clip and yanks the strap forward. "Buckle up, Skye." Nathan shuts her door and makes his way around the truck and settles into the driver's seat.

"Where are we headed?" she asks. The truck's engine grumbles under the hood, a sleeping giant waking.

"A fire road I know of about an hour from here."

"That far?" She can mentally hear the clock ticking down the time.

"Not far. Slow going. We have to take back roads."

He shifts the truck into gear and eases off the brake, his eyes on the rearview mirror, checking the trailer behind them. Satisfied it's hitched and the snowmobile strapped on, he clips on his belt and drives.

"The road is closed to the public this time of year, but I know the ranger on duty," he explains, reaching for the climate control. "Are you warm enough?"

"I am now." Warm air blows in her face. She adjusts the vents and slips off her jacket, folding it on her lap.

"Seat warmer button's here if you need it." He points at the dial, then rubs his hands together and blows into his cupped palms. "Ready for some fun?"

"Ready to talk?"

He laughs, shaking his head. "Ease up, Skye. There will be plenty of time for that later."

They drive for an hour over narrow, pothole-laden back roads until they reach the end of one, the road barricaded with a steel barrier gate. Yellow paint peels off the tubular post, and a NO TRESPASSING sign hangs askew by one bolted corner. Beyond the gate is a decent snowpack. Nathan turns the truck around so that the trailer faces the barrier. He cuts the engine.

"Are you sure this is okay?" she asks, looking

out the rear window. The road on the other side, hidden under the snow, disappears into a dense thicket of trees.

"Yep." He reaches into the back and drops the shell pants on Ella's lap. "Put these on. I'll unload the sled." He hops from the truck. Cold air wafts inside, swapping places with the cab's heat. He pokes his head back inside. "Got gloves?"

She waves her black leather, cashmere-lined gloves. Had she known she'd be spending this much time outdoors, she would have brought her ski gloves.

"Those'll do." He grins, schoolboy giddy, and slams the door.

Ella watches him out the back window, moving about the trailer, releasing latches. Before she thinks to put on the shell, he has the snowmobile down the ramp.

Facing back around, she jams one leg into the shell. Nathan bangs on her window and she jumps with a squeak. "Holy—"

"Hurry up."

"Slow your roll, dude," she grumbles. Someone's a tad too excited to play with his toys.

Sixty seconds later, jacket and gloves on, she hops from the truck and waddles to the snowmobile, holding the shell pants at her waist. She feels ridiculous. Bending over, she folds up the hems. Nathan hands her a helmet when she straightens back up.

"We're really doing this?" She side-eyes the sleek black helmet with a reflective lens.

"Sure, why not?"

"I can't talk to you with this on." She inspects the helmet. Nathan fires up the snowmobile and revs the motor. "Or over that," she yells.

"Yes, you can," he shoots back. He points to the communication device inside the helmet. "But you're not asking questions. I have to focus on driving." He straps on his helmet.

She scowls and puts on her own.

"Play first. Talk later. Hop on, Skye." His voice fills her head. He pats the seat behind him.

Ignoring the double entendre of his words, she straddles the seat.

"Hold on." Nathan's voice comes over the com.

She grasps his waist.

"Tighter or you'll fall off." He tugs her arms so that her chest is plastered to his back and her thighs tightly flank his. She bites her bottom lip to keep from groaning out loud. Holy moly, the fucker planned this.

"Here we go."

Nathan maneuvers the vehicle through a narrow opening and then they're off, soaring across the flat, white landscape. Ella shrieks with delight and the guilt she briefly felt earlier evaporates. Through the com, she can hear Nathan's answering whoop of excitement.

When she was a sophomore in high school,

Ella started dating a senior named Mike Tate, the same boy she was with the night Grace took her life. Ella broke up with Mike a few days after her best friend's death. Guilt drove her to end their relationship, even though she was still into him. But she shouldn't have been with him that night. She should have been with Grace. Looking back, though, Mike might have been the first boy she loved, and if it wasn't him she loved, it was the rush she got when she was with him.

Mike owned a 2004 lime-green Kawasaki Ninja, spoiled ass that he was. The motorcycle purred with unbridled power when he let it fly down the freeway, weaving in and out of traffic, taking Ella for the joyride of her life. There was something exhilarating about her body breaking through the wind and the horsepower vibrating between her legs while going at top speed. Skating just inside of control.

Ella just now realizes that she hasn't experienced such freedom since riding with Mike. Not even with Damien. And she hasn't realized she missed this—craved it—until Nathan flies them over an embankment, catching air.

Laughing, she hugs him tighter. This is what he seeks when he free-climbs cliffs. This is the rush he chases when he skydives. This is what he wanted to share with Stephanie and she rejected it. She rejected him.

Did he find that rush with her?

CHAPTER 18

Ella forces herself to be present, to enjoy the ride. To not dwell on what she might have once felt for him or what he might have once meant to her.

They ride the ungroomed terrain for a couple of hours, and when the tank nears empty, they return to the truck. Laughing, knuckle-bumping, and high-fiving, they banter about the ride and muse over the spectacular views they captured through the trees. Ella snaps photos of Nathan and his sled, as he likes to refer to his snowmobile. Sled on steroids is more like it. She'll use the pictures for the article since Rebecca didn't assign a photographer. Nathan's request. Ella only.

Nathan loads the snowmobile onto the trailer and straps it down. They pile into the truck's cab and shut their doors at the same time.

"That was fun," she says, breathless. She sets her camera on the dash and pulls off her gloves.

Nathan tosses his gloves aside and reaches behind him over the seat. "I brought hot chocolate. Want some?" He shows her the metal thermos.

"You're prepared. Is it laced?"

He snorts a laugh. "No. I have to drive." He pours two cups.

She blows across the surface of her drink. Steam moistens her nose. She takes a tentative sip. Rich chocolate with a cinnamon bite fills her mouth. "This is good." Though she could have used a shot of whiskey to soothe the adrenaline pulsing through her. It might quell her craving to crawl onto Nathan's lap. Or . . .

It could lower her resistance, and that wouldn't be good at all.

Nathan presses the ignition button and lets the truck idle. Warm air circulates in the cab and Ella sheds her coat. A faint echo of her dream touches her mind. She doesn't remember the specifics. The images are elusive, but the feelings are there. Arousal, need, and a burning desire to reach across the center console and touch Nathan overtake her. If she kisses him, would it feel familiar? Would touching him so intimately be strong enough to trigger her memories?

She hates that she yearns for him in the way a married woman shouldn't.

Nathan watches her, and his brow creases. "What?"

She finishes her hot chocolate and places the empty cup in the cup holder. She might as well ask. "Did we sleep together last summer?"

Nathan sputters his hot chocolate. He lets out a nervous laugh, then looks at her. His expression says it all. The longing and regret. And hope.

Shit.

Why would he invite her up here? Does he expect to start something up again?

Hello? They're married. To other people.

But that didn't stop them before.

"Why am I here?" she asks him.

"I promised to take you snowmobiling."

When did he promise that? Why make such a promise when they never should have gotten involved in the first place? And where were they for such a question to come up? It had been the middle of the summer.

She has so many questions, but his answer isn't the right one for her question.

"You know that's not what I'm asking."

Nathan finishes his drink and sets the cup on the dash. He shifts in his seat, angling his body so that one arm is draped over the steering wheel. "We hiked for five days. You spent another nine at my place."

Nine days at his place. Two weeks total. Fourteen days. Half a month. However she spins it, it was quite a bit of time.

Where was Damien during all this?

London. He told her she joined him there after the ten days she spent on assignment.

She lied to him and Davie about the amount of time she spent on the assignment. Same with Rebecca. She'd told them ten days, Rebecca five. Why?

Despite the self-disgust, she can't ignore one

thing: blocked memories or not, she's still very attracted to Nathan.

"We got to be very close," Nathan quietly acknowledges.

"You still haven't answered my question."

He takes a beat before he does. "I got an email from Rebecca's assistant a couple of months ago. Late January, I think. She was feeling me out about my interest in pursuing the exclusive again. I wasn't going to call, and it took me a long time before I did, but . . . " He sighs. "You're here now because I wanted to see you."

"Hell, Nathan. My being here better be about more than you missing me. And don't even think about pulling the exclusive again. You do and I might lose my job."

"I won't." He raises a hand. She gives him a hard look. "Swear. I'm not expecting anything out of this. What happened between us before just happened. I didn't plan on it. For Christ's sake, my son died and my wife wanted to divorce me. She *still* wants a divorce. The last thing on my mind last summer was—" He stalls, his attention pulled elsewhere. He points at the windshield. A green truck approaches.

"It's Ted," Nathan says when he can make out the driver. He eases down his window when Ted stops his truck alongside Nathan's. "Afternoon, Ted."

Ella's gaze darts to the dashboard clock: 12:06 p.m. The morning has flown by.

"Good to see you, Nathan." Ted's hazel eyes land on Ella. "Afternoon."

Nathan gestures at Ella. "This is my friend Ella. Ella, Ranger Ted Berringer."

She waves. "Hello."

"How's Sue?" Nathan asks.

"She's good. She's home with Alex. He's been fighting the flu."

"Tell her hi for me. Hope your son gets better soon. What brings you out here?"

Ted glances beyond the barrier gate. "The department received reports of gunfire. My guess is some jackass illegally hunting. Hear anything?"

"Nope." Nathan looks at Ella. "You?"

She shakes her head.

"We were just leaving."

Ella narrows her eyes at him. No, they weren't. They were in the middle of a conversation and she wants to finish it.

"I'll just check the gate." Ted gets out of his truck. "You know, Sue's going to ask if I invited you to dinner when I tell her I ran into you."

"Don't tell her." Nathan smirks.

"Yeah, that won't fly. What do you say? Dinner at our place after Alex recoups? Or are you still playing the crazy recluse in the woods?" Ted's tone is teasing, but he's right—Nathan needs to be around other people.

Before she can think otherwise, Ella nudges his shoulder. "You should go."

"Listen to the lady. Come on over. Scotch is on me."

"I guess I'll be there. Call when you've got a date." His voice is slightly irritated.

If Ted noticed, he doesn't comment on it. He grins. "Will do. By the way, it's good to see you finally shaved. That mountain man beard was scaring the tourists."

"It was a disguise," Nathan grumbles. "I had to buy groceries."

"Worst disguise ever. Nice to meet you, Ella."

"You too, Ted."

Nathan shifts the truck into drive.

"You shaved for me." She grins.

Nathan doesn't comment. They drive back to his place in silence and Ella wonders if she stepped over the line. It isn't her place to interfere in his personal life. It's not right of her to force him into public when he's not emotionally ready.

As Nathan pulls up his driveway, Ella turns to him, an apology on her tongue. But Nathan is glaring out the windshield. Ella looks in the same direction.

A Toyota Corolla takes up the space beside Ella's Range Rover, and the owner of the car is sitting on the porch. He stands and waves. Ella recognizes him immediately, and she doubts this is a social visit.

"Why is Miles Jorgenson at your house?"

Nathan shoots her a look. "You know him?"

"Of him. We met once at a media awards banquet."

Miles Jorgenson and Ella run in the same circles. He's a seasoned contributor to numerous magazines, mainly *Outside*. Known for his provocative stories about engaging, outdoor-oriented personalities, Miles is relentless, with a paparazzi-style persistence when in pursuit of a story. It appears he's after Nathan's.

"Why's he here?"

Nathan cuts the engine and sighs.

Ella's stomach plummets. "Did you offer him an interview, too?"

"No, I didn't," he says sharply. "Although considering everything, maybe—"

"Don't even finish that thought," she says. Nathan's story is hers. Too many people at *Luxe Avenue* are counting on her to see this through. "How do you know this guy?"

Remote and unlisted, the only way to locate Nathan's property is to have the address. And to get that, Nathan would have to have given it out.

"We collaborated on several articles about the Tahoe region."

"I know, I read them. That doesn't explain why he's here. My understanding is that you gave my magazine the exclusive."

"I did. It's just—"

"Damn you, Nathan. You yanked this story

from me once. You swore back there you'd see this through."

"Miles has been after me since I quit *Off the Grid!* Don't worry. My story's yours. Let me see what he wants. He's a friend. This could be a social visit. I drink beers with the guy," he says.

Nathan opens his door. Ella scrambles out hers. They meet at the front of the truck.

"Go inside. I'll be there in a few." Nathan tries to hand her his keys.

She balks at them. "I'll stay, thanks."

"Ella." Irritation ices her name. "I gave you my word."

"You did, and I appreciate that. But I happen to know journalists. They'll sweet-talk your life's history out of you."

Nathan folds his arms. "Tell me about it."

"I don't trust Miles any more than a pack of wolves that'd wander onto your property."

"That would never happen. Bears maybe. Wolves are rare up here, and if they weren't, Fred and Bing's incessant barking"—he scowls at his dogs yapping and howling in the window—"would scare them off."

"Then why's Miles still here?" She grins.

Nathan throws his head back and laughs. "You've got me." He pockets his keys with a smile.

Miles approaches and she sees the moment he recognizes her. His eyes narrow.

Nathan shakes his hand. "Good to see you, man."

"You too, Nate," Miles greets. He turns to Ella and extends a hand. "Ella," he says, his tone cool. "It's been a while."

Fourteen months to be precise. They were introduced through a mutual colleague at the California Press Club Journalism Awards Gala. Ella doesn't have a personal opinion about Miles and assumes he's a decent person. Professionally, she respects him and admires his tenacity to go after a story. Until today. Today he's competition.

She grasps the hand he offers. "Good to see you again."

"No, it isn't." He sees right through her. "What are you doing here?" he asks, glancing from her to Nathan and back.

"I asked her to come. She's working on a piece about me."

Miles recoils. "You gave the exclusive to *Luxe Avenue*? Their readers aren't your audience. We've talked about this. Running with them won't do a thing for your career."

"That career's over. You know that."

"My advice as your friend? The longer you hide out up here, the less chance your audience will be there when you come back. You'll be a has-been."

Nathan bristles. "I'm not going back."

"What about—" Miles slides his gaze to

Ella. He shifts closer to Nathan and, lowering his voice, says, "What about that thing we discussed?"

Ella rolls her eyes. "I can hear you."

"He's talking about my concept for another reality show," Nathan explains to her.

"Dude," Miles says with disappointment.

"I have nothing to hide from her. She'll know everything by the time we're done. And I scrapped it."

Miles shakes his head, falls back a step. "Unbelievable. It had so much potential."

"My concern. Hey, Miles, great to see you. Ella and I are on a tight schedule. Are you going to be around next week?"

"Yeah, want me to swing by?"

"Nah, I'll meet you at the Tavern. I'll bring you up to speed over a beer."

"Nathan," Ella starts to object. He shouldn't be sharing anything about their discussions, at least not until the article's published.

Miles looks at Ella. He has something to say and doesn't want to say it in front of her. Nathan touches her shoulder. "Would you give us a moment?" He shows her his keys.

Reluctantly, she takes them.

"I won't be long."

Nathan leads Miles to his car, where they converse, heads close and voices lowered. After a few moments, they shake hands and Nathan claps

Miles on the shoulder. Miles gets into his car and Nathan returns to her side.

"Couldn't head inside, could you?"

There was no way she was going inside while Miles was still on Nathan's property.

"Why did you promise to bring him up to speed?" she asks when Miles leaves. "You signed a contract with us. You shouldn't be talking about it."

"I'm not sharing anything with him." Nathan sinks his hands into his front pockets. "He needed something to chew on or he wouldn't have left, not with you here."

"Do I have anything to worry about?"

"No." He shakes his head and gently touches her arm. "Will you stay? Dinner's cooking in the Crock-Pot. We can spend the rest of the afternoon on the assignment, see if we can finish this up."

"Thanks. I'd like that." She waves her phone. "I have to make a few calls first. Do you mind?"

"I'll unhitch the trailer and meet you inside."

CHAPTER 19

Ella settles inside her car, grateful that Nathan's Wi-Fi is strong enough to reach out here, and checks her phone. Eight missed calls from Damien. She'll get to him later, because right now, she needs to call her editor.

"Talk to me, Ella," Rebecca greets.

"We have a problem. Nathan leaves for Alaska tomorrow."

"Wrap it up, then. Use your notes from before. Can you get a draft to me by Monday?"

Five days.

"There've been some, ah . . . developments." Like she doesn't have her notes or her memory, developments. "Miles Jorgenson showed up today. He's pissed Nathan gave us the exclusive. Apparently, they're friends."

"Nathan signed a contract. He can't talk with anyone until we go to print."

"I know, but I don't trust Miles, not around a story this big."

"What are you saying?"

"I want to go to Alaska with Nathan. I'll wrap up the interview there. He's heli-skiing so I can get some great action shots for the article."

"Nathan agreed to this?"

"Yes." Lie. But she should be able to convince

him to invite her along now that she's convinced they had an affair. She wants the details. Nathan also owes her. He agreed to help her with her memories when she first got here.

"Go then," Rebecca agrees. "I'll give you until Thursday, but that's a hard deadline."

She victory-punches the air. "You'll have it in your in-box first thing."

"Paul was in my office asking about it this morning. Both our jobs are riding on you getting this right. We had to scramble last summer. Don't let me down again."

"You have my word."

She ends the call with Rebecca and calls Damien. He answers after the second ring.

"Where are you? I've been trying to reach you all day." Gravelly and urgent, Damien's voice rumbles over the phone. She knows he won't be happy with what she has to tell him, but it's such a relief to finally hear his voice.

"Still in Truckee with Nathan Donovan. The coverage is really bad up here. I only just got Wi-Fi again a few minutes ago."

"I've been worried." Ella feels the impact of his words. It pulls at her. His frustration that she's far from him and unreachable.

She could say the same about him. She hasn't heard from him since his cryptic text message yesterday morning. *Everything's going to shit.*

"How's the internal investigation coming along?"

He sighs, and she pictures him standing by the large front window in the bedroom of their darkened London flat, staring out into the night sky. Scrubbing a hand over his mop of hair, the city lights reflecting in his eyes, his sleep pants riding low on his hips, the perfect V of his lower abs disappearing beneath the waistband. They can see Buckingham Palace from their Kings Gate apartment. To the east, the Thames glitters under the lights of the London Eye.

"Legal department's casting a wider net and we've brought in our IT security team," he explains. "This is bigger than we thought, El. It doesn't stop at the client list or with one employee."

"Do you still suspect your dad's behind this?"

He takes a beat. "My gut tells me yes but the employees involved that we've identified aren't talking yet. We're keeping this on the down-low until we've collected as much evidence as we can. I can't get into specifics, you know that. My attorneys will shit if they find out I've told you anything. But I trust you'll keep this between us. The last thing we need is for the media to catch wind of it. When's your flight? I miss you, and . . . we need to talk."

"Of course, you want to talk now," she snaps, the words escaping before she can lock them down. "So here's a question for you: Did I sleep with Nathan?" She swears he knew she had an affair with Nathan and he didn't tell her. He didn't stop her. Yeah, he tried, but looking back, his efforts were weak. Doesn't he care about her? What about their marriage? Anger pours through her.

"I'll answer that but not over the phone."

Ella lets the arm holding her phone fall into her lap. *Are you freaking kidding me?*

She puts the phone back to her ear. "Do you know how pissed off I am?" she asks. "Why now? Why didn't you tell me last November or every other time I've asked what happened?"

Say it, Damien, she silently wills. She wants him to admit it out loud. *Say, "You fucked Nathan."*

"Not. Over. The. Phone," he clips, irritated. "I'm not getting into this with you when you're with him and eight time zones away from me."

"If you can't give me a straight answer, I mean . . . fuck."

What kind of marriage do they have if they can't talk?

Reality check. The kind where she cheated on him. Self-loathing is a rusty weight in her stomach, making her queasy.

"You won't like what I have to tell you. I don't know how you'll take it and I want to be there with you when you hear me out. I can't risk—" He takes a few beats before he speaks again, and when he does, he sounds so forlorn that Ella

218

wonders—not for the first time—exactly *what* happened between them before the accident.

"We weren't supposed to find ourselves back here."

Back where? Pissed off and uncommunicative?

If he'd been straight with her from the beginning, they wouldn't have found themselves in this predicament in the first place. Him in London, finally willing to talk, and her on a mountain half a world away. With her ex-lover, apparently.

"I blame you, Damien. Whatever happens with Nathan, I blame you. You got us into this mess."

Had she known she had an affair with Nathan before Rebecca called about the assignment, she would have declined it on the spot. Fuck her job. Not when it interferes with her marriage. But it's too late. She's committed. Her boss's job is on the line. Her job is on the line. The Jordan Talbots of the world are pining for her assignments. Nathan *is* the one with the key to unlock her mind. She's sure of it. Only he can tell her exactly what they did together. Only he can show her what they meant to one another and why. Only then will she be able to figure out why she's forgotten him.

"Ella." Damien says her name in warning.

"Nathan leaves for Alaska tomorrow, and if I can convince him, I'm going with. I need another day or so to wrap up this assignment."

"You what?" he bellows.

"My deadline's Thursday. I'll catch a flight to Heathrow when I put the article to bed."

"Goddamn it, Ella."

"I don't see a point—"

"To what?" he snaps, cutting her off.

She sighs, closing her eyes, weary of the secrets and cryptic talk. The circles they've been running around each other like loops of coding. She was going to say that she doesn't see any point in continuing their conversation. But those aren't the words that leave her mouth. She doesn't know exactly what she's thinking until the two-letter word eases off her tongue.

"Us," she whispers.

"You don't mean that."

She doesn't. But they'll deal with it when she gets to London. Because he doesn't want to talk "Over. The. Phone."

"I have to go." She ends the call, silences her phone, and lets her forehead fall to the steering wheel.

Everything has gone to shit.

Ella spends another ten minutes chilling in her car. That conversation did not go as planned. More like a backward spiral into the shallow end of a pool. She has so many questions. But she knows she'll get the answers from Damien when she joins him in London. For now, she's with Nathan, and he's holding a whole other set of answers for her.

Unfolding from her car, she takes a deep breath of crisp mountain air, tosses back her hair, and straightens her shoulders. She treks across the yard and lets herself into Nathan's house.

Inside, Fred and Bing rush over to greet her. Happy with the pats and scratches she doles out, they return to their pillow beds. A fire roars in the wide stone hearth, and stew bubbles in the Crock-Pot. The mouthwatering aroma of roasted meat and onions saturates the large, open living space.

Nathan is at the wet bar. He has changed into jeans and a fitted, long-sleeved blue shirt, the Squaw Valley ski resort logo above the outline of his pectoral. Ella wonders if there's a Tahoe resort shirt he doesn't own. She also wonders at her reaction to seeing him so casually dressed and laid-back, barefoot and freshly combed. He looks too damned good.

He mixes her a gin and tonic. "You look like you need it."

"I do. Thank you." Who cares that it's mid-afternoon? She sips her drink, relishing the cool juniper flavor. "How'd you know I like G&Ts?"

"It's your go-to drink. You had me mix them for you last time," he says, pouring himself a bourbon over ice.

"Now you're not playing fair."

His brows lift. "How so?"

"You know more about me than I do you."

"Not really, Ella. You *do* know everything about me," he says in a tone that leaves Ella wondering how much he'd come to care for her.

A flush rises up her neck and she delicately clears her throat. "Maybe I did at one point, but now . . ."—she shows him the voice recorder, determined to stay focused—"let's get down to business. I have a deadline and you have a story to tell."

His expression cools. He gestures to the seating area before the fire. She sits beside him, leaving a comfortable, professional distance between them, and sets the recorder on the coffee table.

Nathan leans forward, forearms resting on his upper legs, just above his knees, the bourbon glass cradled in his wide hands. "Where do you want to begin?"

"With Stephanie."

He sips his liquor. "All right," he says slowly. "What do you want to know?"

"Let's talk about your marriage. The early years. Were they ever good?"

"Aren't all marriages good in the beginning?"

"I'm sure most can be. I want to hear about yours."

"We were one of the good ones," Nathan confirms. "For a few years." His gaze drifts to the fire. Flames dance, reflecting in his eyes as he slips back in time. "For a while, it was me and Steph."

"You loved her."

"Ridiculously so. We were inseparable before we moved to Colorado. I couldn't do anything wrong in her eyes. But like all good things, we came to an end. I'd be filming an episode and couldn't wait to get home. Then I'd be home with her and couldn't wait to get back out there." His eyes skip to the recorder.

"Forget it's there," she encourages.

"That's not what worries me."

"I don't share my recordings. With anyone."

"But you lose them," he accuses.

Ella takes a sharp inhale through her nose. "No. I deleted them." She wouldn't have lost them. She isn't that careless. "I guess I got rid of them because we killed the article." But even deleting them isn't something she'd do. "Do you want to tell me why you changed your mind? Why give us the exclusive only to pull it?" Maybe his reasons will help her understand why she doesn't have any files left from the first interview. She holds his gaze. He slowly shakes his head.

"Later." He apathetically points at the recorder. "Let's get back to Steph." He launches into the story about their media-frenzied wedding in New York. She was gorgeous, a gem wrapped in ivory silk amid a sea of flashing lights.

Reporters crowded the sidewalk outside Le Parker Meridien, where they held their wedding reception in the Estrela Penthouse. Three-sixty-degree views of New York, with Central Park as the backdrop to the wedding party table. You can't beat that.

"I read about your wedding. The grand scale of it, the location, everything, surprised me. I pegged you as more of an intimate affair at a remote lodge type of groom."

"Steph wanted it. She was in publicity and thought the exposure would be good for my career. I was shooting the final season of *Survival of the Unfittest* and was in the preliminary concept phases of *Off the Grid!* I needed to keep the networks interested in me."

Survival of the Unfittest was Nathan's first adventure reality series where participants were put in unsuspected survivalist scenarios, such as a plane crash in the desert or a broken-down car high in the Rockies in the middle of a snowstorm. The first thirty minutes of the episode set up the situation, and under the watchful eye of the crew and on-location experts to ensure no one seriously injured themselves, they followed the participants as they tried to survive the scenario using their limited knowledge and skills. About thirty minutes in the hour-long episode, when it became obvious to viewers that the chances of surviving were minimal, Nathan would step in.

He'd guide the participants from the scenario setup to safety, showing where they'd made poor decisions and what to do instead. Ella read the series premise. She didn't have time to catch any episodes before this interview.

Nathan continues his story, sharing that he and Steph lived in New York for several years, and once the house he was having built for them in Colorado was finished, they moved. Nathan was between series and, for the most part, was home more than he was away. The best day of his life was the birth of his son, Carson.

"When did your marriage sour?" she asks.

"There wasn't any one specific moment. You start to pick up on things. She didn't look at me the same way anymore. She found fault with the most mundane things I did. She resented me when I went away and didn't want to be around me when I was home."

Ella thinks of her marriage. She and Damien rarely argue. Their heated discussion on the phone was unusual for them, but then, their relationship has been tense since November. From what she can remember of the six months prior to her accident, they seemed fine. She can't recall anything abnormal. She still felt an excited rush when he came home from work, and they could barely keep their hands off one another when they'd spent time away. But where do they stand now that she has this secret about her and Nathan? Is it even a secret? Ella would bet Damien knows or he wouldn't have asked her to ditch the interview.

"I'm sure she hated everything about me," Nathan says, still talking. "When I tried to be the person she wanted, it wasn't enough. I was the idiot who didn't see what was really happening with her. She was afraid of being alone."

"Alone in the remote wilderness where you lived, or alone without you and your support?"

"Both."

"What happened?"

"I came home from shooting an episode to find she'd moved out with Carson."

Nathan looks so devastated. She can't resist touching him and reaches a hand over to his back, offering comfort. She feels the heat of him through his shirt and it sends a ripple up her arm, warming inside her chest. She aches for his loss.

"When was this?" she asks gently.

"Two months before Carson died."

"How old was he?"

"Nine."

Nathan swallows roughly. He hangs his head and grips the back of his neck.

"Let's get back to Steph," Ella says quietly, giving him a chance to regroup. "Yesterday you mentioned she found being married to you— what's the word you used? Taxing?"

He nods.

"But she was afraid of being left alone?"

"She worried whenever I left the house. I'd go out to buy groceries and she worried. I'd take a walk and she worried. She worried most when I left to film a challenge on my show."

"She thought you'd injure or kill yourself."

He nods. "What I did was dangerous. I should have listened to her and stopped a long time ago." Remorse is a leaden weight in his voice.

"Can you tell me about Carson?" she asks cautiously, steering the conversation back to his son. He knows they have to go there, to his dark place. She hopes he's ready. If not, she may have to backtrack again and try a different angle. Revisit the topic of his son later this evening.

Nathan tosses back the remainder of his bourbon and leaves the glass on the table. Ella's inclined to offer him a refill, but she doesn't want to disturb the moment.

"Carson was a great kid," he says thickly. "He was adventurous like me. You would have liked him." He rubs his face, stares for a moment into the fire between his fingers, then drops his hands. "Every so often, I'd take Carson on location with me. He'd hang with the set crew and trail Jeff everywhere. Jeff was one of my cameramen. Then, when we'd get home, Carson would recreate the challenges he saw on my episodes, on a much smaller scale."

"Can you give me an example?"

Nathan thinks for a moment, then his face lights up. "He once filled a dirt pit with water and drove his motorized toy jeep through the mud. He'd seen me drive a Renegade through a river. He'd do stuff like that. Make a mess in the yard. Steph would have to hose him off before she allowed him back into the house."

Ella shares his smile. "Carson had an imagination."

His smile turns sad. "A big one."

"You were proud of him."

"Yes, of course."

"And Stephanie?"

"She feared Carson would turn out like me, daring and reckless. She knew right away we were wired the same. Carson was always getting into or doing something she considered dangerous. I didn't mind. I had a great relationship with my dad. I wanted Carson to have that with me.

"Carson lived to have fun, but he lived hard. Steph was always cleaning scrapes, wrapping wrists, or icing a knee. She told me more than once he was going to get himself killed. I'd laugh it off and tell her to chill. He's a boy. Let him have his fun. She didn't like that answer. She left and she took my son. She thought that without her and Carson, I'd consider changing my ways so I wouldn't be such a bad influence. It's ironic, you know? The same woman who was hoping for the most publicity possible at our wedding so I could get another TV gig was now asking me to stop doing what I do."

"So did you? Change your ways, that is?"

He shakes his head. "The opposite. After they left, I'd free-fall past the safety threshold. I'd wait until the last possible moment to pull my chute. I'd take my motorbike off-trail without any idea of the terrain in front of me. I did stupid, stupid shit. Luck's the only reason I'm alive."

"I highly doubt that. I'm sure skill has a lot to do with it. But that makes me wonder." She takes a breath before asking, "Were you trying to kill yourself?"

"I was trying to feel alive. I felt dead after Steph took Carson away. Worse after he died."

"Is that why you canceled the series? Why not just take a hiatus?"

The timer in the kitchen dings. Nathan blinks and Ella startles. She pushes out a breath and scoots away from Nathan. So absorbed in his story, she hadn't noticed that she'd inched closer to him, close enough that their thighs were touching.

Nathan glances in the direction of the kitchen.

"We should take a break," Ella suggests.

"Yeah," he says, standing.

Ella is glad he agreed because she needs one, too.

She collapses against the couch cushions, her gaze trailing Nathan as he moves to the kitchen, her mind on Simon. What would he have been like as a kid? Would he have been adventurous and rebellious? Or would he have been more studious and reserved?

She wishes she'd had the chance to find out.

CHAPTER 20

They indulge in a meal of savory venison stew. Their discussion earlier affected Nathan more than Ella anticipated. Seventeen months after his son's death and Nathan still has a difficult time talking about him. In one sitting, anyway. Ella fears that bringing up his son again tonight and delving into his reasons for canceling his series might entice Nathan to retreat. He'll clam up, shut down, even run. Everything he's been doing since Carson's death. Dashing her hopes to get an invite to Alaska. She's going to need it if she wants to get more time with him.

So she compliments the meal and flatters his sense of fashion. She strokes his ego and teasingly comments on his arrogance.

"You think I'm cocky?"

"No." She laughs the word. "You're exceedingly self-confident."

"See? You said it. I'm cocky."

She laughs again, shaking her head. "No, there's a difference. A falsely inflated ego—"

"Falsely?" he blisters.

She holds up a hand, trying not to laugh more. "Don't interrupt me. A falsely inflated ego is not the same as genuine self-confidence. A solid belief in your abilities. Absolute trust in your skills. When you have that, which you do, yeah, you go out and test your limits. Here's where you're different from those idiots in the YouTube videos riding their dirt bikes off someone's roof. I know you told me that you pushed your limits after Stephanie left, but on-screen, you seem to have a solid concept of your limits. You know when to pull back. You know when to cut off a challenge midstunt because it'll get you killed. Remember that prime-time game-show host you had on your show? What was his name?" She rapidly snaps her fingers and points at Nathan. "Thad Fillmore."

Nathan's lip curls. "That guy's an ass. He almost got us killed."

"Right. The challenge was to drive a jeep across a wide crocodile-infested riverbed. But it wasn't the crocs that had you worried. It was the weather. You kept squinting at the sky, which couldn't have been bluer had you painted it."

"You noticed that?" Nathan remarks, impressed.

"I studied you while I watched. Anyway . . ." She waves a hand to get back on point. "Thad badgered you to get on with the challenge, but you kept stalling. I had to replay the segment a few times because you were muttering something about a change in the air. It smelled different to you. You told Thad you were concerned about a flash flood. Thad laughed and pointed at the sky. He called you a phony—"

A short, sarcastic laugh pops from Nathan. "That's putting it mildly."

"Your editor was kind enough to bleep out his more colorful language. But Thad got in your face. I thought for sure you'd punch him. I was disappointed when you didn't." She grins.

"I wanted to."

"But you didn't. You kept your cool."

He smirks. "Feel free to add self-restraint to my growing list of attributes."

"Aren't you funny?" She wags a finger at him, enjoying their conversation entirely too much. "I think there were eight minutes left in the show when the camera finally panned in the direction you'd been looking the entire episode. It wasn't the sky overhead that bothered you. It was the thunderclouds upriver. Sure enough, the last five minutes of the episode showed the river rising rapidly and overflowing while you, Thad, and your crew observed from higher ground. The best part of the episode was the close-up of Thad's sheet-white face. It said it all. He would have drowned had you let him cross."

"I would have lost several of my crew that day. We were in a wide ravine. A quick escape would have been near to impossible."

"Don't you see, though? You might operate at full throttle, but from your audience's perspective, you never lose sight of the risks."

Nathan rests his forearms on the table, leaning forward. "What's your point, Skye?"

"My point is, Stephanie didn't see the cautious side of you." Whereas Ella does. She's seeing a lot. There's more to him than the thrill-seeking junkie with good looks. He is considerate and attentive, loves hard, and punishes himself just as hard. And Ella finds him entirely too fascinating and enticing than is professionally acceptable. But then, Nathan's giving her what Damien's withheld of late. Conversation—fun banter and deep reflection.

"Are you going to put that in the article?" Nathan asks.

"I think it's worth showing readers, I mean . . . Steph, that you value life more than the next thrill."

He slowly nods. He doesn't say it, but his expression tells Ella he appreciates her perspective. He's just as fascinated with their discussion. So she takes the opportunity to point their conversation north.

"Tell me about Alaska."

"Alaska." He pushes back in his chair and a smile spreads across his face. "Off the Grid 2.0."

"You're returning to television?" Blow her over. She didn't see that coming.

"No, nothing like that," he clarifies. "I'm launching an elite adventure company, where the tours will be tailored to the traveler's destination preference, skill set, and budget. Private tours. No cameras allowed except those my clients bring. I doubt I'll ever do television again." He shrugs.

"I'm meeting with the owner of a heli-skiing outfit to broker a deal. I want discounts for my clients in exchange for exclusivity—I only do trips of that nature through them. In return, they get my endorsement and additional promotion on my site."

"Sounds like a great venture," she says. "You leave tomorrow morning?"

"Day after. I pack and prep tomorrow. Drop the dogs off at the kennel."

She lifts her chin and studies him. "So the recluse is going skiing. You haven't completely given up on pushing your limits. Heli-skiing isn't for the faint of heart."

"I'll never give up skiing. I've eased up, though."

"Eased up? You realize you're talking about being helicoptered onto a mountain, right?"

"Yeah, I know. But I'm controlled and cautious." He lifts a brow, his expression teasing.

A phone rings. Nathan leans on his hip and pulls out his cell phone from his back pocket. He glances at the screen, frowns, then lifts his eyes to her. "Excuse me. I have to take this."

He gets up from the table, answering the phone as he closes the sliding glass door behind him.

"Nathan Donovan," Ella hears him answer before the door closes, cutting him off. He faces inside the house and she can see his frown deepen to a scowl.

Ella pushes out a breath. Who's the caller? Hopefully it's nothing serious. Getting an invite to Alaska will be near impossible if this is bad news.

Rising from the table, she clears their empty bowls and rinses them in the sink. It doesn't take long for Nathan to come back inside. He slams the slider behind him. Energy rolls off him. Cheeks reddened either from the cold or anger, he taps his phone against his thigh, agitated.

"What is it?" she asks.

"Come with me."

"To Alaska?"

He nods.

"Yes. I'd love to," she blurts, not giving him a chance to think twice. She grins. That was easy.

Nathan tosses his phone on the counter. He approaches her, brushing his thumb across his lower lip, his expression pensive. He stops close enough that Ella is forced to look up at him. She can smell the cool evening air on him. It quickens her heartbeat, deepens her breathing.

"I wasn't planning on inviting you," he says in a gruff tone.

"Too late. I'm tagging along. You can't change your mind."

"I won't. I want you to come. I've been enjoying our time together. You?"

236

"Professionally speaking? It's been an adventure."

He smiles easily, the right side of his mouth pulling up a little higher than the left. "And personally?"

Warmth inches up her neck. She can imagine the blush he sees and wishes she could stop it.

"Yes," she whispers.

He smiles, pleased. "Let's call it a night then. We can wrap this up in Alaska."

"My thoughts exactly," she says, shifting back into business mode. "I have to get up early in the morning and do some shopping. I didn't pack for Alaska."

"I'll join you. I have to pick up a few items at Alpine Mountaineering in town." He touches her hair, moving aside a wisp that had fallen over her eye. "Check out of your hotel in the morning. Stay here tomorrow night."

"With you?" Her face heats.

"Ah, no," he says with a nervous laugh. "I have a guest room. We're flying out of Reno first thing. It'll save us time in the morning to drive straight there from here."

"What flight? I'll book my ticket."

"I'll take care of it."

"Nathan," she says. "This is business. *Luxe Avenue* will foot my bill. I'll give you my credit card number."

"No way, I want the miles." He flashes an

impish grin, but Ella gives him a look. "Fine. I'll email the bill to your editor. The magazine can reimburse me. Agreed?"

Ella relaxes a little. "Okay."

"Good. Then it's settled. I'll meet up with you in town tomorrow morning."

"Indeed." Though she does wonder exactly what they settled.

CHAPTER 21

"Too thick." Nathan takes the liberty of removing the pair of socks Ella added to her shopping basket.

"News flash. I get cold easily." She tosses the socks back in her basket.

As planned, she checked out of her hotel after breakfast. Nathan texted the location of Alpine Mountaineering, adding that he'd meet her there.

Nathan wears another one of his button-down flannels under a hunter-green jacket. A beat-up vintage Northstar-at-Tahoe cap is on his head. Oakley aviators hang from the collar of his heather-gray undershirt. His rugged handsomeness, his subtle aloe-soap-and-pine scent, and his nearness—most especially his nearness—keep drawing her eye. She can't seem to get her fill of him.

Nathan replaces the socks, dropping a different pair in the basket.

"Aren't those a little thin for where we're going?" she observes.

"They'll be fine. Believe it or not, they're designed to keep your feet warmer and allow them to breathe. You'll sweat in those others, then that sweat will chill in the Alaskan climate and your toes will freeze."

"If you say so." She skims the label of the pair he selected.

"We had an in-depth discussion about socks last summer."

"Did we? Sounds fascinating."

"It was a surprisingly thorough conversation. We covered the need for ventilation zones and stretch recovery. Don't you hate it when the elastic fails?"

"We're talking about socks, right?" She eyes him as she digs through the discount sock bin.

"Absolutely. Socks bunched at the ankle is the worst sort of inconvenience midhike."

"The horror." She gives him an exaggerated shiver. "What about seams? Were you one of those kids who wouldn't put on his shoes until the sock seams laid exactly right over your toes?"

"That was me to a T. Good news, though. These socks have no seams." He dangles another pair in front of her face. She snatches them and drops them in her basket.

"Tell me, Nathan," she begins, moving on to the coatrack. Her quilted coat and the hiking jacket she doesn't remember leaving at Nathan's house won't cut it in Alaska's Pacific coast windchill. "What else did we talk about?"

He removes his jacket and hooks it over his arm. Thinks for a moment. "Your brother. How's his app coming along?"

"Come Over Rover? Great. He's found an

investor." She pushes aside coats on the rack. Selecting one at random, she shows Nathan.

"Try it on," he suggests, and she does. The thick blue parka, lined with sheep's wool with a faux trimmed hood, fits well. Flipping up the hood, she extends her arms and turns full circle. "Well?" she asks.

"You remind me of a toddler stuffed into a snowsuit."

She laughs. "Good. It'll keep me warm."

"Excuse me, are you Nathan Donovan?" asks a young woman neither of them had seen approach. Two friends flank her. All three are decked in knit snow caps and snowboard pants that bunch at their ankles. Sun-kissed cheeks and windburned noses with a defined outline in the shape of their ski goggles adorn their ChapStick-commercial perfect faces.

Nathan looks to Ella. She can tell he wants to say no, but he pastes on a smile and forces out an "I am."

"I loved your show," she gushes. "May we take a selfie with you?"

She has her phone out with the camera app open before she finishes her question.

"I'm going to pay for these." Ella points at her basket. "Meet you up front."

Nathan barely acknowledges her. The woman already has her arm around him, and the other two women are pulling out their phones.

By the time the salesclerk rings up and bags Ella's items, a small gathering has formed around Nathan. They demand autographs and selfies. They want to know when his next series starts. Where does he live? Is he vacationing in Truckee? Who's the woman he's with? Does that mean he and Stephanie aren't getting back together? Are they going to have another kid since Carson died?

Nathan's face pales and Ella's stomach lurches. The nerve of some people. A staff member tries dispersing the crowd, but they are all over him. Nathan has been off the grid for too long. Everyone is too caught up in getting his attention and the scoop on his next move.

His gaze meets hers over their heads. A sheen of sweat shines his forehead. Ella would expect that a celebrity with his degree of popularity would be used to this level of exposure and have the charisma to step away from the crowd graciously. She'd seen Steve Young do it on numerous occasions while shopping at Stanford Shopping Center when she was growing up. But Nathan is backed into a corner, trapped between the coatrack and sock bin. He looks like he's about to panic.

"Excuse me." Ella pushes between a heavyset woman and an adolescent boy and wraps an arm around Nathan's waist. "Nathan, darling. We're going to be late."

"Sorry, peeps. Gotta bounce." Nathan's arm drops around her shoulders. Phones click in their faces. He looks at her with relief.

Threading her fingers through his and keeping his arm tight around her, she maneuvers them through racks of clothes and out the emergency exit in back. An alarm blares when Nathan shoves open the door. They don't stop until they reach her car in the parking lot. Releasing his hand and her breath, she searches for her keys.

"That was so bizarre," she says on a laugh, and the laugh builds. She can't stop herself and sags against the car.

Nathan just smiles, waiting for the moment to pass.

"All right, you've had your fun," he says when Ella settles down.

"Whew, I needed that." She exhales, holding her ribs, then grins up at him. "Admit it, I was totally your bodyguard."

He chuckles, shaking his head. "Cutest bodyguard ever." They share a smile, then Ella sobers.

"Is it always like that for you?" His fans had even made her feel claustrophobic.

"When I get caught out in public, yes," he says, his pale face slowly returning to its normal shade of winter tan. He shoves his hands into his pockets. "Thanks for that."

"You're welcome. Why didn't you tell them you had to leave or something?"

"I tried following you to the checkout counter, but . . . Confession?" Nathan lifts his cap and tunnels his fingers into his hair. His hand shakes. "I get anxious in a crowd. It's why I left New York."

"Oh. I'm sorry." She shouldn't have left him. "Did I know that about you?" He might have told her before. She might have witnessed it before.

He shakes his head. "I've never mentioned it to anyone. It's only bad when people get into my space and I don't have a way out."

Nathan's expression is strained. He sounds perturbed, and for the first time, Ella catches a glimpse of what his life has been like. No wonder he plays the part of a hermit and grew a beard so that he could move about town incognito.

"I shouldn't have left you. I'm sorry it got out of control in there."

"It wasn't too bad. I should be used to it by now, but . . ." He shrugs. "The outdoors, that's my game. Best forewarn you, though: don't be surprised if those shots show up on social media."

Ella swears, thinking of how they must have looked leaving, arms wrapped around each other, and the way Nathan had looked at her when she came to his rescue. The photos his fans took will go viral.

Nathan slides on his Oakleys. He glances back at the store's entrance. "I'll come back later when it's less crowded." Only then does she realize he dropped his basket of items somewhere in the store.

"Where are you headed now?" she asks.

"The kennel. You?"

"I got what I needed. I guess I'll find a coffee shop somewhere and organize my notes from yesterday until you're ready to head back to your place."

Nathan removes a key from his key chain. "Here. You can work at the house."

"Thanks." She takes the key.

"The guest room is on the main level, across from the bathroom. It's ready for you. Towels are out. I'll pick up something for dinner and meet you at home later."

He briefly touches her shoulder, then heads for his truck. As she settles into the driver's seat, it dawns on Ella that he doesn't seem at all fazed that their faces could be plastered across social media, where the photos can be picked up by *Access Hollywood* and ETonline. *Gah!* Or TMZ, the worst of the bunch. Grocery store tabloid on television.

Hugging the steering wheel, Ella drops her head and groans. Why did she call him "darling"? Nathan was panicking. She acted on impulse. She can imagine TMZ's headline: Grieving Celebrity

Adventurer Dumps Mother of His Deceased Son for Lifestyle Journalist.

She's such a moron. But in her defense, she did for him what anyone with a conscience would have done to get him out of an alarming situation. She did what she would have done for her husband.

Damien.

Fuck.

He has no patience for entertainment news and social media, so he doesn't read it. But any of his employees would recognize her and forward the link to the photos. She needs to call him so that he can get his PR department on this fast. She needs to tell him that her relationship with Nathan is, well . . . It's not what he thinks.

But her call goes straight to voice mail. It's early evening in London and he's likely in meetings. Unless . . . he's still upset with her after yesterday's call and ignoring her, which is a real possibility. She leaves a brief message, then drives to Nathan's.

Ella's on the deck taking photos when Nathan joins her that evening. At the sound of the door, she turns and snaps a photo, startling him. He'd shucked his jacket and cap inside and made a visit to the fridge. He shows her two open beers, closing the door behind him. She snaps another photo.

"Stop," he says, coming to stand by her at the rail. A faint smile shows her he doesn't actually mind.

"Just a few more. My editor needs them for the article. It's either me or she sends a photographer with us to Alaska."

He puts down the beers. "Snap away, Skye."

She goes to work, posing him one way, directing him to tilt his head another way. Of course, he's a natural in front of the camera. About fifteen minutes into the session, Ella lifts the camera and catches movement behind Nathan. "Look," she whispers, pointing.

Nathan turns around. A doe and her fawn traverse the yard.

"They're a couple of my regulars." He glances back at Ella and motions for her to come stand beside him. "They cut through my property this time most evenings. I think they rest over there." He points beyond the tree line.

"She's beautiful."

They watch the deer nibble leaves. Above them, the bright blue of the sky has darkened to deep shades of pink and lavender. Gray clouds and jet streams are chalk streaks, interweaving. Smoke clings to the air. Nathan must have started a fire. The woods surrounding them are surprisingly quiet. Ella feels at peace, which is probably why she doesn't move away when Nathan puts his arm around her. She leans into him.

When the doe disappears into the thicket, her fawn follows. A touch of sadness falls over Ella. Her hand trails to her pelvis and hovers over her C-section scar.

"What do you remember most about your son?" she asks softly.

Nathan releases a long sigh. His arm falls from her shoulders. He grabs a beer and takes a swig.

"He was always doing something. Building, crafting, calculating."

"Did he want to be an engineer?"

"And an astronaut, and a lawyer, and the president of the United States. But don't all kids when they're young?"

She shrugs. She wouldn't know. Would Simon have wanted to travel to space? Or would he have been a programmer like his father? A writer like her? She'll wonder about the answers for the rest of her life.

"The thing about Carson is that he could demolish whatever he was working on ten times faster than he'd built it. It was like a switch flipped. Totally engrossed in his project one moment and kicking boards and throwing bolts the next.

"Once we built a tree house together, just a small fort about fifteen feet or so above the ground. It had a platform with rails and one-by-fours we'd nailed into the trunk to use as a ladder. Very old school."

"It sounds perfect."

"It was, once we finished. But while we were building, I had Carson work on the bottom three rungs. I showed him how to nail the boards into the trunk so we wouldn't damage the tree. Well, he couldn't get the nail in the way he wanted to, and rather than asking for my help, he started swinging the hammer around like Thor. Before I could climb down from the platform, he climbed up the metal ladder I'd been using and destroyed half the rungs I'd nailed into the tree above him. His temper flared so quickly and I used to hate that. It drove me mad when he got that frustrated and irrational. But it's one of the things I miss most about him. He would have learned to channel that energy into testing his own limits. I did. I'll never . . ." Nathan falters. He swallows and tries again. "I'll never get to witness that."

He brushes the back of his hand against Ella's lower belly. The gesture is tender and endearing but sudden and unexpected. She recoils.

"I'm sorry." He lowers his hand and looks at her, his eyes full of grief, compassion, and sympathy. "I can't imagine not remembering Carson, the good times and those frustrating moments. I can't fathom what you're going through."

Ella looks away, and all the emotions she read about other women experiencing with late-term miscarriages, all the emotions she's sought to feel, all the ones she envied Damien going through, are suddenly there. Real. Intense. And in her face. She can barely breathe.

"Ella," Nathan whispers, touching her cheek.

"Don't." She jerks her head away. It's all too much. Confused about her growing attraction toward Nathan, devastated she can't remember carrying Simon, and disappointed her husband wouldn't share his grief with her the way Nathan has been, Ella feels overwhelmed. She needs a moment alone.

Grabbing her camera, she says, "I'm going to get ready for dinner."

"Ella."

The way Nathan speaks her name stops her.

"You asked me yesterday why I canceled my series. I didn't give you an answer."

"No, you didn't." She senses he wants to get this off his chest, but she can't handle any more heartbreak, not when she's about to fall apart. "Can we talk about this tomorrow? If you don't mind."

He takes a beat. "Yeah, sure. We can talk tomorrow."

She nods and retreats inside.

CHAPTER 22

"I updated Scott about our flight change. He'll pick us up at the airport tomorrow," Nathan explains when he gets off the phone with the owner of Backcountry Descents, the heli-skiing adventure company Nathan had hoped to meet with over dinner. But their connection in Seattle to Anchorage was delayed due to weather and they missed their last connection, a forty-five-minute flight to Cordova.

"Let's find a couple rooms for the night," Ella suggests.

"Good idea. I'll take care of it."

They take a cab to a nearby hotel where Nathan had called and reserved two rooms. They agree to meet in the lobby restaurant after they check in and shower. Ella's determined to finish Nathan's interview tonight, because once it's out of the way, she can focus on them. One way or another, she intends to find out what happened last summer.

In her room, Ella checks her phone. Damien still hasn't returned the call she placed last evening. After her talk with Nathan on the deck, she didn't care that she ended their call the other day on absolutely the wrong foot. Still, overwhelmed with emotions about the miscarriage, she needed to hear her husband's voice.

She's about to try him again when a text with an image buzzes in from Davie:

Nice arm candy. Damien know?

Gawd. Here they go.

Ella sinks onto the bed and studies the photo: Nathan and her, arm in arm, eyes hooked on one another. To Ella, he looks relieved. To everyone else? His expression can easily be misinterpreted as someone in love, which is exactly how the tabloids will spin their articles.

Ella fires back a text. It's not what you think.

Davie's reply is immediate. I know it's not. But it's gone viral. TMZ identified you.

Crap.

Davie texts a link. Ella would rather hurl her phone into the trash than open the website, but she needs to know what she's up against. She clicks the link and reads: Nathan Donovan Is Back on the Grid—Caught Shopping with New Girlfriend.

The article goes on to explain how Nathan Donovan was spotted shopping with someone whom witnesses described as a possible girl-friend. TMZ identified her as staff writer Ella Skye with *Luxe Avenue*, who happens to be married to Damien Russell, CEO of Phantom Defense Networks. The article includes a photo of the *Inc.* magazine issue that featured Damien on the cover. Nathan and Ella seemed quite cozy according to those who observed their interaction. The article speculates what this means for Nathan's marriage and if his appearance in public is a sign that he has another survivalist series in the works.

This is bad. So bad. Worse than Ella anticipated. While Rebecca will probably see this as free press leading up to the exclusive, Damien won't.

Davie texts. **Where are you?**

Alaska with Nathan, Ella replies. **Finishing up the assignment.**

A text buzzes in from Nathan. He's on his way downstairs.

Ella looks skyward, praying for a moment to breathe. Everything's happening at once.

Gotta run. Chat later, she texts Davie. She then texts Damien—**Call me!**—and slides her phone into her back pocket.

Downstairs, Nathan has tucked himself against the wall near the hostess desk. He wears a beat-up cap. Chin down, face shadowed, he tries to be nondescript as he surfs his phone. The dining room is packed and the waiting area full. A couple of guests have already figured out who Nathan is and have their phones out. They not-so-discreetly take his picture.

"Hey," she says, coming up to stand in front of him to block prying eyes and photo ops.

"Hey." He smiles tightly and pockets his

phone. He crosses his arms and uncrosses them. Anxious.

She motions for him to lean down. "Do you want to get room service?" She speaks into his ear over the din of conversation and pulse of bass thumping through the restaurant's speakers.

"Yes." He puts his hand on her back and follows her to the bank of elevators.

"Crowds really bother you."

He stabs the button for his floor. "More than they used to. Price of being a hermit, I guess."

"Anything I can do to help?"

"You already have. I realized last night that talking helps. I'd forgotten about that. I didn't feel that gnawing guilt when I woke this morning."

"That's great. Did it not help last time?"

"Yes, but I haven't talked with anyone about Carson since last summer with you."

Ella briefly touches his arm, grateful he's chosen to share with her. Everyone should have someone they can talk to. She wishes Damien had shared what happened between them last November.

The elevator dings and doors open. Ella follows him to his room, where they order dinner and eat a light meal. After Nathan puts the tray of dirty dishes in the hallway, Ella silences her phone, asking Nathan to do the same, so that they aren't interrupted. She sets up her recorder on the table and invites him to sit beside her on the couch.

"Ready?" she asks when he sits down.

"Ready," he acknowledges, replenishing their wine.

Ella turns on the device, and for the next two hours, they talk about his son and Stephanie. He admits divorcing Stephanie is inevitable. It doesn't make him happy, but it's getting easier to live with the idea that he and Steph are better off without each other.

But his mood changes when they veer back to his childhood. He speaks candidly, with reverence and adoration about his parents. He misses his father and plans to visit his mother in San Diego soon. He hasn't seen her in more than a year and wants to go surfing.

"My face is the only part of me that's seen the sun in seventeen months."

Ella laughs. "Where have you surfed, aside from San Diego?"

"Many places, but my favorites are Hawaii and Australia."

"Ever been to Half Moon Bay for the Mavericks?"

"No, but I have a ton of respect for big wave surfers."

"You'll jump out of airplanes, hike K2, and heli-ski in Alaska, but you won't face down a thirty-foot wall of water?"

"Hell, no," he says, laughing. "Limits, Skye. I know mine."

She smiles and glances at the voice recorder. The red light blinks. It's getting late and they have a long day tomorrow, but there's one last thing they must discuss.

"Let's talk about the day your son died," she says in a measured voice.

Nathan folds his hands in his lap. "All right."

"Do you think you can walk me through that day?"

He takes a moment, then nods.

"I was on location," he says, shifting on the couch. He runs Ella through his morning, how he spoke with Carson on the phone. His son had watched the wingsuit flying episode the night before and couldn't stop talking about it. Carson convinced Nathan to take him flying when he was old enough. Nathan promised he would, and Carson said he was going to practice so that he'd be ready.

"I should have taken him seriously. By practice, I figured he meant . . ."

"Meant what?" Ella prompts when he doesn't say anything for a moment.

"A good father would have told his son how much he loves him and that he'd be home soon, right?" He looks at her beseechingly and Ella feels herself nodding. "I didn't do that. My mind was elsewhere. We were filming that day and I had to mentally get into the zone. Justin Turner, the actor who starred in that sci-fi blockbuster last summer?"

"*Titan Rising?* Yes, I know who he is."

"He was my celebrity guest. He's a kick-ass mountain biker and we were riding some steep and narrow routes that day in Moab. So, yeah, I needed to focus. What I should have done was listen to Carson. I should have called back." He rakes his fingers through his hair, then leans forward and rubs his face. "This never gets easier."

Ella rests a hand on Nathan's thigh. "What doesn't? Talking about Carson?"

Face hidden in his hands, he nods.

"How did he die, Nathan?" she asks gently.

He lifts his head and looks pointedly at her. "Wrong question. Ask me why I canceled the series."

"Okay," Ella says, unsure as to where he's going with this. "Why did you cancel your series?"

"Carson died after watching one of my episodes, the wingsuit flying one I told you about. My guest and I glided off cliffs. Flying like that is one of the best thrills I've experienced. I remember looking directly into the camera and telling my viewers, 'If there's anything you should do before you die, it's wingsuit gliding. Put that on your bucket list.'

"After he got off the phone with me, Carson crafted a makeshift flight suit. He climbed the giant pine in his grandmother's backyard where he was living at the time with Steph. He was intent on flying, just like his dad, and he jumped."

"Oh, my god." Ella gasps into her hand and grasps his forearm at the same time.

"He shattered both legs and hit his head. Steph found him unconscious at the base of the tree." He pinches the inside corners of his eyes, squeezing them shut, and exhales roughly through his nose. "He never woke up."

Tears flow down Ella's cheeks. For Steph to find their child broken and unconscious? She has no words. She wipes her face with her palms, sniffling. The noise catches Nathan's attention. He looks directly at her.

"Do you see why I canceled the series? Do you see why I never want to go back to television again? My son mimicked my stunts. I'm positive there are other kids out there doing the same. I don't want their injuries, their deaths, on my conscience. One death, my son's death, is one too many. What you need to understand, what I want you to get across in this article, is what Steph has known all along. I *am* to blame. My son's death is on me."

Nathan stands. He strides past her and goes to the window. Bottled energy pulses through him. He fidgets, tapping the window with his knuckle, the force increasing with each knock. He makes a fist, and for a horrifying second, Ella fears he'll thrust his arm through the glass.

"Nathan."

He turns around. Their eyes meet and something unspoken passes between them. Ella disregards she's here on assignment. She dismisses the fact that they're both married. And she stops resisting the urge to comfort him the way he needs. Turning off the recorder, she goes to him.

Tension vibrates from his body when she stands before him. She touches his arm, rests a hand on his cheek. "Nathan," she whispers.

He threads his fingers in her hair. "What is it about you?" he murmurs.

She doesn't know. His touch doesn't seem familiar, but it feels safe and right.

That alone should scare Ella more than anything, but she doesn't move away. Instead, she draws closer.

Nathan leans down until their lips are a breath apart, and even though Ella knows what's coming next, she doesn't feel any guilt, only the desire to ease his heartache.

They kiss, more chaste than deep, and it doesn't last long.

Nathan rests his cheek against hers. "Stay with me tonight," he murmurs. "Let me just hold you."

"Okay," she whispers and kisses his neck. Because for now, that's what he needs. It's what she needs, too.

She slips off her shoes and lies down, fully clothed, on the bed. Nathan turns off the lights and, after removing his own shoes, joins her on the bed, drawing a blanket over them and her into his arms.

"Thank you," he whispers, dropping soft kisses in her hair, light and airy, and soon, Ella feels herself drifting off, thinking of their conversation about his son. Hopefully, tonight he can find some peace.

Ella wakes in a darkened room, foreign with unfamiliar scents. She lies on her side and slowly, like pausing a TV show to take in the scene's details, waits for her eyes to adjust.

Nathan's hotel room. Nathan's bed. Nathan beside her.

Light spills from the bathroom and onto the bed in a blanket of molten gold. Nathan breathes steadily, watching her.

"Hey," she says.

"Hi."

He gently touches her face, gliding his thumb along her lower lip.

"How long have you been awake?" she asks.

"Not long."

"What time is it?"

"Two a.m., I think."

He trails his hand lower, his fingertips lightly dancing along the curve of her neck, the neckline of her shirt. He stops at the top button and their eyes meet, his questioning. His lips part.

"Yes," she whispers before he can ask. She wants this. She wants him.

He leans into her and tenderly, gently, presses his lips to hers. That's all it takes, that one light touch to ignite what's been simmering between them, what's always been there.

They shed their clothes, fumbling with zippers and buttons, kissing, touching, and discovering. When he presses Ella to her back and settles between her legs, she expects him to plunge into her and drive them to the edge with the same ferocity she witnessed him display in his episodes. But as he's done since she arrived at his house earlier in the week, he surprises her. He takes his time. Savors her. Worships the curves and planes of her body, pushing her higher until she peaks.

Before she can catch her breath, Nathan's forearms frame her head as he supports his weight. He grasps her hands, threading his fingers with hers. "You okay?"

"Very."

They share a smile and then Nathan eases into her, all the way, and stills. Ella releases a steady moan. *God, he feels so good.*

But she needs more.

She squeezes his hands and, planting her feet on the mattress, attempts to raise her hips. He doesn't budge.

"Move," she grunts. She needs pressure. There. She aches.

Nathan rocks into her. He moves with purpose, searching for a connection. And Ella's right there with him.

Aurous light highlights the rigid angles of his face, heightens the blue in his eyes, which hold on to hers.

"I wish you remembered us." Spoken against her lips.

So does Ella.

She looks inward, hoping, praying, this might be what it takes to lift the veil in her mind. But she doesn't remember. Being with him in this way isn't familiar. Just different. So different from Damien. Nathan's broader, heavier. His scent sharper, provocative and arousing.

"El."

Her name is a breath of air and she feels a sting behind her eyes.

Nathan's making love to her as though they belong together. How could she ever have forgotten what it feels like to be with him? How could she have forgotten him?

Wrapping her arms and legs around him, she gives herself over to her feelings. She gives herself over to him. And soon, they're crashing, falling. Tumbling into bliss.

Afterward, once they've cleaned up and turned off the bathroom light, Nathan curves his body along the back of hers. He holds her hand.

This isn't good, Ella thinks, because it feels too good.

Sex with Nathan didn't unblock her memories of him. What it did do, however, was make her question her own feelings. How easily she could fall for him, which only makes her more determined to learn the truth.

What happened between them last summer? Did she leave, or did he send her away?

Ella gives his hand a squeeze. "We have to talk," she whispers in the darkness.

"I know. Tomorrow." He nips her shoulder, kisses away the sting, and promptly falls asleep. But when she wakes in the morning, the bed is empty.

Ella sits up, anxious. Nathan's duffel and ski bags are still in the room, but he's not. He probably went to fetch coffee. She flops back on the pillow and looks at her phone to check the time. Numerous notifications display from Damien.

Damien.

Guilt sours in her stomach. She can't bring herself to read his texts, not when she's still in Nathan's bed with his scent all over her.

She'll deal later, she reasons, looking at the time. They have several hours before they have to leave for the airport. She needs those hours to skim through last night's recording and organize her thoughts. Tossing aside the sheets, Ella quickly dresses, leaving Nathan's room and, god willing, her guilt behind.

Nathan knocks on her door around noon.

"May I come in?" he asks when she opens the door. He sounds exhausted, and he looks just as bone-weary, a contrast to Ella, who's been in work mode. She rubs the back of her neck, tense from leaning over her keyboard.

"Sure." She opens the door wider and he glides past, carrying with him the scents of Anchorage—oil, fish, and ice. His nose is red and cheeks rosy. He's been out in the cold for some time.

"Everything okay?" she asks, her mind on last night. Does he regret what happened? Surprisingly, she feels more relaxed than she has in months. Probably because she's been productively working and not dwelling on the possible consequences. Her phone, loaded with Damien's unread texts, is burning a hole in her back pocket.

"Yep . . . um. No. Not really."

He glances down at his jacket as though surprised it's still on. He shrugs it off and tosses it on the bed.

"Where'd you go this morning?" She was disappointed he wasn't there when she woke up. He promised they'd talk in the morning.

"I went for a walk. I've been on the phone since it woke me. Steph's attorney called, then I called mine." He plants his hands on his waist and exhales. "I'm going to sign the divorce papers."

Ella blinks in surprise. "You sure that's what you want to do?" Nathan has been separated for over a year. She wonders if last night has anything to do with his decision.

He shrugs. "Our marriage was over long before Carson died. And no"—he gives her a look—"this has nothing to do with what happened between us. What *is* happening. I made my decision about Steph months ago."

"But I thought the article—"

"It was never about getting her back." He closes the distance between them. "It's about getting her forgiveness."

"Oh." She frowns. She'd been so sure of his motivations and he'd never corrected her. She looks at her black socks, her feet almost toe-to-toe with Nathan's boots. The way she sees it, Nathan doesn't need Stephanie's forgiveness. He needs to forgive himself. But self-forgiveness can't be forced. She knows that firsthand. Grace died nearly twenty years ago and Ella still feels guilty about the way it happened.

Nathan cradles her head, tilting up her face. His eyes search hers. "What about us? Are we good?"

"Yes. We're good." They share a smile.

"I'm sorry I wasn't there when you woke. I wanted to spend the morning making love to you."

"And talking," she reminds him.

He rests his forehead on hers. "Yes, talking. I want to do that, too. Tonight, promise. Meanwhile . . ." He dives in for a quick, hard kiss, pulling away on a moan. "We have a plane to catch. Only flight out of here today. As much as I want to drag you back into bed, we can't miss it." He looks at the clock. "Meet you in the lobby in twenty?"

She agrees. Grabbing his jacket, he steals another kiss and leaves her to pack.

CHAPTER 23

Surrounded by the glacial peaks of the Chugach Mountains, Cordova is a quaint coastal town in Southeast Alaska. Ella's weather app tells her the temp's in the low forties, but the air nips and the wind bites. Cold and damp, it feels like it's in the thirties. Ella bundles her jacket around her as they step outside to meet their ride.

Scott Burgess, the owner and operator of Backcountry Descents, is there to meet them. A wiry man with a sun-bronzed face and chapped hands, he shakes Nathan's hand vigorously, clearly delighted to have *the* Nathan Donovan joining him. He's even more enthusiastic when Nathan introduces Ella, explaining that she's writing a feature on him for *Luxe Avenue*. Scott isn't the least bit shy asking for a mention.

"You can find whatever you need to know about our operation on our website. But please"—he presses his palms flat together—"ask me anything."

"Will do," Ella says, all but lunging into her seat when Scott slides open the courtesy van's door, desperate to get out of the cold. Nathan sits in the front passenger seat.

Scott loads their gear and luggage into the back and settles in the driver's seat, popping his arm over the seatback so that he can face both her and Nathan.

"So, friends, we have a situation. This season's been epic. The lodge is at capacity. I don't have an extra room. The one we booked for you"—he nods at Nathan—"can sleep four. You got a queen and a pullout sofa. I've secured a room at the B&B in case"—he looks at Ella—"you prefer separate rooms. I mention this now because we drive through town and can drop off your stuff before we make our way to the lodge."

Nathan shrugs a shoulder. "I don't mind sharing if you don't."

"As long as you take the couch," Ella quips. After last night, it would be hard for her not to share a room with him.

"Great, then let's get you guys to the lodge." Scott shifts the van into gear.

"How's tomorrow looking? Think we'll get on the mountain?" Nathan asks as they leave the airport.

"We'll know in the morning, but it looks promising. I expect we can get in eight or so drops." For Ella's benefit, Scott goes on to explain that with a fleet of three helicopters and over a thousand square miles of terrain that boasts runs upward to eighteen hundred vertical feet at fifty-five-degree inclines, weather must be constantly monitored for the safety of his pilots, guides, and guests. Any red flags in the weather pattern or risk of avalanche and it's a down day. No flying.

"Is it even safe?"

"Heli-skiing? It wouldn't be the most epic of skiing experiences if it was," Scott retorts and Nathan grins. He gets it. Skiing fresh lines down a glacial mountain face comes with heavy consequences. But for thrill-seekers of big-mountain skiing, heli-skiing delivers. It's the pinnacle of the recreational sport.

"Have you heli-skied before?" Ella asks Nathan.

"Twice. Silverton in Colorado and Ruby Ridge in Nevada. This is my first trip to Alaska."

"You're in for a treat, friend," Scott promises.

Ella's done her share of black diamond runs, but what Scott's described sounds pretty dicey. Nathan might be an expert skier, but she's nervous for him. She also wants to watch. She'll ask him later if he can secure a spot for her on the copter. On *Luxe*'s dime, of course.

Backcountry Descents is ten minutes north of the airport and right on the water. The outfit used to be an old cannery and houses a lodge, helipad, and hangar. Scott tells them they have a restaurant on-site for their meals, and to finish off their days, the facility has hot tubs and saunas.

He parks the van and they get out. "Why don't you guys get settled in your room. Dinner's not for another hour but come down and have a beer. I'll introduce you to my crew."

"Sounds good." Nathan shoulders Ella's bag when she reaches for it. "I got it."

"Thanks," she says. A wall of ice-sharp wind coming off the channel barrels into her back. "My gosh, it's cold."

Scott grins. He unloads Nathan's duffel and one of his two ski bags.

"Let's get the lady inside." Nathan grabs his other bag. Ella couldn't agree more.

They follow Scott into the heated lodge. It feels like heaven. Nathan checks them into their room.

The sun doesn't set for another hour, but the light is waning. Ella turns on the lamps in their small room. The queen bed and sofa eat up the floor space, which doesn't give her and Nathan much room to move around once they set down their gear. The room's style and color are tired but comfortable.

"You really don't mind sharing?" Ella asks Nathan when he finishes in the bathroom. Aside from the inconvenience of having the courtesy van shuffle her back and forth to an inn in town, she doesn't want to be too far removed from Nathan, not when they need to have one final conversation.

"No, what about you? You're the one who's married." His tone is teasing, but Ella detects a note of ire. He doesn't like that she's attached.

"So are you," she points out.

"Not for much longer." He eases in on her, lifts a hand to her jaw. His long, wide fingers thread loosely in her hair. "You once told me you'd leave Damien for me," he murmurs.

Her head draws back quickly.

"I fell in love with you last summer." He whispers the confession.

"What?"

"How could I not? You spent almost a week with me on a trail living in the dirt and didn't complain once. You ski, you run, you'll get on the back of a snowmobile and have a blast. I bet you'd heli-ski if you were mentally and physically conditioned to do it. You, Ella Skye, love adrenaline as much as me.

"But more than that, you're fun to be with. You're witty and intelligent. We can have a deep conversation one moment and the next you're telling me off. And the sex! Whoa." He laughs the word, hands flaring out. "It's mind-blowing with you. Last night was only a taste of what it was like between us before. Just wait until we get back into the groove."

Her cheeks heat. She wants him to stop talking. His words are too much. "Nathan—"

"I still love you," he admits. "And I know somewhere in that head of yours, you feel the same. You told me."

She what?

She steps back, needing a moment to process.

He lets his arm drop. "You seem surprised."

"That's an understatement." Her heart pounds in her throat. A sinking, hollow sensation expands in her chest. "Why are you telling me this now?"

"I didn't mean to upset you."

"I suddenly have the impression a lot of what I've been waiting to hear from you will be upsetting." My god. She fell in love with another man. Worse, she was going to leave her beautiful, magnificent husband. The man she loves.

The man she just cheated on. Again, she thinks begrudgingly.

A wise woman would get back in the van and return to the airport, fly to London, and be with her husband. Never tell him about any of this. But she doesn't want to leave. Hearing Nathan tell her she loved him and was going to leave Damien is shocking, but it does explain things. Namely, how easily she's falling for him. Then again, the same thing happened with Damien. Ella falls hard and she falls fast. She just wants to love and be loved.

She's all sorts of screwed.

Nathan is standing there, looking as though he's holding his breath.

He should have told her everything the first night she arrived. But like Damien, he bit his tongue.

Bite your tongue.

There's that phrase again.

Ella narrows her gaze. Nathan watches her cautiously. "Is this why you've held out on me? You're afraid of how I'll react?"

"No." He forces out a breath. "Okay. A little. But I wanted you to know where I'm coming from when we do talk. I don't want to lose you again," he confesses.

Her first thought is that she doesn't want to lose him, too. But that isn't right. She doesn't want to let him go. She doesn't want to leave him. More than anything, she's confused. She needs time and space to think.

Rising to her toes, she kisses his neck, his jaw, his mouth. "Go," she whispers against his lips. "We'll talk tonight."

Nathan leaves to meet with Scott, and later, Ella joins them for dinner. Afterward, while Nathan finishes up downstairs, she goes back to the room to continue work on the article. By 10:00 p.m., Nathan hasn't returned. Exhausted, Ella shuts her laptop and climbs into bed.

What must be an hour or so later, she wakes as Nathan eases into bed. He spoons her, his warm breath dusting her shoulder. He traces his thumb along the scar over her pelvis. She clasps his fingers, stilling his touch.

He buries his face in the crook of her neck and murmurs something incoherent. From the tone, it sounds like an apology.

She twists her head in his direction. "What?"

He kisses her shoulder. "Do you think you'll try again?"

She feels his hand, still over her scar.

"To have kids?" she asks. "I don't know. I'd like to." But Damien hasn't wanted to talk about it. And she doesn't want to think about Damien while in another man's bed. Right now, she doesn't want to think at all.

Rotating in Nathan's arms, she pushes him to his back and straddles his hips. He's ready, and she takes him inside. His hands palm her breasts.

"You're beautiful."

"You can't see me." The room's pitch-black. She can barely make out the outline of his face.

"I can feel you."

She can feel him, too. Everywhere, which is exactly what she wants. To feel. This moment. In the dark.

With Nathan.

CHAPTER 24

"Ella."

She groans, burrowing under the covers.

"Ella." Nathan nudges her shoulder.

Her eyelids flutter. The room sits in darkness but her internal clock tells her it's morning.

Nathan turns on the bedside lamp. She groans again, burying her face in the pillow. "Turn it off."

"Wake up, Skye."

Her eyes snap open at the order. Nathan grins. Energy radiates off him.

"What?" she grumbles, her voice hoarse, drowsy.

"We've been cleared to fly. I secured a spot for you on the heli."

"You did?" She sits up and tosses off the covers. "Why didn't you say so in the first place?"

Nathan stands, moving out of her way. Already dressed for skiing, he can't stop grinning.

"Excited much?" She picks through her clothes, selecting items. Ella mentioned last night that if there was room, she wanted to ride with them. She'd photograph him heli-skiing for the article.

She glances over her shoulder at Nathan. He's inspecting his gear. "I can't believe I didn't hear you get dressed."

"I wore you out last night."

She raises her eyes to the ceiling. "Yeah, right. That must be it."

"You were snoring."

"I don't snore."

"You were making little squeaky noises," he says, pinching his fingers together.

"I don't squeak." She whips his upper back with her shirt and locks herself in the bathroom to change.

They meet Scott and another guide for breakfast, and after, they sit through what Ella believes is the longest, most detailed safety presentation she's ever heard. It lasts an hour, covering everything from loading and unloading from the helicopter, skiing conditions, avalanche preparedness, and the importance of listening to their guides. Their word is final. Disregarding the rules means an immediate extraction from the mountain and return to base without a refund. Each guide is trained as an EMT and every skier is outfitted with a radio to communicate with their guides.

When it comes time to load into the helicopter, Ella sits up front between Cam, the pilot, and Trey, one of their guides. In the rear are Scott, Nathan, and a Canadian couple from Whistler who are over the moon to be skiing alongside Nathan Donovan. Nathan graciously poses for pictures before they board the helicopter. Scott loads the skis and poles into a cargo carrier that looks like a rescue basket attached above the landing skid. He climbs aboard and they're off, lifting, up and over a stark white landscape.

The ride is bumpy but the views are magnificent, the mountains majestic, and Ella can't help but feel the skiers' excitement. Her heart races and palms sweat as they climb in elevation, following the lay of the land as it rises from the channel and up. Ella smiles broadly, thrilled she can witness Nathan in action. She waves at him over her shoulder and he gives her a thumbs-up.

Basically, the helicopter is a chairlift. The first drop is eight minutes from base, and each successive drop is a two- to four-minute flight apart until they return to the lodge. The entire trip takes no more than ninety minutes. Depending how things go, Scott hopes they can get in seven rides. That's seven landings on various ridges—which aren't true landings, but a hover inches above the surface—and seven pickups with fly time in between.

Skiers will ride downhill one at a time, from safe zone to safe zone, until they meet up at the pickup zone, or PZ, as Cam calls it, at the end of the run. Scott will lead, followed by Nathan, then the Canadian couple. Trey will bring up the rear.

After the first drop-off, Cam comes over the com. He and Ella are the only two with headsets in the helicopter so that they can communicate over the whir of the helicopter's rudder and blades while the others ski.

"We'll do a flyby so you can watch."

The heli dives down the mountainside and Ella's stomach shoots up into her throat. But she waves her thanks to Cam and gets her camera ready.

As Scott explained during the safety meeting, the skiers take off one at a time. Scott descends first, cutting across the pristine mountainside, digging his poles into the fresh snowpack. He's fast. Full speed ahead, until he skids to a stop at the first safety zone, a spot about one-third of the way down.

Nathan follows, full throttle. Ella's heart pounds in her throat. A fresh layer of nervous perspiration blooms across the back of her neck, yet she has her camera ready and takes a ton of photos.

When Nathan reaches Scott, the Canadian couple follows, then Trey, until eventually, they all reach the PZ. Scott comes over the com, giving Cam the signal they're ready for a pickup.

Nathan loads first and their eyes meet. She can tell he wants to tell her how epically awesome it was, but his words would only get lost in the noise of the copter. Instead, they share a smile. He'll tell her all about it when they get back to base.

They follow this pattern for another three drops, until they reach the highest ridge of the day, where they'll be able to cut lines in a sixteen-hundred-foot run at almost a fifty-degree angle. After they unload at the LZ, landing zone, Scott gives the signal and Cam lifts off. They fly down the mountainside and cut a wide circle so that Ella can watch. Scott takes off, and when he reaches the first safety zone, she has her camera ready.

Nathan descends the mountainside, following Scott's trail. Ella lifts her camera and the good vibe inside the helicopter plummets. Cam swears.

Ella lowers her camera and looks around, thinking something's wrong with the helicopter. But Cam's attention isn't on the controls. It's locked outside.

Ella looks in the same direction and gasps. Her chest clenches as her mind tries to catch up with what she's seeing. Scott, skiing for his life, with Nathan right behind. The entire mountainside has ripped out from under them. Avalanche. And the wave of snowpack is gaining on Nathan.

Scott, who has a couple hundred yards on Nathan, quickly skis out of the avalanche's path. He radios in to Cam. "You seeing this?"

"Yep. Coming in." Cam closes in on the mountain, ready for the pickup when they'll need it. "Ski, you bastard," Cam mutters into the com. There isn't anything he or Ella can do but watch in silent horror as Nathan tries to outski the rushing snow.

Ella realizes that watching an avalanche as it's happening is a whole different game than playing a YouTube video where she can speed ahead to skip the horrific parts or stop it and walk away. She couldn't look away even if she tried. She can only watch, stunned speechless, as Nathan points his skis downhill and furiously digs in his poles to get away. But the avalanche consumes him, and suddenly, he's tumbling, flipping head over skis, over and over and over.

The last thing Ella hears before Nathan disappears under a white sheet are Scott's clipped words over the com. "He's heavy. Going down hard."

"You keep that up and we won't get any sleep."

After spending the afternoon at the medical clinic and a better part of the evening downstairs with Scott and his crew as they exchanged tales of their own near-death experiences, Ella finally has Nathan alone in their room. He's whole, he's alive, and she can't stop touching him. His body isn't having issues reacting to her ministrations either.

"Sorry." She adjusts his flannel sleep pants so that the elastic waistband doesn't press into the large contusion on his left hip.

Aside from a couple of bruised ribs, some contusions, and a dislocated shoulder, compliments of an old motorbike injury, Nathan survived the avalanche unscathed. On the grand scale of avalanches, it was minor. Just a shelf of snow that broke off, triggered on Nathan's descent. As soon as the snowpack had slowed and Nathan stopped sliding, he radioed to Scott that he was okay, even dug himself out before Scott could ski to him. Nathan was already standing and talking about the burn in his shoulder before the Canadian couple and Trey skied down the mountainside after him.

A lot of things come into play to trigger an avalanche, but Scott thinks this one happened because the fresh powder fell onto a section of harder packed snow.

Small avalanche or not, it's not something Ella wants to witness again. Her hands shake as she helps Nathan into his shirt since his arm's in a sling. No wonder Stephanie worried for Nathan. She can't imagine feeling this way every time he left the house.

Ella tugs his shirt to his waist and Nathan sinks onto the bed. "I ache."

So does she. Dead center in her chest.

She bites into her lower lip and distracts herself by adjusting the bedcovers over Nathan. Between the business deal with Scott, his pending divorce, and his injuries, Nathan has enough to contend with. The last thing he needs is a blubbering mess hovering over him.

But she can't help it. The scene on the mountain keeps replaying in her head. Nathan tumbling, on the wrong side of control, disappearing, buried alive under a layer of snow. Who cares if those layers were only inches of loosely packed powder and all he had to do was lift his head and shake off the snow? It was still scary to witness. A tear glides down her cheek, and another slides and clings to her chin. Nathan watches her curiously. Embarrassed, she turns away and wipes her face.

"Hey," he murmurs.

She turns back to him, dragging her sleeve-covered fist across her cheekbone.

"Come here." Nathan stretches his arm across the pillow, inviting her into bed.

She slides under the covers and snuggles up against him, mindful of his bruises. He smells of the hospital, antiseptic and bleach, and she's unexpectedly taken back to the morning she forgot Simon, those same smells fresh in her nose. She buries her face into his shirt and cries.

"Why do you do these things?"

He lifts a hand to her hair, massages the back of her head. "I want to feel alive."

Heli-skiing, wingsuit flying, even speedgliding, a crazy-insane parachuting and skiing mash-up. He's done so much and even though he told her during their sessions that he wishes he could do more—Everest, BASE jumping, and Antarctica trekking, to name a few—he swore to himself that he was done. But now that he is divorcing Stephanie and has had a taste of the extreme again after a long hiatus, Ella wonders if he'll be able to abstain.

"Is it worth getting yourself killed in the process?"

The words are out before she can think otherwise. Nathan tenses underneath her. She already knows why. It's something Stephanie would have said to him.

"You aren't thirty years old anymore," she risks saying. "Actually, you're closer to forty than thirty," she says, trying for levity.

"I know." Nathan's expression softens, and he chuckles. Then he groans. "Ouch." Laughing and sore ribs. Not a good mix. "Thanks for pointing out my age, Skye."

"Anytime, old man." She props her chin on his chest and smiles. At thirty-seven, he's still in mighty fine shape.

"There's something else I know," he says, his voice sounding sluggish, his eyelids drooping as the painkillers kick in.

"What's that?" she murmurs.

"You make me feel alive."

CHAPTER 25

Nathan wakes Ella with his mouth. He lavishes kisses on her bare breasts. He skims his teeth along her ribs, nips her hip, then kisses her scar.

Self-conscious yet curious about his interest, Ella leans up on her elbows.

"What is your fascination with my scar?" she asks drowsily.

Nathan lifts his head and their eyes meet. He rolls to his back and lies beside her.

"Nathan?"

He drapes his uninjured arm over his eyes.

Ella pushes down her sleep shirt and sits up. "Talk to me."

He peeks at her from under his arm. "You want to do this now? I'm bruised, battered, and drugged."

"Don't be a baby." She playfully nudges him. Physically, he's the toughest guy she knows. "Did you take a pill this morning?"

"I was going to, but I got distracted." He reaches for her breasts.

She smacks away his hand. "Focus. You. Me. Last summer." She's done waiting.

"You're on your walkabout on the PCT, and after months of being pestered by various media outlets for your story, you decide to give *Luxe*

Avenue the exclusive," she summarizes. "You call Rebecca, she sends me. You double back and meet me at the Squaw Valley parking lot. We backpack for five days, and then what? What did we do?"

"Gawd, Skye. It's early. Can I at least shower and dress first? Coffee sounds real good."

Ella glances at the clock. Seven a.m. If they go downstairs for coffee, Nathan will get sucked into conversation with Scott or any one of the other guides or guests. It could be hours before she gets him alone again.

She shakes her head. "No, now. Let's get this over with so I can go write. I'm on deadline. What did we do on the PCT?"

"Okay, fine. We hiked and we talked."

"About what?"

He pinches the bridge of his nose and closes his eyes. "I don't know. A lot of what we rehashed this week."

She frowns. "That can't be all."

His eyebrows rise and hands flip as if saying what else does she expect?

A lot more.

There is a significant reason she agreed to go home with him.

Nathan watches her.

"Well . . . what happened next?" she prompts.

"Something unexpected." He opens his eyes, letting his hand flop onto his belly. "I fell for you. I invited you to my place, and you helped me work through my guilt."

"Yeah, I got that, but I feel like there's something here I'm missing. Did you pull the article because we were involved?" she asks, holding his hand in her lap.

But that doesn't explain why he came back to *Luxe Avenue* with the exclusive.

Nathan rubs the side of his nose, glances at the ceiling.

Ella feels a twinge in her chest. Something's off here. Nathan must sense the moment her mood shifts, because his grip on her hand tightens, brutally so.

"Don't leave," he rasps.

Any other time, that rasp in his voice would have her mentally undressing him. Not today, though.

"Let go, please."

"I love you, Ella. Don't leave me."

I don't want to lose you again.

His words to her two days ago.

Clarity rings clearly.

Ella never was going to leave Damien for Nathan. She left Nathan.

Suddenly, everything comes together. Nathan fell for her. She might have cared for him. She was extremely attracted to him. But she doesn't believe she fell in love with him. Her plan from the beginning was to return to San Francisco, write the article, and submit it to her editor. To be with Damien and to leave Nathan.

Nathan had only been a fling for her, hadn't he?

Ella recalls Nathan's interest in Damien.

How's Damien handling this?

This has nothing to do with her miscarriage. It has to do with Ella spending time with Nathan. Because Damien knew about last summer's affair. And Nathan knows he knows. How?

"You blackmailed me." Nathan's eyes flare with heat as Ella yanks free her hand. She scoots back on the bed. "The only way you'd let the article run was if I agreed to leave Damien. But I didn't, so you threatened to tell Damien about our affair unless I killed the assignment. That's how you convinced me."

She shakes her head. "No, there's got to be more," she thinks out loud, gasping when it hits her. "You threatened to tell my boss about us. That's how you convinced me."

If Rebecca knew she slept with Nathan while on the job, Ella would have lost more than the exclusive assignment. She would have lost her position at *Luxe Avenue*. Blacklisted from getting hired at any credible publication.

Then why is she back on this assignment?

"If you weren't going to let the article run, why'd you call Rebecca again?"

Nathan snickers. A low, disrespectful noise that heightens the chill Ella felt a moment ago. He then grimaces because his ribs hurt and slowly rolls to his side. He leans up onto his good elbow. "I didn't plan this." He motions between them. "It sort of happened. To say I was shocked you agreed to see me is an understatement. I swear to god I didn't know about your memory loss."

But he took advantage of it. If he could woo her, appeal to her on the grounds of their common losses, she might fall for him, and this time, she'd stay.

She almost did fall for him.

"Why did you call Rebecca?"

"Because, Ella . . ." He takes a long beat. "I've been worried about you since you lost our son."

CHAPTER 26

"Whoa." Ella backs off the bed, pointing her finger at Nathan. "Stop right there. Not. Cool. Simon—"

"Was mine."

A sinking, drifting sensation floods her. She stumbles back, hand pressed to her stomach.

"Did I tell you he was yours?"

"No. I ran into you by accident in Reno last October." He sits, protecting his ribs with one hand, supporting his weight on the bed with his good arm. "It was obvious you were pregnant. You told me you were nineteen weeks along. That put you with me in Truckee, so I asked."

"How presumptuous of you. I'm married."

"You sure aren't acting like it."

Ella sees red. "Bastard." Like he's one to talk.

"My question was valid, but you never answered me. I had the right to know. I still have that right." He pushes off the bed and slowly stands. He hisses through his teeth, his muscles tight and sore from yesterday's fall. "I kept calling you. I wanted a paternity test, but you blocked me."

"You stalked me?"

"I loved you. I wanted to be involved in Simon's life. *My* son's life," he says. "Tell me,

Ella." He makes a move toward her. "Was he mine?"

"Enough!" Ella cuts her hand through the air. "I've heard enough." After everything she's been through. After the loss he's suffered, grief has him grasping at straws for anyone he can claim as his own. It certainly won't be Simon. The nerve of him to assume her baby was his.

Ella looks wildly around the room. The dull morning light between the cracks of the curtain panels. The rumpled bedsheets.

Oh, my god. What has she done? What is she doing here? With him?

Going to her luggage, Ella yanks on a pair of jeans.

"You called me right before your accident."

She stills.

"I think you were about to tell me but we got cut off."

She squeezes her eyes shut to block out his words. But she can't. They're there, and they want to be heard. Mulled over. Considered.

Ella lifts off her sleep shirt and puts on her bra. She tries to put on a clean shirt but her arms shake so badly she keeps dropping it.

Nathan's voice lowers. She can feel him standing right behind her, the disturbance of air when he says, "I tried reaching you for days after you called. I was worried about you. Rebecca told me you had an accident. I called her when

I couldn't get hold of you. I visited you in the hospital."

"What?" Ella finally pulls on her shirt and swings around. Her mind stumbles back to her last day in the hospital, to Nurse Jillian, who told her about the commotion the previous day. To the argument between Damien and her that Andrew had mentioned. That argument must have been over Nathan. That commotion must have been between Nathan and Damien. Damien wouldn't have allowed him to visit her.

Stuffing her sleep shirt into her bag, Ella packs furiously. She's tough. Usually she can handle the worst sorts of stories about human nature. But this reality, *her* reality? What Nathan's done to her? What *she's* done to Damien? It's too much. She has to get out of here.

"What are you doing?" Nathan asks. He winces, his hand still clutched to his ribs.

"What does it look like? I'm leaving."

"You can't do that," he says.

"Watch me."

Nathan's expression darkens. The temperature in the room nose-dives.

"You. Bitch."

Ella snaps to attention. "Excuse me?"

"You got your story and now you're bailing."

"That's not why I'm leaving and you know it." She zips her luggage closed.

"Why then? You didn't like what you heard? Not what you expected?"

"I don't know what I expected. Certainly not this."

"Then try this on for size," he says, following her to the bathroom. "Screw and ditch is your MO. That's how you get your interviews. You did it with me last summer, and you did it with that actor Michael Leed. You got him to spill about his affair with his male costar. You met Senator Burmeister at a fundraiser, a man you'd been trying to nab an interview with for months, charmed the shit out of him, and fucked him. Next thing you knew, his secretary is calling to set up an exclusive with *Luxe Avenue*. And Damien! Of course, you stayed with him, but you fucked him the night you met because you wanted his story. You told me *a lot* last summer, Skye, and it wasn't all pretty."

She slaps him, the crack of bone on flesh startling. She's never hit anyone. But then, she's never been as angry as she is with Nathan. He barely flinches, but the blue in his eyes cools, two icebergs that chill her to the bone.

"I'd say that's the meds talking, but you didn't take any this morning."

"That's the truth talking." He growls the words. "I'm only repeating what you told me last summer."

"Why on earth would I tell you any of that?" His words burn.

"Beats me, babe. We got real close. Maybe you felt compelled to confess all your shit."

His accusations are insulting and demeaning, designed and delivered to hurt. But what hurts more is that Nathan is telling the truth, as disgusting as he's made her sound. Ella remembers the interviews, but they were pre-Damien.

As for Simon, Ella doesn't know what's the truth and what are lies. What she does know is that she can't trust Nathan. She made a horrible mistake coming to Alaska.

Scooping up her cosmetics and toiletries, she pushes by him and dumps them in her luggage. She's still shaking so badly that she almost drops her laptop when she picks it up.

"Didn't you find it easy getting into bed with me? Guilt-free, I might add. You'll do whatever it takes to get your story."

She slams her laptop into her bag.

"I honestly thought I was different than your other lays."

There's so much venom in his voice that his words stop her on her way to the door. "For what it's worth, you were different. I did care about you. But I also fucked you to see if it triggered my memories. Clearly it didn't work."

Partial truth. She wants him hurting as badly as he hurt her.

Nathan stumbles back, sinking onto the bed.

She grips the doorknob.

"Ella." He speaks her name quietly.

She stops at the door but doesn't turn around.

He sighs. "I'll call the airline for you. Get you on the next flight out of here."

"Thank you," she says and leaves.

After a long flight to Reno with two layovers, a Lyft to Nathan's house to get her car, and a four-hour drive down the mountain and into the bright lights of the city, Ella arrives home shortly before dawn. Damien's standing in the hallway when she enters, drawn to the door by the sound of her key unlocking the bolt. His hair stands on end from the repeated abuse of his hands raking through the thick locks. His clothes, a navy shirt and gray sweatpants, look like they've been slept in for days. He tightly grips his phone, watching her through bloodshot eyes as though his entire world just walked through the door.

"You're home," he says, relieved.

"So are you," she says, unable to contain her surprise. "When did you get here?"

"Saturday morning. I would have flown to Alaska, but . . ." He takes a cautious step toward her. Stops. Looks at the phone in his hand, then at her. "I didn't know where you were."

Because Nathan kept their travel arrangements under his name and credit card, at his insistence,

294

which Ella agreed to, thinking nothing of it. Otherwise, Damien would have been able to track her through her purchases.

The knot in her stomach tightens. She'd been so gullible and trusting in her desperation for answers. Her desire to feel what it was like to carry and lose Simon so that she could mourn with Damien.

And here he is, home for her, when he should be in London, working to save his company.

"What about the investigation?"

"You're more important. I was going to call the authorities." His expression is pained. "You weren't answering my calls."

Shamefully, she ignored them. He'd hear her voice and then he'd know. She betrayed him.

Tears well and then spill over. The guilt that was absent when she followed Nathan to Alaska, joined him in his bed, and started feeling *something* for him arrives with a vengeance. It claws to the surface, digging and scratching. This must be how Grace's father felt when he confessed his affair to her mother. And in this moment, she can understand why he did it. It's suffocating.

"Ella." He speaks her name with reverence.

"I—I'm sorry," she stutters, her lungs shuttering on the exhale.

She drops her luggage. He drops his phone. Then Damien has her in his arms and his mouth is on hers. He threads both hands in her hair and cradles her head. He kisses her. A possessive, powerful, breath-stealing kiss. Words are impossible. Her confession disappears in a muffled whimper.

Damien's hands move to her hips and his fingers dig into her flesh. He keeps her flush against him and they do what they do best when there's too much to say and they don't know how to say it. They fuck. Rough, angry sex. Against the wall. Bent over the couch. In the middle of their California king, where their bodies mellow into tender lovemaking. Until finally, in the golden hours of dawn, they crash into slumber, limbs entwined.

CHAPTER 27

Three Years Ago

"What an epic day," Ella said, following Damien into their suite. California had been in its fourth year of drought and the mountains were dry. Damien had surprised her with a spontaneous trip to Vail. It was their first Thanksgiving holiday together and Ella was more than fine with getting out of the city. Anything so that they wouldn't have to celebrate the gluttonous holiday.

"I haven't skied on snow like this for years." Damien took Ella's boots from her hands and set them on the floor beside their skis that he'd carried up to the room.

"Where should we go for dinner?" Ella asked, shedding her jacket. She tossed it on the bed along with her knit cap and ski gloves.

"I thought we'd order in." Damien slowly unzipped Ella's hoodie and skimmed the backs of his fingers down her sternum. Ella's breath caught. "You know, just the two of us, some candlelight, a nice bottle of Zin." His hand trailed lower and cupped her breast.

"Sounds heavenly," Ella said, leaning into him. There was a two-person tub in the bathroom. They'd skied hard today. Her legs felt like jelly.

She could use a good soak. And a good fuck, she realized as Damien's hand dipped below the waist of her ski pants.

But a knock on the door shattered the moment.

"Later," Damien promised, pressing a teasing kiss against her lips.

"Who's here?"

"Room service."

"Dinner already? When did you order?"

He just smiled and opened the door. A young man in the black-and-white hotel staff uniform wheeled in a cart. Ella saw a bottle of wine, glasses, and four metal domes.

"Where to, sir?" the attendant asked.

"By the window. We can watch the snow fall," Damien said, looking at Ella, then frowning when he caught her expression. He came over to stand by her.

"Everything all right?" he asked, his voice just loud enough for her to hear.

Ella slowly shook her head. She held a hand to her throat, just above the knot she was having trouble swallowing past. She'd caught a whiff of the food under the domes when the cart wheeled by.

"Would you like me to uncork the wine?" The attendant spoke quietly.

"No, I'll do it," Damien answered, not taking his eyes off her. "Talk to me, El. You don't look well."

"Of course, sir." The attendant removed the domes and Ella peeked over Damien's shoulder to see. On the table was a small roasted turkey, barely larger than a chicken, and all the dressings that came with a Thanksgiving meal at a five-star resort hotel. Mashed potatoes and savory gravy, cranberry relish, string beans with caramelized onions, and an assortment of root vegetables: parsnips, carrots, and sweet potatoes. Damien had gone all out. Steam rose from the plates and the smell of roasted turkey overwhelmed Ella. Warm, juicy, and nasty.

Her stomach roiled and she gagged. Cupping a hand over her mouth, Ella ran to the bathroom, barely making it to the toilet. What had to be less than a minute later, Ella heard the hotel suite door close, then felt Damien's presence in the bathroom. He knelt beside her. His strong hands gently scooped her hair, holding it away from her face.

Ella's stomach had emptied and her throat was raw. She felt like she'd been run over by a snowplow.

"I'm sorry," she said, hoarse. She'd ruined the romantic meal he'd planned.

"Don't be." He handed her a towel. She blotted her face. "Did you eat something earlier?"

He thought she had food poisoning. She shook her head. "I don't like turkey."

He smiled. "That's quite a reaction for

something you don't like. Sure you aren't allergic? I've heard that the smell of something can be strong enough to—"

She shook her head. She wasn't allergic to turkey, but she owed Damien an explanation. The smell of turkey was a powerful reminder of the worst day of Ella's life. She hadn't eaten turkey since she was six. She hadn't celebrated Thanksgiving since then either.

"My parents died on Thanksgiving."

"God, El, I'm sorry. I wish I'd known."

Damien knew her parents had died when she was a kid, but she hadn't gone into details. She hadn't seen a point. Damien was estranged from his parents and hers were gone. They just didn't talk about them.

But she now owed him an explanation as to why she despised the holiday, especially if they were going to spend the rest of them together. That dinner hadn't been cheap, and she felt awful that she'd ruined his plans.

He handed her a glass of water.

"Thanks," she said after swishing and spitting into the sink. "I hate Thanksgiving."

"I gathered that," he said on a laugh. "Wait here, then we'll talk."

Damien left the bathroom, closing the door behind him. Ella heard the clang of dishes, the squeak of wheels, and the hotel room door open and shut. He returned a moment later, holding

300

out a hand for hers. He led her into the room and Ella noticed the cart was gone. The window was also cracked and the heater circulating, diffusing the smell. Tears beaded in the corners of her eyes. "I'm sorry." She felt stupid and silly. She couldn't believe she threw up. It had been years since she'd had such a strong reaction to the smell.

"Don't be. We'll order steaks later. Feel up to having a glass of wine?" She nodded and he uncorked the bottle, pouring their glasses. Giving her one, he raised his in a toast. "Happy Un-Thanksgiving."

Watery laughter bubbled from Ella. "Happy Un-Thanksgiving."

Damien settled onto the love seat and patted the cushion for her to join him. He draped a blanket over their laps and his arm around her shoulders. For a short time, they drank their wine and watched the snow fall. She knew he was waiting for her to tell him why they'd never celebrate Thanksgiving, and she loved him even more for not pushing her. But she was ready to talk.

"I don't remember much about my parents, mostly what Aunt Kathy told me. But I do remember that they argued, a lot. Well, Mom argued. Dad just took it. Aunt Kathy said he loved my mom above anyone else and that he tried hard to keep her happy. Anyway, Mom got pregnant with me in high school. Her parents wanted her to get an abortion and threatened to donate the college tuition they'd saved for her to a charity."

"I take it some random charity received a hefty donation since you're here with me." Damien gave her shoulder a squeeze.

"It did. And Mom made the situation worse by marrying my dad. My grandparents disowned her."

"Ouch."

"Aunt Kathy felt my mom was better off without them. They weren't nice people. But my mom took it hard. I think she loved my dad at one time, but she definitely came to resent him.

"I was six and Andrew four when we went to Aunt Kathy's for Thanksgiving that year. We'd go every year. She practically raised my dad after his parents died. But that year, my parents drank all day, and so did my aunt. She passed out before we left that night; otherwise, I'd like to think she would have told my parents to spend the night.

"We spent the day playing games and my parents at least acted civilly toward each other. I remember the five of us playing charades. That was fun. But the more they drank, the more Mom bickered. By the time we got into the car, they were both smashed and my mom was spewing such hateful things at my dad."

"He drove drunk with two kids in the car?" Damien asked, aghast.

Ella nodded. "It wasn't the first time, but that night I think he just wanted to get home and pass out so that he didn't have to listen to my mom anymore." She paused and gulped her wine. Liquid courage.

Damien rubbed her back. She offered him a weak smile. "This isn't easy."

"You don't have to tell me everything. We can wait."

She shook her head. "No, I want to." She sipped more wine, then set down the glass. "My mom was so mean to him, but I think my dad believed she still loved him. Either that, or he hoped that she would again one day. But—and I remember this vividly—while we were driving home, my mom shouted that she wanted a divorce. Then she said that she never did love him, even in the beginning, and that she only married him to piss off her parents. Whether it was that specifically or a culmination of her abuse, she broke him. He started crying and the car started swerving. Andrew and I were screaming. There was construction on the freeway, and to this day, I don't know if it was an accident or if it was intentional, but he drove the car straight into the back of a parked flatbed truck. The last thing I remember is the crunch of metal and glass shattering. And the pipes on the flatbed. I remember those. They cut into the car and punched into my parents."

Damien looked at her, stunned. "Fuck me."

"Yeah, that about sums it up."

Damien pulled her into his arms. "I'm sorry you had to witness that."

"Me too. That's why turkey makes me gag. The smell always triggers images of the wreck."

"I can imagine."

"I guess it's a good thing we aren't planning to have kids. They'd hate not celebrating Thanksgiving." Ella tried to joke, but it only made her sadder.

"Whether we had kids or not, we don't have to celebrate anything you don't want to," Damien said solemnly.

They sat quietly for a few moments, lost in their own thoughts, before Ella said, almost hesitantly, "I blame my mom."

"For what?"

"Their deaths. I think she could have left it at telling my dad she wanted a divorce. She didn't have to get into all the stuff about not loving him. She was more honest than she needed to be. They'd still be alive if she hadn't told him that. Her admission broke him, and that's what killed them."

Damien looked at her oddly.

"What?" she asked.

"You said something similar when you told me about Grace. You said you blamed her suicide on her dad. If he hadn't confessed to an affair, her parents wouldn't have divorced, and Grace wouldn't have committed suicide."

"I do believe that."

"Huh." He rubbed his jaw. "Do you feel the same about us?"

"What do you mean?"

"Do you think there are things we shouldn't share with each other?"

Ella's chest tightened, but she smiled. "Are you hiding something from me, Damien?"

He looked at the glass in his hand. "Nothing of import."

She nudged his shoulder. "Are you trying to tell me that you hate turkey, too?"

He laughed. "No."

Ella grinned before sobering. She thought of the one thing she desired almost as much as she wanted Damien. A baby girl. She brought his hand to her lips and kissed the inside of his wrist, letting her mouth linger on his skin. Then she met his eyes. "If it's something that could hurt our marriage, then no, maybe we shouldn't share it. I'd hate for us to not work out. I want to spend the rest of my life with you, Damien."

"Me too."

CHAPTER 28

Ella wakes at noon craving coffee and pancakes drenched in maple syrup. The sun is out, a perfect spring day. The blue bay will be speckled with white sails should she get up and look out the window. But she's tight and deliciously sore from her and Damien's predawn aerobics, and rolling over and burrowing under the covers sounds like a perfect way to spend the day. She stretches. A lingering arousal clings to her. Damien's scent clings to her.

Ella extends an arm across the bed. Damien's side is empty. Knowing him, he's been up for hours. Probably already went for a run.

She sits up in bed and startles when she sees Damien in the corner armchair, fully dressed in faded jeans and a blue Henley. Hair damp from a recent shower. He watches her with a stony expression. She pulls the sheets around herself, feeling self-conscious under the weight of his stare.

"How long have you been up?" she asks.

"A few hours."

"How long have you been sitting there?"

"Same."

Ella moistens her lips and slowly nods. She's not sure what to say, where to begin. But Damien does.

"I saw the photo." The one on the internet.

Ella's heart sinks, heavy with guilt.

"Do you have any idea how that made me feel? Seeing the two of you together like that? Why would you do that to us?"

"It's not what you—"

"You're looking at him the same way you look at me," he interjects, voice raised. "What does he mean to you?"

Nothing! she wants to shout. But she doesn't really know that.

She shakes her head.

"Do you love him?" he asks, his voice flat.

Her head snaps up. "No!"

"Did you sleep with him?"

Ella opens her mouth to object. But the denial falls flat on her tongue. She looks down at her lap. "I thought it would trigger my memories." Half truth. The last thing she wants Damien to hear is how she couldn't resist consoling Nathan. She couldn't resist him.

Damien taps the chair with his index finger. Ella glances back up at him and he sighs heavily. "That's on me. I should have told you about him. I shouldn't have—" He plucks at a loose thread on the chair's arm.

"You shouldn't have what?"

He smooths the suede fabric where he plucked off the thread. "I shouldn't have listened to you."

"Me? About what?"

"At the hospital. I promised that no matter how often you asked or how difficult it would be not to say anything, that I wouldn't tell you what happened. You made me promise to lie to you if I had to. Throw you off course when I needed to, because you knew you would ask questions. I agreed to do whatever it took so that you and I could start over. Pretend that the seven months before the accident never happened."

"What are you talking about?"

"Your memory loss. It's intentional. You did it to yourself."

Ella's mouth falls open for a beat. She then laughs, tossing her head back. "You aren't serious?" she says when she can get the words out.

"I'm dead serious." He doesn't smile.

Ella stops laughing. "Impossible." She did her research on selective memory loss after Dr. Allington's diagnosis. Motivated forgetting, the purposeful repression of memories on a conscious level, is highly questionable. It's a theory. Unproven, from what Ella read. There is still much scientists and psychologists don't understand when it comes to memories.

Ella slides off the bed and walks to their closet.

"What're you doing?" Damien asks.

"Getting dressed." She isn't going to sit and listen to this nonsense. The nerve of him to blame her. He's the one who's avoided talking about the accident and Simon. If Damien can't own the reasons for his silence, she doesn't want any part of this conversation.

She yanks on panties and yoga pants, straps on a sports bra, and tugs on a tank top. Marlene should have an afternoon hot yoga class on today's schedule at her studio. Ella needs to get out of the house and sweat out her angst.

After brushing her teeth and twisting her hair into a messy bun, she returns. Damien hasn't moved.

"I'm going to make coffee. When I get back, I expect the truth from you, not this crap about intentional memory loss."

His jaw ticks. "I am telling the truth."

"Do you hear yourself? Do you seriously expect me to believe I chose to forget our baby?"

"You weren't supposed to forget Simon."

She goes cold. He said the same thing to her in the hospital. Ella remembers that. She remembers his anger. He didn't believe her then. He thought she was pretending.

"Last summer, you interviewed an actress named Amira Silvers. For whatever reason, the article didn't go to print. But she wanted to forget something that happened when she was a kid and had found a doctor who was helping her suppress the memories. Dr. Irwin Whitely is a cognitive scientist doing cutting-edge research in the areas of memory control and motivated forgetting. You approached him to get his story. You wanted to write a feature on his groundbreaking research. You interviewed him last August in Reno."

Reno. She ran into Nathan in Reno. But that was in October.

"Show me this doctor," she demands.

Damien stands and retrieves his phone from his back pocket. He brings up the website to Dr. Whitely's lab and gives Ella his phone.

Ella skims through the site's pages, speed-reading sections of Dr. Whitely's research. The lab is a neuroscience research center focused on studying the mechanisms that underlie memory control. Most people, especially as they age, want to improve their ability to retain and retrieve memories. But this facility, with the use of advanced techniques and a diagnostic approach, doesn't just center on improving the ability to retrieve memories. It aims to control the retrieval process, training individuals to consciously and deliberately do the opposite of retrieving memories. It rewires the brain to block specific memories, on purpose, at the individual's will. The lab claims that once the mind has been conditioned to intervene in the memory retrieval process, which takes multiple sessions, all an individual would need to do to consciously repress a person or event from memory is to apply a string of unique code, a formula of words, that has been programmed into the brain. The same process works to reverse the effects.

"Did this guy do something to me?" Ella asks, returning his phone.

"Dr. Whitely? You agreed to be one of his test subjects. I don't think you intentionally set out to forget anything specific, it was just research on your part. You wanted a better understanding of his methods. Twice a week for two and a half months, you drove to Reno. He taught you how to suppress specific memories about someone you know or something that happened to you. The theory behind it is that by virtually wiping someone from your mind, you wipe out everything associated with that person. You told me he intends to use his research as therapy for people who were abused as kids. They could forget what happened to them. After we lost Simon, you told me in the hospital that Dr. Whitely had given you the tools to forget everything that happened, and you wanted to forget Nathan specifically. For the sake of us, I agreed to help you."

She did forget Nathan and everything associated with him. Meeting him. Interviewing him. Sleeping with him. Her pregnancy.

Simon is mine.

Tears well in her eyes. She squeezes them shut. She forgot her pregnancy because she forgot everything associated with Nathan. Why hadn't

311

she thought that through? How stupid could she have been, and for Damien to go along with her?

Wiping her eyes, she clears her throat and turns around. "Nathan said some things to me. He claims Simon was his."

Damien's face falls.

"Damien?" Her voice comes out as a thin whisper. "Is it true?"

"I'm not Simon's biological father."

Ella has the sudden urge to run to the bathroom and vomit.

"Did I know?"

He slowly shakes his head, his eyes dropping to the floor. "I don't think so. If you knew, you didn't tell me."

"You don't think so? Then how did you know Simon wasn't yours?"

Damien sighs. He stares at the floor.

"Damien?"

His gaze meets hers. "I'm sterile."

Ella's mouth falls open. She blinks. "You're sterile?"

He nods. "I found out in my early twenties. Anna had trouble conceiving so we both got checked out. She was fine. I wasn't."

Ella's heart goes out to Damien. Her big, strong, larger-than-life Damien. So ashamed and embarrassed that he'd kept the truth from her. He hadn't been honest with her.

She guessed it was easier for him to say he

doesn't ever want kids than to admit he could never have them.

Which pisses her off even more. How dare he assume she would have walked away from him. Did he think so little of her? Unlike Anna, she never would have left him.

"Did I know that you were sterile?"

"Yes. I told you the day of the accident. Right before you got in the car."

We need to talk.

The words she remembered in the hospital but couldn't quite grasp.

Ella stumbles back. Of course. He must have told her out of guilt, unable to live with his secret any longer. He'd known all along he wasn't the father.

Ella can picture it clearly. Damien would have accused her of cheating on him. And he would have been right. But still.

"You let me believe you were the father. How could you?" Ella accuses, voice rising.

"You wanted a baby," Damien fires back. "You have no idea what it feels like to not be able to give you that. I will never, ever be able to create life with you."

"You were going to raise Simon as your own?"

"Yes."

"And let me believe he was yours?"

"Yes!"

"For the rest of our lives?"

"Yes, dammit!" He kicks the ottoman. It flips over. "And I could have done it," he bellows, stabbing his chest with a finger. "Donovan and I are the same. Same coloring. Same height. We even look the same. No one would question that Simon wasn't mine."

"You're crazy."

"No! Not crazy. In love. With you. I'm so fucking in love with you, El. I didn't want to lose you over something I couldn't give you."

Ella sinks onto the edge of the bed, facing Damien. Her rage burns hot yet her heart breaks for him. The fact he kept his secret from her for so long tells how ashamed he is. He bit his tongue.

Damien lifts his head. "I wanted to adopt. Anna did not. She married a coworker six months after our divorce finalized. Her first daughter was born five months later."

She wants to ask more about his marriage. She's realizing there's much about him she's let slide by. Important aspects of his past they haven't discussed. People and events that have shaped him into the individual he is now. Those are conversations they need to have, but they'll have to wait.

Right now, she needs to get to the heart of where they'd gone wrong.

CHAPTER 29

"I'm going to make coffee. Do you want one?" She needs time to let everything sink in. Damien could use the break, too. She can tell it wasn't an easy admission for him.

The same man who's appeared on the covers of *Entrepreneur* and *Business Insider*, quoted in countless other articles and publications as an IT security and business strategist expert, sees himself as inadequate. He probably believes she'd love him less, even leave him like his first wife, had he told her. Damien follows Ella to the kitchen. She boils water and pours it over the coffee grounds. Damien adds a splash of whiskey to their mugs. They stand beside each other, hips leaning against the marble-capped center island. She takes her first sip, feels the sharp prickly warmth of the whiskey as it coats her tongue and washes down her throat.

"Do you remember the first time we saw this kitchen?" Damien asks as he glides his hand on the countertop.

She watches his fingers touch the cool stone and feels a blush spread across her chest and up her neck. She remembers the feel of the marble against the bare skin of her thighs, the pressure of his fingers digging into her hips.

"Yes," she says. She wants to take his hand in hers but senses he doesn't want her touch. She cheated on him, twice. Guilt leaves a bitter taste in her mouth the coffee can't wash down.

"Do you remember what I said to you?"

She nods. The memory is so clear. "I want us to always come back here and find each other."

"I still feel that way."

Ella moistens her lips, tasting whiskey and coffee. "Then why didn't you stop me when I told you *Luxe Avenue* was putting me back on the Donovan exclusive?"

"I did." Damien sets aside his mug. "I mean, I tried. I asked you to come to London, remember?"

"You asked me to ditch my interview. Why didn't you just come out and tell me about him?"

"You're right. I should have. But I was distracted. The internal investigation has been a total nightmare and it's taken so much of my time. I tried to stop you after our last phone call."

"What call?" Ella asks but at the same time the answer comes to her. The argument they had after Nathan had taken her snowmobiling. The call when she'd told Damien she was going to Alaska. Clarity appears out of nowhere and she draws back a step.

"You called Nathan that night." The phone call that came just as they'd finished dinner. Nathan had stepped out onto his deck to take the call, only to return agitated.

"I couldn't reach you."

"I was conducting an interview. I silenced my phone. And if you recall, I wasn't too happy with you at the moment."

"I figured, so I called Donovan instead. I wanted to remind him of the restraining order I threatened him with when he showed up at the hospital. I thought he would pull the exclusive and you'd fly to London."

Damien called and threatened him. Nathan must have seen his chances of convincing Ella to be with him slipping away at that phone call.

The whiskey sours in Ella's stomach. She sets down her mug and tucks loose wisps of hair behind her ear. "Nathan hadn't invited me to Alaska yet when you called. I don't think he would have, but he did right after he hung up with you," Ella softly confesses.

Before Ella can blink, Damien hurls his mug into the sink. Pottery shatters. Coffee splatters against the backsplash and cabinets.

He grasps the counter's edge with both hands, his back to Ella, and it takes a moment for her to realize he's crying. Silent sobs that draw out her own tears. She gently lays a hand on his back. He's perspiring. She can feel the damp heat of him through his cotton shirt.

"Damien, love. Tell me what's wrong."

"What's wrong?" he asks in a voice thick with self-loathing. "I am. I keep fucking us up."

"No, no, no. That's not true. I made mistakes, too. Big ones. Whatever's happening with us is on us both. And we're going to fix this together."

"We can't," he says, pinching the tears from his eyes. He turns to her. "I don't think we can."

"What do you mean? We can. We'll talk this through and come up with a solution. We'll learn from our mistakes. We'll be honest from now on. I promise."

Damien slowly shakes his head. "You can't deny love."

"I'm not. I love you. I love you so much," she says, grasping his arms.

"I'm not talking about me." He cups her face.

Ella shakes her head hard. "I don't love him. I don't. I swear."

He turns away and lets go of her. "The photo."

"Means nothing! Nathan means nothing. I don't love him." She's crying now, desperate for Damien to believe her.

"I think you do. You just blocked it out. What happens when your memories come back?"

"I don't want them to, I swear," she says, shocked by her own admission. The truth about the months leading up to her accident is worse than she could ever imagine.

"He can give you a child, Ella. I can't."

He looks past her, toward the entryway.

Ella follows his gaze and sees what he's been up to while she slept in. A large roller case and a garment bag wait at the door.

He's leaving her.

"No!" She grasps his fingers and holds his hand to her breasts. "I love you, Damien. You're it for me. You're the one that I want."

"But you also want a child. That's what you told me on our trip."

"Which trip?"

"The Maldives. You said you wanted to start trying for kids. I wasn't prepared to tell you about my . . . issue. I convinced you to table the discussion until we got home. But then—"

Ella's shoulders drop. "I went on assignment for Nathan's article. You flew to London where I joined you afterward and—"

"And several weeks later you found out you were pregnant. You were overjoyed. I knew it wasn't mine, but I couldn't take that happiness away from you. You know us—reuniting in London—you would have thought it was mine." He lays a gentle kiss on her forehead. "I don't know why you left Nathan last summer, but you chose to stay with me. And you chose me again at the hospital. You told me you could fix our mistakes. You said you knew how to suppress your memories of Nathan. You'd block your memory of the night of the accident, when we argued and I told you about my sterility. You

319

didn't want to feel anything for Nathan. You didn't want to remember I was sterile, and you wanted to still believe that I didn't want kids. You described it as 'cleaning the slate.' We could start over. Go back to the way we were. But it didn't work, Ella. You ended up right back in his arms."

She squeezes her eyes shut. "I'm so sorry."

"I believe you love me. You might love him, too. But I won't share you. I doubt Nathan will either." He tucks an errant strand of hair, now moist from her tears, behind her ear. "I love you, Ella." He kisses her lips and moves away.

"No!" Ella follows him into the entryway. "You can't leave me!"

He steps into his loafers, pockets his wallet, and picks up his keys. He removes one of the two flash drives from his key chain, takes her hand, and closes her fingers around the drive. "This is yours. You'll find all two thousand eighty-two files I removed from your laptop."

Ella opens her hand and stares at the little red drive. "You scrubbed my computer?"

"And your phone and cloud accounts. You asked me to. It was part of the promise I made to you. You didn't want access to anything that chanced you remembering Nathan."

"I guess we didn't anticipate him reoffering the exclusive to his story," she says, glum.

Damien doesn't comment. He takes a breath.

"I also wiped *Luxe Avenue*'s servers of any correspondence between you and your editor about him in case you asked your boss for anything."

She flinches. "You hacked into *Luxe*?"

"It's what I do, El. I protect what's mine."

"Then why are you leaving me?"

He swings the garment bag over his shoulder. "I'm not leaving you. I'm letting you go."

CHAPTER 30

Ella nurses a mug of cold, bitter coffee and stares out the kitchen window into the gray afternoon. The city and bay are there, but she can't make out anything other than the faint outline of nearby buildings. Off in the distance, the foghorns at the middle and south span of the Golden Gate Bridge blare their warning, the sound forlorn, echoing off the city's cold, sunless shores.

It's been over twenty-four hours since Damien walked out their front door. He didn't leave her. He let her go, like a drab outfit discarded at the donation center. Somehow it makes their parting that much worse. It evaporates the sliver of hope for them he tried to instill in her.

Do you remember the first time we saw this kitchen? Do you remember what I said to you?

How are they supposed to come back here and find each other when he's already gone?

Dejected, Ella hasn't slept, showered, or eaten anything other than dry toast last night. She's stewing in guilt and that's what she deserves.

She hasn't opened her laptop to finish the article that Rebecca's expecting in her in-box tomorrow. She also hasn't returned any phone calls. And there have been plenty. Rebecca's left two messages. One, she's sending a photographer to Anchorage to meet up with Nathan to shoot the cover. And two, she wants an update from Ella ASAP. If she misses tomorrow's deadline, she'll leave the entire team scrambling.

Nathan's called four times since she landed in Reno. The first three were hang-ups when she didn't answer. The last call, he left a message, an apology. He shouldn't have said those things about the way she conducts her assignments. They were gross exaggerations.

What about her telling him that she loved him? Was that a gross exaggeration, too?

Nathan and Damien don't seem to think so.

Davie has also called. She left a message reminding Ella about her client's art exhibit tonight. And finally, Andrew. She let his call go to voice mail, and when she eventually listens to it, it makes her smile more than she has in the past day. He has a date tomorrow night. He's been seeing someone for a couple of months and it's getting serious. Can Ella meet him at Westfield Centre? Shopping for a new outfit makes him want to stab his eyeballs. But he also wants to make an impression. This girl, she's different from the others.

Just as Ella finishes listening to Andrew's message, Damien calls. She answers his on the first ring.

In a dry, measured tone, Damien tells her his plans. He's staying at the Embarcadero Hyatt

Regency. The internal investigation at PDN is keeping him in town. He'll let her know if he has to fly overseas. Otherwise, he'll give her his address once he finds a more permanent place and figures out what he's going to do.

Not them, she notices. Not us or we.

He. Him. Alone.

Ella wants to cry into her coffee, but the tears won't come. She's married and in love with her husband. She wouldn't have slept with Nathan unless she had good reason.

The Maldives.

Her mind keeps circling back to that.

Damien mentioned an argument they'd had while on vacation, of which Ella has no recollection. But she can speculate. For whatever reason, on that trip, she told him she wanted to start a family, but he brushed her off. Ella then slept with Nathan because she'd been infuriated with Damien, disillusioned about their marriage. Crushed she couldn't convince him to have kids.

So she lashed out. She wanted to hurt Damien the way he'd hurt her. It's what she does. After her parents' deaths, she destroyed her mom's Lladró collection, and she did something similar after Grace's death. Grace's dad had asked Ella for photos of his daughter to use at the funeral. Rather than saying no, Ella ripped every photo she had of Grace, including the pages in her yearbook. Seething, she put the torn pieces in a shoebox and left them on Grace's mother's porch, where her dad was sleeping on the couch while in town to bury his daughter. Spite and rage drove her to hurt Stan because she blamed him for Grace's death. In the end, though, Ella only hurt herself. The only photos she has of her best friend are in her memory.

Of course, she has to consider the other reason she slept with Nathan.

She fell in love.

Behind her on the marble counter sits the thumb drive. That drive has the answers, perhaps the key to everything. Yet every time she reaches for it, she hesitates. Damien's words come back, haunting her: *Are you sure you want to remember?*

No, she's not.

There's a reason she made herself forget. Because . . .

No memories, no emotions.

A coward's way out.

Stop being one, Ella reprimands herself. She needs to deal with this now, or else she'll never fix what's broken between her and Damien.

Ella pours her coffee in the sink, leaving a brown spiderweb stain on the porcelain, and grabs the thumb drive. In her office, she boots up her laptop and plugs in the drive. Two thousand eighty-two items display in the window that pops open. Folders, files, transcribed recordings, and photos. Forgotten moments, even days, from the seven months prior to her accident if she's counting her and Damien's time in the Maldives.

She picks through the files, opening random documents. Notes from her first interview with Nathan reveal they covered the same topics, proving Nathan hadn't lied to her. Surprisingly, there's a fully drafted article, similar in style and direction to the one she started the other day in Alaska. That's comforting, and a huge help considering her deadline. But the photo she opens next is not.

Nathan stands shirtless, waist deep in water, his bare back to the camera. Her cheeks heat. She quickly closes the file and opens the next.

Nathan sits cross-legged on the ground, the front of him cast in the glow of firelight. His expression is reflective. From the look of this photo alone, Nathan hasn't changed much between interviews. He still broods. Self-disgust still simmers just below his surface. Guilt has him living a solitary existence.

Ella risks clicking open several more photos, none of which are incriminating or make her too uneasy about her relationship with Nathan. Though she's overcome with the same feelings she had while looking at the photos of her pregnant self after her accident. The pictures don't feel like they belong to her.

Ella clicks through the files on Amira Silvers,

the celebrity she interviewed last August. She doesn't remember the interview, but Amira was the one who referred Ella to Dr. Irwin Whitely. Again, another draft article that wasn't forwarded to Rebecca, along with eight recordings. Notes suggest Rebecca killed the article. The magazine didn't have the space that month. But before the cancellation, the interview had been conducted over the course of three hours in a single day. Eight recordings tell her there were plenty of stops and starts during their discussion. What did they talk about off the record?

Ella closes out the Silvers folder and opens the Irwin Whitely folder, also on this thumb drive. It is extensive. She opens the first document and starts reading. Several hours into her search she comes across a brief mention of a code to unblock memories, a trace that the mind follows to retrieve a specific memory or idea, even a miniscule fact that's been stored.

Ella pushes back from her desk with a whoop of relief. There it is. Now all she has to do is find the file with her code.

Several hours later, when Ella is deep into her notes, her phone vibrates on her desk. Ella jerks, startled. Davie's face glows on the screen. She snatches up her phone.

"The opening is in an hour. Are you coming or not?" Davie asks after Ella apologizes for not getting back to her earlier.

Ella looks at the time. Six o'clock p.m. She hasn't showered, and her stomach has decided it's no longer feeling sorry for itself. It growls. She glances back at the laptop. There are plenty more files to pick through, at least two months' worth, and she still has an article to finish tonight. But she also needs some air.

"I'll be a little late, but yes, I'll be there."

"Fantastic. See you then."

CHAPTER 31

Located directly on the Embarcadero Promenade and under the Bay Bridge, the Pier 24 Photography gallery has beautiful views of the bay. But viewing photographs is not Ella's idea of a great evening out, especially in her current frame of mind. She finds the showing, a retrospective of California architecture, from the adobe shacks built by the missionaries to the Spanish Colonial Revival bungalows and Eichler tract homes of suburbia, seriously boring. And two champagnes and a handful of passed hors d'oeuvres later, Ella is ready to leave. She sets down her glass and looks for the ladies' room. After a quick pee and fresh lipstick application, she's going to call an Uber. But she spots Davie waving at her, the gorgeous photographer, her client, at her side.

Davie weaves through the crowd, making her way over to Ella. Davie looks stunning, as always, in a shimmering navy-blue tunic and gold lamé Roman sandals. Ella feels like a fraud in her jade-green wrap and nude heels. But she's smart enough to blame that feeling on her current mood. She's depressed and rejected. Guilty on all counts.

She should have stayed home. Nathan's article

is due to Rebecca tomorrow. She'd promised her it would be first thing, but as long as she sends it by midnight, she's still within her deadline. Though it's probably a good thing she isn't working on it right now. Exhausted and snippy, who knows what she'd write?

Stifling a yawn behind a hand, Ella quickly pastes on a smile and takes the hand the photographer, Flynn Hershberger, offers. His jet-black, glossy curls meet at the top of his black mock turtleneck and Ella can't help smirking. He looks like a young Steve Jobs. Flynn envelops Ella's hand with both of his. "Our exquisite friend Davie tells me you write for *Luxe Avenue*." His eyes flash. "I can't wait to read what you think of my work."

Ella raises her brows. She glances at Davie, who shrugs.

Ella slips her hand from Flynn's. "I'm sure Davie will let you know when that happens. Great show, Flynn. I wish you luck. If you'll excuse me." She smiles graciously and parts company.

Davie catches up with her on the way to the restroom. "Sorry about that. This is Flynn's biggest exhibition to date and it's attracting a lot of media attention. He just assumed—"

Ella flicks her wrist, waving aside the apology, and pushes open the restroom door. "No worries. I get it." She tucks into a stall.

"Do you want to go across the street and grab a cocktail?" Davie asks when they meet back up at the sink.

Alcohol is the last thing Ella needs. "I can't. I have to finish Nathan's article."

Davie pouts. "Lucky you. Spending time with two delicious men. That god of a husband of yours and that fine specimen you get to write about."

Normally, Ella would laugh. This time, her stomach turns.

"Tell Damien I said hello. How is he, by the way? I haven't seen him in a while."

"I don't know. He left." Ella dries her hands.

"For London?"

"No. Me." Ella drags her Bobbi Brown stick across her bottom lip. Her eyes meet Davie's stunned expression in the mirror.

Ella drops the lipstick into her clutch. "Simon wasn't his."

Davie's mouth hangs open. "What the hell, Ella? When did this happen? How did this happen? Oh, my god, don't tell me." But her mind clicks and sets an answer. She mouths, "Nathan?"

Ella nods.

"Damn, girl." Davie's eyes are huge.

Ella yanks a towel from the dispenser and dabs the corners of her eyes and roughly exhales through pursed lips. "He left yesterday. But it started last summer. Maybe before that. I don't know. I can't remember."

"You poor thing. I can't believe you didn't text me!" Davie gives her head a hard shake and holds up both hands. "Screw the article. We're having drinks, and you're telling me everything."

They find a bar around the corner and order appetizers. Ella tells her everything she knows from what Damien and Nathan told her and what she read earlier in the day. Everything except the news about Damien's sterility. That would betray his confidence, and it's not her secret to tell.

Three dry martinis for Davie and two ice waters for Ella later, Ella wraps up the seven months before the accident. She glances at the time on her phone. Ten o'clock p.m. She's going to be up all night without a clue how she'll string ten thousand words together. She can barely think straight.

Davie downs the remnants of her martini and slides the glass aside. "Remember when you first came home from the hospital and asked me if you'd said anything to me while you were there that might have seemed odd? I didn't think it worth mentioning, but after everything you just told me, it might be important."

A muscle twinges in Ella's chest. "What is it?"

Davie leans forward. "You told me you wished you never told Damien that you wanted a baby. I figured you wished that because you were sad about everything that happened with the accident and Simon. Do you think you . . ."

Davie continues talking but Ella tunes her out. Hands trembling, she realizes what she did. Ella didn't set out to forget Nathan. She wanted to forget that she has always wanted a child. She wanted to believe that, like Damien, she didn't want kids either.

CHAPTER 32

Panic! at the Disco's "Say Amen" blares in Ella's ear. Buried deep in the depths of her comforter and sheets, she thrusts out an arm and roots around for her phone, snatching it off the nightstand.

"Hello?" she groans.

"Where are you? I've been waiting for thirty minutes," Andrew barks into the phone. Stress adds irritation to his tone. He really hates shopping for clothes.

Ella peeks at the clock. One fourteen p.m. She had texted him last night that she'd meet him today but had forgotten to set her alarm. "I'm coming. Give me twenty." She tosses aside the covers and drags herself to the bathroom.

"You're still asleep?"

Not just asleep, but seriously passed out. She slept through two alarms. She vaguely recalls slapping the snooze button on her clock.

It was 5:00 a.m. when she finally toppled into bed, unable to keep her eyes open and head up any longer. Thank goodness she found the article she drafted last summer. Otherwise she doubts she'd manage tonight's deadline.

Ella meets up with Andrew at the Espresso Bar in the Westfield San Francisco Centre. Bundled in a thick hoodie, jeans, and Ugg boots, with a trucker's cap covering her still damp hair, Ella whips off her reflective Ray-Bans and Andrew grins.

"Rough night?"

"Long night writing. Coffee first." She points at the bar.

With one vanilla latte with a double shot of espresso in hand, Ella turns to her brother. "Okay. Show me what you've picked out so far."

He shows her his empty hands. "I got nothing."

"Nothing? What have you been doing for the past hour?"

"Waiting for you."

"You're hopeless. Come on."

Giving him a nudge, Ella leads her brother up the escalator to the men's furnishings floor in Nordstrom. "Tell me about this girl," she says, sipping her coffee.

"Corey?" Andrew's face lights up. He leans a hip on the moving rail. "She's cool. Nah, that's not right. She's real." His grin spreads. "There's nothing fake about her, if you know what I mean." His brows waggle.

"Stop." Ella smacks her brother's chest. "Gross."

Andrew's expression sobers. "She isn't like most women I've dated."

"You mean she has a brain?" she lobs.

"High expectations," he returns. "A lot of people

I work with want big rewards for minimal work. Not Corey. She works her ass off." He cringes and clears his throat. "Sorry. I mean she's driven. She's earned everything she's been offered. She's genuine with people. Just an all-around great lady."

"You've been dating for two months? I can't believe you haven't told me about her."

"She works in marketing at Talbert & Dean."

Ella's brow furrows. "Isn't T&D the investor in your app?"

"Mm-hmm."

"Ah."

"We've been keeping it under the radar, but now that we're getting serious, we don't want to hide anymore. Aunt Kathy always said, 'Honesty's the best policy,' right?" He nudges her in the ribs.

"You could have told me."

"I wanted to but . . ." He shrugs. "You've been dealing with your own stuff. I didn't want to add to it."

The escalator drops them off on the men's floor. Ella touches his upper arm. "I'm happy for you."

"Thanks. I can't wait for you to meet her."

"Me too. Where are you taking her tonight?"

Andrew slides his fingertips into the front pockets of his jeans. "Dunno. Dinner? Maybe a jazz club after?"

"Impressive. My little bro is growing up."

"Bound to happen at some point." He snorts a laugh. "Might as well start acting my age."

"Nah, I like you the way you are. Let's see what we can do with you." She taps her chin, taking in Andrew's SpongeBob shirt, unzipped hoodie, faded baggy jeans, and Converse sneakers. His hair is a mess even by cute surfer-boy standards, and his facial hair is long past trimmed and contoured.

"What you need is a button-down shirt and dark wash jeans. I'm going to insist they're fitted." She points at his baggy rear. "A blazer of some sort would be nice, too."

Andrew blanches at the mention of the coat.

"Oh, come on. A few nice pieces in your wardrobe won't kill you. First, we need to get you cleaned up. Then we'll find an outfit."

An hour later, after a shampoo, trim, and shave at the salon on the other end of the mall, Ella walks Andrew through the various sections of the men's department, picking shirts and jeans along the way. A stylist latches on to Andrew at one point, selecting her suggestions from the racks of tailored jackets. Arms full, she escorts them to a large dressing room. Ella settles onto a leather bench, sipping her second latte, which she'd purchased on the way back from the salon. As Andrew strips to his boxer briefs, everything Ella has avoided thinking about since her conversation with Davie suddenly starts pounding around her brain.

She glances at her phone. No calls or texts

from Damien. Nothing from Nathan either. She owes him a call and the truth. But Damien is her priority. She just needs to get Nathan's article off her list.

Andrew pushes an arm into a blue-checked shirt. He already stepped into a pair of Citizens of Humanity dark wash jeans. So much better than the saggy Levi's she would bet he sleeps, works, and eats in. He nods at Ella's phone. "Expecting a call?"

"No, why?" She drops the phone into her purse.

"No reason other than you can't stop looking at it. Is this shirt supposed to be this tight?" He swings his arms, crossing them over his chest, then jutting back his elbows.

"It's extraslim. Here." Ella sifts through the pile of shirts she brought in. "Same shirt, one size up. I'm glad you've got a girlfriend. You've been spending too much time alone at the gym." His chest is wider and biceps larger than she remembers.

"That's why I have a girlfriend." He grins.

Andrew has the look of their father: brown eyes, sandy-blond hair, divot in his chin, and deep creases in his cheeks when he smiles. She knows this more from photos than from memory. Both she and Andrew are older than their parents were when they passed, Ella by almost ten years.

"Do you think of Mom and Dad much?"

"That's a weird question." Andrew tosses aside

the shirt he just tried on and takes the one Ella hands him.

"Looking at you now, I was reminded of Dad."

"You look like Mom. She was pretty."

"Is that a compliment?"

Andrew winks at her, buttoning the shirt.

Ella never gave it much thought, but she does wear her hair in the same long, straight style as her mom. Their coloring and build are also similar.

"Do you wonder if they would have stayed married?"

"I don't wonder. I know they wouldn't have lasted. They argued too much." He pauses in buttoning the shirt. "The accident was my first vivid memory. I heard what Mom said to Dad about how she didn't love him. When a guy hears that from his wife, I dunno." He lets his arms fall against his sides. "It's hard to come back from that. Truth?"

"Truth."

"I think that's why I've never gotten serious with anyone until Corey. I didn't want to find myself so hopelessly in love and wake up one morning to find out she never loved me back. Arguing's one thing. You can always kiss and make up. Own up to mistakes and forgive. But once you stop loving the person you've pledged your life to? How do you come back from that? I don't think you can."

He turns his back to the mirror and, with a glance over his shoulder, inspects the shirt.

"When did you know you loved Damien?" he asks.

"The night we met."

"How did you know?"

She taps her chest. "I felt it here." Still does.

"That's how I feel with Corey. She kind of had a rough childhood, but she's been open with me about her past. I've done the same with her, and I try to be honest about everything. I don't like keeping secrets."

"Unlike Mom and Dad."

"For real. Those two had communication issues. How's everything going with you and Damien?"

Ella feels her face pale. "Fine, why?" She isn't ready to delve into her marital problems. What would Andrew say if he knew Damien left her because she'd had an affair? Not once, but twice. That's one secret she isn't divulging with him.

"No reason other than you rarely bring up Mom and Dad."

"They've been on my mind lately." Hard not to have them there when her own marriage is imploding. She did exactly what her mother had done. The same could be said for Grace's dad. Ella had a secret, and by the time she'd confessed that she genuinely wanted a child, the truth was enough to set her and Damien on course to where they are today: hurt, betrayed, and living under separate roofs.

Would she and Damien have married if she'd been honest with him from the beginning? That time at the soccer field when he asked if she wanted kids, what would he have done if she had said yes? Would he have been honest with her in return? Would he have told her he was sterile? She wonders if Andrew might be onto something. Maybe she and Damien can have a second chance if they truly start over, the right way this time, without any intentional memory suppression.

"What about kids?" she asks.

"What about them?" Andrew gives her an arm so that she can button the cuff.

"Do you want them?"

"Sheesh, Ella. We've only been on a few dates."

Ella buttons the cuff on the other sleeve. "Not with Corey. In general."

"I haven't thought about it much. Yeah, maybe."

"What if you found out your wife couldn't have kids?"

Andrew turns away from the mirror to face Ella. "Can you still . . . ?" He chokes on the question.

"Yes, I can still have kids, or so I've been told." Lynn had said so.

Andrew exhales with relief. "A little nephew or niece would be cool."

His words bring on a touch of sadness. She looks briefly at the pile of shirts Andrew has yet to try on. Hopefully, one day, she can give him a nephew or niece. If she's lucky, one of each.

"What about you, though? Would you adopt if you found out your wife couldn't have them or if something happened to you?"

"Yes," he says without hesitation.

"Why?"

"Simple. I'd want to experience everything I can with the woman I loved, including raising a child. Just because the kid doesn't have my blood doesn't mean I'd love him any less."

Ella's heart swells. "You're a good man, Andrew."

"That may be so, but I'm a lousy brother. I hate this shirt."

"Oh." Ella blinks, surprised. "It looks good on you."

He shakes his head.

She gestures at the pile. "There are others you can try."

"No. I don't like button-downs. Sorry, but they're not me. Be right back." Andrew dashes from the dressing room, and less than five minutes later, he's back. Hurriedly, he unbuttons the shirt and pulls on a black MadeWorn graphic T-shirt with the AC/DC logo.

Ella grimaces. "Really?"

Andrew beams. "Really."

He swaps out the brown loafers Ella made him wear while trying on the designer jeans with his beat-up Converse sneakers. Thankfully, he keeps on the dark wash jeans while sorting through the blazers the stylist left in the room. Landing on a black tweed, he yanks it off the hanger and puts it on, turning to Ella, arms out.

"What do you think?"

"Nice. A little cas for dinner and jazz, you think?"

"Yeah, but this is me. Corey's been honest about who she is and I want to do the same. No pretenses, no secrets. What she sees is what she gets, and if she doesn't like it, well, that's her problem."

Ella leans back against the dressing room wall. "She'll love it. She'll love you and whatever you decide to do together. Good for you for being up-front with her from the get-go."

"I'm scrapping my dinner and jazz club plans. I think I'll take her to Lucky Strike, then the Metreon."

Ella grins. "Bowling and a movie." A date right up Andrew's alley. "You and Corey will have a blast."

"Think so?"

"Know so, because she'll be with you." Ella stands and helps her brother out of the blazer. "Go pay for these so you can get ready for your date. When you want to introduce us, Damien and I would love to have you and Corey over for dinner."

"Thanks for your help today. I know you're busy and all with your deadline."

"No, thank you." Andrew showed her what she should have done with Damien since day one. But first, someone else needs her honesty.

CHAPTER 33

One Week Later
Mid-April 2019

She thought about meeting him at a café near Union Square. She considered a restaurant off Highway 80, somewhere in Roseville, midway between them. He doesn't like crowds and she doesn't want to draw attention and invite media speculation. The photo of her and Nathan at Alpine Mountaineering might be last week's news, but it's still circulating. It surfaced in her news feed just yesterday morning. In the end, Ella settled on going to him.

A patchwork of snow decorates the ground around Nathan's house like a winter quilt. The scent of pine and dirt with a hint of woodsmoke saturates the cool afternoon air. Nathan meets her on his porch, decked in his standard issue of jeans, boots, and a flannel shirt.

"Hi," he says when she reaches the top step.

"Hi." She musters a smile, keeping a polite distance. Despite how they left things in Alaska, she still wants to feel his arms around her. But that's not why she's here.

"About Alaska," she begins, ready to get this over with. She has a flight to catch. She also doesn't trust herself around him.

"I'm sorry," he says in earnest.

"Me too."

A breeze ruffles her hair. Nathan smooths it away from her face. His touch is fleeting, unexpected, and her body reacts immediately. He smiles, knowing exactly what he's doing to her.

"Do you want to come inside?" he invites, gesturing at the door behind him.

"Sure. I promise not to take up too much of your time."

She follows him into the house. Fred and Bing greet her with lolling tongues and wagging tails. Ella doles out some affection before they wander over to the fireplace and collapse on their pillow beds, resuming their afternoon nap.

"Coffee?" Nathan asks.

"No, thanks."

He gestures at the sectional. He settles into the chair opposite her. A restless energy rolls off him.

"So, um . . . why are you here?" he asks.

"I finished your article. My editor has it now. The issue's printing as we speak. You'll be on the cover." She fishes in her shoulder bag for the manila folder she brought with her. Rising from her seat, she gives it to him. "I wanted you to read it before it hit the newsstands."

"You could have emailed it," he says, taking the folder.

True, but she didn't write it to appeal to Stephanie as Nathan had wanted. She wrote it for him, and she wants him to know that before the magazine is published.

Nathan flips open the folder and skims the title page. Adventure's End: A Grieving Father's Tribute to His Son. He snaps the folder closed and tosses it aside.

"Aren't you going to read it?"

"Later." He regards her coolly. "I want to talk about us."

"Us? There can't be an us." She holds up a hand when his mouth parts and continues before he can challenge her. "I'm sorry about Alaska and everything that I let happen between us, but we're married to other people."

"I'm divorcing my wife. I want to be with you."

"I don't know what promises I made to you before, but I'm not leaving my husband. I love him."

"And me? Do you . . ." He falters, looks down at the floor before trying again. "Do you love me?"

"I . . ." She stops, catching herself before she says the words *I don't love you.* Almost the exact words her mom shouted at her dad that fateful Thanksgiving night.

Bite your tongue, Ella.

Nathan watches her expectantly. Ella realizes there's no easy way to tell him. There's never an easy way when it comes to matters of the heart, especially when one's heart is being worn

347

on his navy-blue flannel sleeve, as in Nathan's case.

Ella chooses her words carefully, and she chooses to be honest. "I care about you, Nathan. I care about you a great deal. More than I should."

He makes a pained sound deep in his throat. "Then why not follow through on it?"

"I can't. I mean, I won't. I believe you when you say I loved you once. But I don't remember how I felt about you. I don't feel that way now." She whispers the last admission.

He watches her quietly. He looks as if he doubts her. She shifts, uncomfortable under his gaze.

Ella looks at her hands in her lap.

"Simon was yours."

When she doesn't hear a response from Nathan, she lifts her head to make sure he heard her. He did. His face has gone white. He squeezes his clasped hands so tightly together that Ella can see the whites of his knuckles from where she sits.

Suddenly, he pushes to his feet and goes to the window. Arms folded over his chest, he keeps his back to her.

"Remember when you told me we ran into each other in Reno? I don't think I knew he was yours then." Ella tries to explain what she's concluded based on what she's been told, careful not to betray her husband's confidence. Nathan doesn't need to know about Damien's sterility. "Damien told me he wasn't the father the same day as my accident. That must have been why I called you."

Nathan crosses the room back to her. "You called me seconds before your accident. We got cut off. I was on the phone with you when . . . God, I'm so sorry. I didn't know you were driving. I would have told you to call me back or find someplace to park so that we could talk. I can't stop thinking that had I simply hung up, Simon would be with us today. Don't you see, Ella? It's my fault he's dead." He's crying now. Reaching for her, he pulls her into his arms. "I'm so sorry. About everything. Can you forgive me?"

For an instant, Ella wants to shove him away. She wants to blame him. For everything. But it's not his fault. She's the one who called him. She's the one who'd been on the phone while driving and not paying attention at the intersection.

Nathan blames himself for both of his sons' deaths. But the weight of Simon's loss isn't for him to carry. It's Ella's and Damien's. It was their lies that got them to where they are today.

Ella steps from his embrace and looks him in the eyes. "The accident wasn't your fault. I shouldn't have called you when I was so upset and driving. I forgive you, but I never blamed you, nor will I ever. Do you think you'll be able to forgive yourself?"

He thumbs away her tears and wipes off his own. "I'm trying."

"Good." Ella nods, sniffling. "That's good." Looking behind her, then on the floor, she grabs her bag and hefts it onto her shoulder.

He clears his throat. "You're leaving?"

"I am. I have a plane to catch."

"Can I see you again?"

She shakes her head. "I don't think so."

He closes his eyes, nodding. He doesn't like her answer, but he doesn't argue. She's right, for both their sakes, and he knows it. Leaning in, he kisses her gently on the lips. "Goodbye, El."

"Bye, Nathan." She turns to leave, then stops. Tipping her head toward the manila folder, she says, "Read it. You'll see how I see you." As a man who loved his wife and as a father who gave his son the best possible life. She won't give Nathan her love, but she can give him her words. Hopefully, through them, he'll find the peace he seeks. The strength to reconcile with himself.

CHAPTER 34

The following day, Ella sits on the stool that gives her the best view in Lobby Bar at the ARIA Resort. She arrived late last night after leaving Nathan's place and checked into the same room Damien had when they first met. She debated meeting at Luna's, but the café often gets too noisy. She also considered inviting Damien home, where they could "find each other again." In the end, Ella decided on Las Vegas. If they're truly going to start over the right way, by being open and honest with each other, she wants to be where it all began.

This time, she's not wearing a revealing slip dress and downing cocktails. The black crepe jumpsuit and cognac-colored wedges are casual and classy, more aligned with her tastes. The glass of ice water sitting on the cocktail napkin is a wiser choice than the bourbon on ice she could go for. She needs to keep a clear head.

Damien texted thirty minutes ago that he had landed. She hasn't seen him in over a week and she can't stop looking around for him. Gamblers gather at tables, tossing dice. Bells ring from slot machines. Techno music pulses like a throbbing vein through the entire floor. She feels the beat inside her rib cage. Her hand shakes when she takes a sip of water. Everything about her marriage and a future with Damien rides on this next hour.

She misses him, even aches for his embrace. She wants to see his smile and hear his voice. There's so much she wants with Damien.

And there he is.

Ella watches him weave through the lounge chairs and her heart races. He's taken off his tie and unbuttoned the top button of his shirt. His suit fits him perfectly and he looks so much like he did when she first saw him here four years ago. She feels as if she's falling in love all over again.

She slides off the stool and slips her arms around him when he reaches her. "I've missed you," she says, resting her cheek against his chest. She breathes in his scent, the starch of his shirt, and the Giorgio Armani cologne she gifted him on their anniversary, and her nerves settle. Just a little.

Damien takes a moment to react, but he finally wraps his arms around her. He rests his cheek on her head.

"El." Her name is a sigh.

She wishes she could stay within the warm confines of his arms for the rest of the day, but there's a reason she asked him to come. She moves out of his embrace and Damien looks at her, wary. "What's going on?"

She didn't tell him anything when she called. Only that she wanted to talk and for him to meet her in Vegas.

"Can I get you a drink, sir?"

The bartender's timing isn't ideal and Damien shoots him an irritated look before tipping his head at Ella's glass. "I'll have what she's having."

"One water coming up."

"Water?" Damien lifts his brows and Ella gives him a slight smile.

"There's so much I have to tell you." She smooths his white shirt with a shaking hand.

Damien stills her hand, holding it to his chest. "You're nervous."

She nods.

"Me too," he says with a hint of a smile.

"You're never nervous."

"This time I am." He lets go of her hand and drinks his water. "Why'd you have me come here? We could have met at home."

Home. Her heart flutters with hope. "I know this will seem over the top, but I have a point. I got us a room. Will you come up with me?"

"Ella, I . . ." He turns his face away, taps a finger on the bar before looking at her again. "I would love nothing more than to take you upstairs and make love with you, but I . . ." He shakes his head, eyes sad. "I can't."

"Oh, no! That's not what I meant," she

exclaims, flustered. "I want to talk, Damien, that's all. No expectations. I brought us here because I'm hoping we can start over, for real this time. No memory manipulation involved."

"Okay," he says, nodding slowly.

"Great." Ella smiles. She gathers her clutch and keycard off the bar and leads them to the bank of elevators. As they walk, Damien's fingertips skim the curve of her lower back, sending a current through her, arousing her. But once they step inside the elevator and the doors slide closed, he pockets his hands. He even maintains a polite distance between them and Ella has to fight the impulse to move closer.

She presses the button to their floor and, once they're there, swipes the keycard against the door latch panel.

"This is the same room," Damien observes when they walk into the suite.

"You remembered."

He shrugs off his jacket. Folding it lengthwise, he lays it on the king bed and looks at Ella. Their eyes catch, and he says, "I remember *everything* about the night we met."

Ella's entire body warms. "Me too," she whispers.

"I . . . ah . . ." He glances at his watch. "My flight leaves at seven."

"Seven?" She looks at the clock. He's only giving them three hours. Two until he has to return to the airport. She was hoping he'd spend the night with her.

"Early morning meeting." He looks at her apologetically.

"Oh, okay. So . . . how's work?" she asks, hating how she feels awkward around her own husband.

He walks to the window, looks down at the Strip. "Fine."

"The investigation?"

"Over," he says, turning back to her. "Thank god."

"Oh! That's great." She wishes she'd known. She would have wanted to be there with him to celebrate. "What did you find out? That's okay if you can't tell me. Corporate confidentiality and all that. I get it." She crosses her arms.

He rubs the back of his neck, lets his arm fall to his side. "I want to tell you, but—"

"Will you tell me why your dad wants to put you out of business?" she blurts. "Will you tell me why you didn't invite them to our wedding or call them on Christmas? Why don't they ever call you on your birthday?"

"Ella," he says, slightly irritated.

"I'm sorry." She pushes out a breath. "That's not how I wanted to start this." She takes a deep breath and refocuses. "There are two things about me I want to share with you. One of them I should have told you when we started dating."

"Why didn't you?" he asks curiously when she pauses.

"After seeing the way my mom treated my dad—she was way too honest about her feelings and it destroyed them—I was scared. I thought if I was honest with you, it would tear us apart. Now I'm hoping my honesty will do the opposite. Bring us closer together."

Damien slides his hands into his pockets. "All right. I'm listening."

"I wasn't truthful when you first asked if I wanted kids. You told me you didn't, and I was afraid that if I said I did, you wouldn't want to be with me. I had already fallen in love with you. I guess I thought I could give up my dream of having kids if it meant I could spend the rest of my life with you."

"But you didn't give it up. You still want kids."

"I do, and I need to tell you why. Do you remember me telling you about my friend Grace?"

"The one who committed suicide?"

"Yes. This probably sounds silly, but we used to play house when we were little. We'd made a pact that when we grew up, we'd name our daughters after each other. I've never told anyone, but Grace left me a suicide note. I found it under my pillow. She asked if I remembered our pact. She then wrote, and I quote: 'Please name your first daughter after me so that I can go knowing you'll never forget me.'

"I could never forget Grace. But I felt so guilty about what happened, and I've always wanted to fulfill her wish."

Ella inhales a shaky breath and she feels tears glide down her cheeks.

"El," Damien says, his voice full of compassion. Coming over to her, he cups her cheek and wipes away the moisture with his thumb. She leans into his hand. It feels so good to have him touch her again. His mouth parts and she holds up a finger.

"I have one more thing to confess."

Damien lowers his arm.

"I didn't just intentionally forget Nathan. I tried to forget that I wanted to have children."

Damien falls back a step. He frowns. "How did you figure that out?"

"Davie told me. I guess I mentioned something to her in the hospital. I'm guessing I thought I could fix our problems if I didn't want kids, like you. Instead, I screwed up and made a total mess of my head. I forgot the wrong things, like Simon. I never would have wanted to forget him.

"I'm sorry for all the trouble I've caused us. And I'm sorry for cheating on you. I didn't mean to hurt you. But it'll never happen again, I promise."

Damien is quiet for several moments and Ella fears the worst. She wants children. He'd wanted them with Anna. Would he want them with her?

If not, what was the point of staying together when they don't want the same thing?

But Damien says something that floors her.

"I had a twin brother."

She blinks. "You did?"

He nods. "I should have told you about him a long time ago. Broderick was the firstborn. He was also my parents' favorite. We were only four when he died in his sleep of a heart defect no one knew about. Anytime I got less than an A on a test or didn't beat my PR in track, my parents would not so subtly weave my brother into the conversation. They'd wonder if Broderick would have beaten my time or scored higher. I could never live up to Broderick's imagined potential. I've competed against my dead brother my entire life for my parents' recognition."

"How could they treat you like that?"

"I was in Broderick's bed when my parents found him. I guess it was easier for them to blame me than accept that their perfect child had a defect."

"They don't think you killed him, do they?"

"No, nothing like that. But there were times I felt they treated me as if I did. I have memories of my brother. I've seen pictures. I loved him. I never could have hurt him." His voice cracks.

"Of course you couldn't. You were only a child."

"My parents had dreams of grandchildren and

were ecstatic when I married Anna. They hoped for twins. When that didn't happen and I told them why, my dad reneged on his offer to hand over CyberSeal when he retired. My punishment for ending the family line. As if I chose to be sterile!

"I didn't see it coming. All the work I'd done for him, my college education, training at his company. It was all for nothing. He demoted me, then told me he was taking the company public. I left before that happened."

Anger fills Ella. "What an asshole. I don't get how parents can cut off their kids," she exclaims, thinking of her mom's parents.

"It happens all the time."

"Well, it shouldn't have happened to you. I don't want you to invite them to dinner, ever."

Damien chokes out a laugh. "No worries there. I met my dad for lunch earlier this week and showed him the evidence we collected against CyberSeal. He claims he didn't know anything about it."

"Do you believe him?"

"No. But I did get him to agree to compensate us for lost revenue in exchange for keeping it out of court. That's publicity his board doesn't want. Had he not agreed, I would have made sure this turned into a media circus and his stock would nose-dive. PDN can take the hit. CyberSeal, being public, can't."

"I'm glad you worked out an arrangement. That must not have been an easy meeting."

"It wasn't." He shoves a hand through his hair, messing the neat waves he styled that morning.

"You must have felt like he was rejecting you all over again. Thank you for being honest with me, Damien."

He presses his lips into a flat line and nods. Restless, he goes to the desk, slides aside a magazine but doesn't really look at it.

"I get why you never told me about your sterility. I imagine it's easier to say you don't want kids than to explain the truth. And I'm sorry about your brother. I can't imagine losing Andrew."

Again, he nods, his eyes downcast. He fans the magazine. Pages flip. Ella wants nothing more than to hold him. For now, though, she tries to lighten the burden he carries.

"I love you, Damien. You don't have to give me kids. Just give me you."

"But you want kids, Ella," he says firmly. "I'm not going to take that away from you."

"So, what? You're just going to give up on us?"

"We have other issues. You cheated on me, twice." He holds up two fingers for emphasis.

Ella's heart sinks and she closes her eyes. "I'll regret that every single day for the rest of my life. I'm so sorry," she says, meeting his gaze.

"Me too." He taps a finger on the desk, and

after a moment, says, "I should have told you I can't have kids."

"Would you, if you could?"

"Ella."

She goes to him and grasps his hands. "Just answer the question, please. Do you want to have kids with me?"

His face crumples. He looks on the brink of tears. "If I could have kids, I wouldn't want anything more than to have them with you," he admits, his voice thick.

Ella squeezes his hands reassuringly. "Same. I want to experience raising a family with you. You don't have to give me a baby. Adopt one with me. We can foster a child or get a donation from a sperm bank. We have so many options, Damien. I don't care what we decide, as long as we decide together and that we stay together."

"You'd do that for me . . . adopt?"

She frowns slightly. "I'm not Anna. Whatever child we bring into our family will be ours." Ella slowly smiles. She cups her hand over his damp cheek. "So yes, Damien. I'd do that for you. I'd do it for us."

He briefly closes his eyes. "I can't tell you what this means to me."

"Hopefully it means you forgive me. For cheating on you and for getting into the car accident. For losing Simon and forgetting about him."

"Losing Simon isn't your fault. Neither is the accident."

She isn't so sure about that, but she needs to hear the words from him. "Please forgive me," she whispers.

"I do," he says without hesitation. "But can you forgive me? I should have told you I was sterile. There were so many times I wanted to tell you, but I thought if I did . . ." He shrugs.

"It wouldn't have changed my mind about marrying you and staying with you if you did."

"Speaking of minds. Do you want your memories back? You mentioned last week you didn't."

Ella thinks for a moment, tapping her lips. "Let me see if I have this straight. We go to the Maldives and I tell you that I want to start a family. But you don't tell me you're sterile, only that you still don't want kids. Right?" She waits for Damien's confirmation and, when he nods, says, "We return home, I go on assignment with Nathan, and you fly to London. I meet up with you two weeks later and several weeks after that realize I'm pregnant. I believe Simon is yours, and you let me think that. Then, for whatever reason—guilt maybe?—you tell me you're sterile, that you're not Simon's father, and that you know I had an affair. This happens on the day of my accident. After dinner, I guess. So far, so good?" He nods again. "We then argue.

362

Upset, I leave the condo, where I call Nathan, presumably to tell him about Simon, but I never get the chance. A truck hits me. And, well . . . we know what happens next."

Damien's jaw ticks.

"Did I get it right?" She looks at him expectantly. His expression is tight and his eyes reflect all the pain she's caused them. But he nods.

"Yes, that's how it happened."

"Then, no. I don't want my memories." She'll miss not having the opportunity to experience the maternal connection with Simon, but she doesn't want to remember her affair with Nathan, the first one, or the hurt she inflicted on Damien.

The pain recedes in his eyes and he smiles, a wide satisfied grin. Ella would say his smile almost looks calculating, but that wouldn't make sense. Her vision is blurry through her tears and distorting everything in the room. Damien's just happy. Super happy they've worked through everything, because he pulls her into his arms and kisses her deeply.

"I love you," he murmurs against her lips. "I love you so much."

When he lifts his head and smiles adoringly at her, she catches the time on the clock. It's almost six o'clock.

"You have to get to the airport," she says, sad he has to leave.

"Or"—he grabs her wrist when she moves toward the door—"I can cancel my flight. And tomorrow's meeting. There's a big bed here, just waiting." He smiles that sexy, wide grin that always makes her breath catch.

"You'd do that for me? Cancel your meeting?"

Damien draws her to him until their bodies are flush. He brushes his lips over hers. "I'd do *anything* to keep you happy, Ella."

CHAPTER 35

INTERVIEW TRANSCRIPT EXCERPT

August 18, 2018
Fairmont Hotel, San Francisco, CA
Interviewer: Ella Skye, Senior Features Writer, *Luxe Avenue* magazine
Interviewee: Amira Silvers, Academy Award–winning Actress

[Continuation of Recording]

Ella: For the record, you've agreed to share with *Luxe Avenue*'s readers what you were going to tell me a moment ago. You said that you know how to forget your husband. So let's pick up where we left off. What do you mean by that? How do you forget Harry? Are you saying you can completely wipe him from your mind? Is that even possible?

Amira: Have you heard of a Dr. Irwin Whitely?

Ella: No.

Amira: He's a cognitive scientist. He's conducting research on memory retrieval and suppression. Specifically, motivated forgetting.

Ella: What's that?

Amira: It's the deliberate suppression of memories. Dr. Sigmund Freud theorized it. Dr. Whitely has discovered how to do it.

Ella: Really? Sounds fascinating.

Amira: Quite. He's looking for more test subjects. I met with him last week. He offered to work with me.

Ella: Are you going to?

Amira: I think so. What about you, Ella? If you could intentionally forget someone, would you?

Ella: Umm . . . I'm not sure.

Amira: What if the person had harmed you?

[Pause]

Amira: Let me rephrase. What about something you did that hurt someone else, something you regret? Imagine the guilt you feel. Imagine eliminating that guilt like this. [Sound of finger snap] Would you block what you did from your memory?

[Pause]

Ella: I'm pregnant.

Amira: Congratulations. How far along?

Ella: Five weeks. I just found out.

Amira: Does your husband know?

Ella: Yes, of course. He's ecstatic. We both are, but . . .

Amira: But?

Ella: Never mind. I shouldn't have said anything.

Amira: Why not? Is something wrong with the baby?

Ella: No, not that. It's . . .

[Pause]

Amira: It's what?

Amira: You can tell me. Ella, darling, there's no one in this room but you and me. Nothing we say gets out that door unless you decide to publish it.

[Pause]

Ella: My husband isn't the father.

Amira: Does he know?

Ella: Yes. He's okay with it. More than okay, surprisingly.

Amira: Interesting. What about the baby's biological father? Does he know?

Ella: No.

[Pause]

Amira: You aren't going to tell him.

Ella: My husband doesn't want me to. I agreed not to at first, but now . . . I don't know.

Amira: You feel guilty keeping your pregnancy from the father.

Ella: Yes. How did you put it? Guilt. It's the devil.

Amira: Mm-hmm. It is. Do you wish you could forget that you told your husband the baby isn't his?

Ella: No. Not that. The opposite.

[Pause]

Amira: [Gasp] You want to forget that the baby isn't your husband's.

Ella: Yes.

Amira: [Low laughter] My, oh my. That is something.

Ella: You don't even know the half of it.

Amira: There's more? Do tell.

Ella: [Expletive]

Amira: What is it?

Ella: We're still recording.

[End Recording]

CHAPTER 36

Six Weeks Later
Late May 2019

Damien sits in his office chair in PDN's San Francisco headquarters. He faces the window that overlooks the murky gray water. The Bay Bridge sprawls below, grappling the shores like an Olympic gymnast doing the splits. On the other side of the bridge, planes take off from the Oakland Airport. They lift into the sky, disappearing into low-lying clouds.

In his hand, he flips a flash drive end over end. A backup to the drive he gave Ella. He always keeps a second copy. It's the nature of his business. Files can crash and data can corrupt in a snap. One string of bad code can erase a lifetime's worth of work. Ella's motivated forgetting was not part of their original plan, the one they devised last summer when she first received the Nathan Donovan assignment on their return from the Maldives.

If there's anything Damien regrets happening on their trip, it's telling Ella about his issue. Unlike what he told her when she got back from Alaska, he had actually revealed his sterility when they were in the Maldives. He told her in a heated reaction to Ella's own confession: she'd admitted that she always wanted kids. She'd forgotten to pack her birth control and thought it would be a good time to try to have a baby. They'd been married for a while. She'd thought maybe, by then, he might be open to the idea. Maybe he'd want to start a family.

Ella had blindsided him. He had no idea she wanted children.

He should have confessed he couldn't give her any before they married. He should have stuck with his usual refrain: he didn't want kids. Because as soon as the confession about his sterility left his mouth, he regretted it. Ella would leave him, just like Anna had.

To his surprise, she didn't. Yes, she was angry he didn't tell her—she felt betrayed. She also didn't speak to him for two days. The longest two days of his life. But she came around, and better yet, she was understanding. She was open to adopting, or they could foster. They could also find a donor. There are a million ways to have a baby, she had said.

A million ways.

And the best way for them came in the form of Nathan Donovan.

Damien's plan was spontaneous, but his wife was on board and it had worked. Perfectly. That was, until Ella let the guilt over what they'd done consume her. Because something had happened while on assignment that neither Ella nor he could have predicted: Ella had fallen in love with Nathan. And after everything he'd been through with Carson, after she found out she was pregnant with Nathan's son, she felt they could no longer deceive him. Nathan had a right to know he was going to be a father.

Damien adamantly disagreed. Nathan could never know the truth. If he did, Simon would no longer belong to Damien and Ella. Nathan would be a part of their family, too. They argued for months until everything came to a head that fateful November evening. Damien distinctly remembers how, after a dinner of pork loin and rice pilaf, Ella said she planned to call Nathan, how she grabbed her car keys and slammed their front door in his face. Then everything changed. The accident. Her emergency C-section. Simon's death. Nathan's audacity to show up at the hospital a few days later and insist on the truth. Was he Simon's biological father?

That night after the hospital staff forcibly removed Nathan, Ella, devastated and racked with guilt, confessed the last thing Damien ever expected to hear from her. She still loved him, but she also loved Nathan.

Ella knew she had to choose, and thankfully, his wife chose him. She then proposed her own plan. She'd intentionally forget Nathan and everything she felt for him, and she knew how to do that. It was the only way she believed they could truly start over.

Damien did what any loving husband would do to help his wife. He went along with her plan. He did what she asked of him. He wouldn't answer her questions about the seven months leading up to the accident, no matter how hard she pressed. He would misdirect and mislead anytime she got close. He would scrub her phone, laptop, and cloud accounts. He even took it one step further on his own and wiped Rebecca's and Nathan's servers of their email exchanges with Ella.

At first, he didn't believe Ella when she told him that she couldn't remember the pregnancy or accident. He had a hard time believing Dr. Whitely's methods would work. But when it became evident she didn't recall his sterility, their argument in the Maldives, or the plan they came up with last summer either, he saw a new opportunity, especially when he noticed that she didn't start back up on birth control after her miscarriage. His wife wanted a baby, and he was determined to give her one. This new plan was his gift to her.

Men like Nathan Donovan are predictable. Damien knew Nathan wouldn't give up until he had Ella's confession about Simon's parentage. He'd be back. And it only took hacking into *Luxe Avenue*'s email server and sending one email to Nathan from Rebecca's assistant's email address for him to show up. It took Nathan over a month to reply, but when he did, all Damien had to do next was lure his unsuspecting wife back into Nathan's bed. Ella could finally get what she'd been wanting most, and Damien would get Ella's lifetime loyalty and devotion. He'd keep her happy.

This time, though, they'd do things differently. By forcing Ella to choose him over Nathan and capitalizing on the guilt Ella would feel from cheating on him, not once but twice, as he let her believe, there was no way in hell, no matter the circumstances, Ella would risk betraying Damien a third time.

Damien can all but guarantee Nathan Donovan is—once and for all—out of the picture. Because Damien Russell doesn't share.

Damien spins his chair to face his desk. He plugs the drive into his computer. A new window opens on his monitor, displaying 2,084 files, exactly two more files than were on the drive he gave Ella. Damien ensured that drive didn't include one of the nine transcription files from her interview with Amira Silvers, where Ella confessed their plan. How disloyal of her. It also didn't include the code for Ella to unblock her memories. The code, Ella once explained to him, that is as unique as the individual's mind it's programmed into.

He doesn't want her to remember last summer's

plan or how guilty she felt about it, else she'd be inclined to confess to Nathan—*again*—and invite him back into their lives. He especially doesn't want her to remember what it felt like to love Nathan. That's why, this time, Ella needed to believe she didn't wrong Nathan. Rather, she cheated on Damien. She needed to believe she's the one at fault. She betrayed him, twice. Guilt will keep her by his side.

See? Loyalty and devotion.

He also doesn't want her to suspect how he took advantage of her memory loss. The internal investigation over CyberSeal's meddling with PDN's trade secrets and client list? It couldn't have happened at a better time. It kept him distanced and made him appear distracted. Ella would have no choice but to seek answers elsewhere. She'd look to get them from Nathan. Because Ella is as ruthless in her pursuit of a story, even if it's her own, as Damien is with a deal. That's why they make the perfect team.

Does he feel guilty letting her believe events unfolded the way she thinks they did? Not at all. If he felt any remorse about any of the decisions he's made or strategies he's devised and implemented, he wouldn't be where he is today: CEO of a top-ten private cybersecurity firm. Husband to a gorgeous, intelligent, and passionate woman. And soon, a father.

Damien erases the files on the drive and shuts

down his computer. He shoulders his jacket, tugs down the cuffs of his shirtsleeves, and straightens his tie. He picks up his biometric briefcase and heads home. His pregnant wife is waiting for him.

CHAPTER 37

Last Summer
The Plan

Damien strides into Ella's office with two steaming mugs of Ethiopian blend. Setting one down within her reach, he leans a hip on her desk and studies her intently. He's been doing that a lot since they returned from vacation, as if trying to anticipate her next move so that he can counter or assist. She knows that he still expects her to leave him. Just like Anna.

"What are you working on?" he asks eventually.

Ella clicks through photos of Nathan Donovan, landing on a headshot from early in his career.

"Rebecca called with a new assignment."

"Nathan Donovan? Isn't he that survivalist guy?"

"Yes and yes. It'll be a cover feature, for sure. Rebecca wants me to spend five days with him."

"Five days," Damien repeats in a flat tone.

He doesn't want her to leave, not with things unsettled between them.

"I think the time apart will be good for us," Ella says quietly. A needed distraction from how messed up their marriage has become. She and Damien could use the distance to think and regroup. To decide if adoption, fostering, or a sperm bank is in their future. Unless their marriage is destined to be childless.

Ella's mouth flattens to a grim line. She rapidly clicks through images. Even if they didn't need the time apart, there's no way Ella's passing up this assignment. It could be the pinnacle of her career.

Ella lands on a recent headshot. She'd be lying if she said she wasn't attracted to Nathan. His ice-blue eyes stare back at her. "He looks like you," she remarks to her husband.

"You think so?"

Damien comes to stand behind Ella. He drops a hand on her shoulder and leans forward to peer at the monitor.

Ella clicks to the next photo. Nathan decked out in a three-piece suit at a charity auction several years back. "You could pass as brothers."

Damien makes a contemplative noise in the back of his throat and straightens.

"What?" she asks.

He doesn't share his thoughts, not right away. His finger strokes the side of his nose as he studies Nathan's image. Ella turns back to the screen and clicks through more pictures.

"Are you still off birth control?"

A sharp intake of breath fills Ella's lungs. She doesn't have to ask why he wants to know. She knows how her husband thinks, what he's thinking. The meaning of his question is clear.

He wants Nathan Donovan to donate his sperm.

Shocked, her mouth falls open. "You aren't seriously . . . you want me to ask him . . . ?" But even as she sputters to get out the question, the idea takes root in her head. And it's damn brilliant.

They can avoid the hassle of searching for a perfect match through sperm banks because Nathan already is one. Not only does he resemble her husband, but he's intelligent and athletic. An entrepreneur. Traits someone like Damien can admire and respect. Traits that could have come from her husband.

But doubt sets in. "I can't ask him to donate his sperm. Nathan just lost his son. He'll never go for it."

"Then don't ask him."

Ella twists around and looks up at him, appalled. "You can't be serious. You aren't suggesting . . . ?" She can't finish the sentence. Because her husband of three years has just suggested that she sleep with another man.

"He doesn't have to know. No one will ever know your baby isn't mine if we don't tell them."

Ella's hands shake. She clasps them in her lap. Charming interview subjects into bed isn't new to her. She did it with Damien when she thought she'd still write his story. But she hasn't done it since, and none of the men she'd slept with beforehand had been an official assignment at the time. She could put her job at risk. Her marriage.

There's also another obstacle. A big one.

"He's married," Ella points out, even though, surprisingly, she isn't finding herself completely opposed to sleeping with Nathan. It's an odd sensation for sure. Nathan isn't the first man she's been attracted to since marrying Damien. But to sleep with him? She'd be cheating on Damien, wouldn't she?

But is it really cheating if Damien suggested it and they get the baby they both want?

Damien points at the image on the monitor. "Caption here says he's separated. His wife left him last summer."

"Doesn't mean he'll sleep with me."

Damien snorts his objection. He grasps Ella's hands. She pictures an infant in those hands, can almost smell her downy head and hear her soft coos. Or his. She'd be happy either way. A certain thrill from what they're planning buzzes through her. She wants a baby in her arms. Her baby.

Damien sits on the desk and lifts her to her feet, fitting her between his legs. He kisses her solidly on the mouth. "I don't make many mistakes," he murmurs against her lips. "But my biggest mistake is not telling you the truth about me. I should have told you before we married, and I'll regret that I didn't until the day I die. I'm sorry, Ella."

"I know," she whispers. She senses the honesty of his words.

He kisses her again and Ella feels the kiss—his love, his regret, his shame—to the tips of her fingers and down to her toes. Relief floods her because their love is strong. Grace's parents didn't have this love. Her parents didn't have their kind of love.

Damien lifts his head and clasps Ella's face. "Let me tell you something about a man like Nathan Donovan. He's hurting. He's lonely. You'll be a ray of sunshine in his life. Just like you were for me. I was also heartbroken and lonely when we met. Make him care for you, like you did with me. The guy won't be able to keep his hands off you. I couldn't."

Ella chews her bottom lip.

"We're a team, Ella. In this and everything else. No matter what, we'll always be a team," Damien negotiates. "You're doing this for us, Ella. I'll never hold it against you."

She slowly shakes her head.

"What?" He taps her lip.

"I'm just thinking." She frowns, looks inward. "I'll have to do more than make him think I care for him. I'm meeting him for an interview. It's business. He'll want to keep it professional unless . . ." She plays with the top button on her husband's shirt.

"Unless what?" Damien prods.

"Nathan needs to believe I've fallen in love with him. I'm going to have to do everything I can to make him fall for me. I also have to check my cycle. I may need to stay longer. Five days might not be enough."

Damien is quiet, but he nods.

Ella hugs him, rests her cheek on his chest. "Please tell me this is going to work and we're going to come out of this together."

He threads his fingers into her hair and brings his lips close to her ear. "It's going to work and we'll come out of this together. I'll make sure of it."

EPILOGUE

"She gets more beautiful every day," Ella says of her three-month-old daughter, Grace Ella, suckling at her breast.

"That's because she takes after her mother." Damien leans down to where Ella sits in the nursery rocker and kisses her temple. He then caresses Grace's crown, ruffling her dark-walnut hair.

Finished with the morning feeding, Ella lifts her daughter to her shoulder and gently pats her back, the organic knit onesie with the corgi print soft under her hand. Davie had purchased the outfit and many others from Peek Kids in the Marina.

"Only the best for my favorite little girl," Davie announced at Ella's baby shower.

Ella has plans to meet Davie for smoothies later in the afternoon. Her best friend adores seeing Grace dressed in the clothes she picked out.

Ella turns her nose into Grace's hair and breathes in her baby's dewy scent. Her heart flutters with love and Grace lets out a belch.

"Oh, my." Ella laughs softly. "She takes after her daddy, too." She grins up at Damien. He simply shakes his head and lifts his eyes to the ceiling.

As for Grace's biological father, Ella hasn't given him much thought these past months. Keeping Nathan at bay stifles the guilt that she gave birth to his child and has no intention of telling him. Her remorse over cheating on Damien twice is enough to keep her devoted to their perfect little family unit. She couldn't bear hurting her husband again by bringing Nathan back into their lives. What if she tells Nathan and he tries to take Grace away from them? Her heart physically hurts at the thought. Losing Grace is unfathomable. She holds on to her daughter a little tighter.

Grace coos and squeaks. Her legs wiggle as she works up another gas bubble. Ella rubs her back, wondering who Damien sees when he looks at Grace's blue-gray eyes, eyes Ella suspects will brighten to an ice-blue. The man his wife slept with or the wife who betrayed him? Hopefully, he sees a bit of himself, thanks to his and Nathan's uncanny resemblance.

Damien hasn't brought up Nathan's name once since she confessed her pregnancy. At first he was infuriated. Betrayed by her yet again. But she quickly promised her baby would be theirs. She wanted Damien to raise it as his own, just like he'd planned to do with Simon. He agreed.

"Here, let me take her." Damien lifts Grace to his chest. He pats her back.

"Don't you have to get to work?" Ella stands, stretching her arms overhead.

"Work can wait." Damien turns toward the crib, paces the room. Ella swears Grace smiles at her over his shoulder and her heart pounds with a protective happiness. One of the best outcomes of Grace's arrival has been the peace Ella's felt over her daughter's namesake's suicide. With the birth and naming of Grace Ella, Ella fulfilled a promise to her childhood best friend. She also gave herself permission to forgive. To forgive Grace for taking her own life. And Grace's father, Stan, for setting it all into motion. She also found within herself the strength to forgive her own mother, which probably has something to do with being a mother herself. Motherhood broadens one's perspective, making room to consider alternative ideas and deciding not to give energy to others. Ella also finally forgave herself. Where and when Grace committed suicide wasn't Ella's fault.

Ella waggles her fingers, getting her daughter's attention. Grace squeals in Damien's ear. He jerks his head to the side.

"If I suffer from hearing loss, it's because of this little bugger." Grace yawns, resting her head on Damien's shoulder, and promptly falls asleep. He gently puts her in her crib. Looking down at his daughter with an expression of adoration and awe, he says, "I can't believe she's ours. I swear I love her more each day."

"Remember that feeling. She'll be an angsty

teenager before you know it and you won't be able to wait to send her off to college."

Damien groans.

"Her orbit will switch from you to makeup, music, and boys."

Damien clasps a hand over his heart. "You're killing me."

Ella kisses his cheek. "Don't worry. She'll always be your little girl."

"Let's hope so." He glances at his watch. "Gotta run. I'm late for my staff meeting. See you tonight, sweetheart."

He kisses Ella goodbye and she retreats to her office. She is still on maternity leave but checks her email every so often. As she anticipated, waiting near the top of her in-box is Dr. Whitely's reply to the email she sent him after Grace's 3:00 a.m. feeding.

Two weeks ago, the doctor sent her an email. He received a new grant. He's entering the next phase of testing. Is Ella available to participate? Is she also still planning to write a feature for *Luxe Avenue*? His team could use the publicity.

For two weeks, Ella debated whether she should reply. She'd told Damien she didn't need her memories because she trusted him to tell her about those lost hours and days in the months leading up to her motivated forgetting. She also feared she was, in fact, in love with Nathan. How would that affect her marriage? Who would she choose? She'd like to believe she'd remain with Damien. But does she truly know that she would? Ella never dreamed she'd make herself forget important moments of her life. She also never imagined cheating on her husband. It makes her question how well she knows herself.

Not only that, but how well does she know her husband?

She'd promised Damien her honesty. Since Las Vegas, she's been honest with him about everything. Everything except that email from Dr. Whitely. Because she's had a niggling feeling in the back of her head.

Ella thinks back to her conversation with Damien in their Las Vegas hotel room and the way he smiled when she told him that she didn't want her memories back. His smile was almost calculating. His expression was one of satisfaction. She excused it as happiness, but maybe she's been lying to herself. That smile has never sat well with her.

There's the way Damien watched her in the months after the accident. Studying her as though contemplating his next move. What had he been thinking about?

And her phone, the one he'd purchased and set up for her after her accident. Her location services had been on the entire time she was with Nathan, and in her settings, under "share my location," an unfamiliar phone number had been approved. Ella suspects Damien knew exactly where she'd been in Alaska.

Everything about those memories has increasingly bothered her. But it was the discovery on her phone just the other week that finally pushed her to log into her laptop early in the morning. Huddled over the bright screen with a blanket draped over her shoulders to ward off the cold night, Ella typed her reply. She told Dr. Whitely that his process worked. She also informed him that she unintentionally blocked too many memories.

Ella looks at the time stamp on Dr. Whitely's response. It was almost immediate. He must have been up late working. She opens the message and reads. He wants her to come in ASAP so that he can evaluate her. He wants to run more tests. Meanwhile, attached is her unique code in the event she's misplaced her file. He assumes she did since she didn't mention that she attempted to retrieve her memories on her own. Probably best that she waits until she can come in, he suggests. Just in case something goes awry again.

Ella drags the cursor across the screen, lets it hover over the file. She's not sure she should open the document. If she does, she won't necessarily apply the code. She's not sure she even knows how. She also promised Damien. She doesn't need her memories. He'll tell her all, and she assumes he already has.

Then again . . .
That niggling feeling.
Has Damien been honest with her?
She double-clicks the attachment.

Author Note

The idea of motivated forgetting started with Friedrich Nietzsche, a German philosopher, and continued with Sigmund Freud and his studies of memory suppression. Today, research labs are studying memory control: the retrieval process and repression of specific memories. As fantastical as Ella's situation seems, the reality of motivated forgetting may be closer than we think. Thank you for reading Ella's story. It was an adventure to write.

Discussion Questions

1. Ella wakes up in the hospital with no memory of her pregnancy or the car accident that caused her to lose her baby. How would you react in a similar situation? Did you suspect then that Damien knew more than he alluded to?

2. Damien is withdrawn and reluctant to talk with Ella about Simon in the weeks following Simon's stillbirth. If you were in Ella's position, would you have pressed Damien to talk or allowed him to heal in his own time?

3. What did you think of Ella's choice to meet with Nathan when he reoffered the exclusive to *Luxe Avenue*?

4. Were you surprised to learn about Simon's parentage? What about Damien's reason for not wanting kids?

5. Did Damien's plan to lure Ella back into Nathan's arms surprise you? What about Damien and Ella's plan from the previous summer? Did it surprise you that she's

complicit? Did it change your opinion of Ella or Damien?

6. What do you think happens after Ella reads the attachment to Dr. Whitely's email?

7. Damien was desperate to keep his wife happy so that she wouldn't leave him, so desperate that he came up with a plan for her to get pregnant. Ella was so desperate to have a child that she agreed to go along with Damien's plan. Have you ever been so desperate to have something that you've lied or cheated to get it? How far would you go to get what you want? Would you do it again?

8. Many themes are addressed in this book: love, lies, deceit, honesty, and trust. Which themes resonated the most with you? What other themes did you find in the story?

9. If you could erase someone from your memory, would you? Who would it be and why? What about a specific event? How do you think that would affect your other memories?

Acknowledgments

I knew the moment the concept of *Last Summer* presented itself to me that the story would be my most challenging project to date. I would be dealing with characters who went against my own moral compass. I'd have to push myself as much as I did them. Not one to shy away, I set about writing what I hope is an unputdownable page-turner that is as entertaining as it is unpredictable. This book is in your hands today because of my agent Gordon Warnock's unwavering support and faith in my storytelling. Thank you, Gordon, for being as enthusiastic about *Last Summer* as I am—and, at times, more so. Your encouragement kept me writing, revising, and polishing, even as the story took a darker turn from the original concept.

From editorial and production to marketing and publicity and everyone in between at Amazon Publishing, thank you, Chris Werner, Danielle Marshall, Nicole Pomeroy, Hai-Yen Mura, Dennelle Catlett, Ashley Vanicek, Mikyla Bruder, Kristin King, and Gabriella Dumpit for believing in me and making *Last Summer* shine. Best team ever!

To Heather Lazare, my developmental editor, for your thorough feedback on where to tighten, heighten, and enhance the plot, pacing, and characters: thank you for helping me realize the story's true form.

Thank you, Cheri Madison, my brilliant copyeditor, for crossing my t's and dotting my i's and understanding my love-hate relationship with commas. *Commas slow the pacing!* My mantra, and I'm sticking to it.

To my wonderful first readers and friends, Barbara Claypole White and Orly Konig, thank you for your honest thoughts about the story and characters. It's amazing what you'll do on my behalf for a bottle of gin and vino.

No book is complete without research. Thank you, Chris Griffin and Maura Mack, for your insight about heli-skiing and Alaska. You convinced this girl to add a similar adventure to her bucket list. I also want to mention Bear Grylls. The information I gathered from his books *Mud, Sweat, and Tears* and *Living Wild* and series *Running Wild* inspired the Nathan Donovan character and his series, *Off the Grid!*

Not to brag, but I have the best top readers. I am beyond grateful for the members of my Tiki Lounge, who not only act as my advance readers but share my book news with their followers and always recommend my books. A special shout-out to Jenny Belk, who came up with the name of Nathan Donovan's survival series, *Off the Grid!* And to Michelle Stuck, who thought of the name for Andrew Skye's start-up, Come Over Rover.

For every blogger, bookstagrammer, and book reviewer: thank you for reading, and thank you for posting your lovely photos and honest thoughts about my books across your social media platforms.

Thank you to my husband, Henry, who still gave me an encouraging pat on the back when I failed miserably to explain the book's premise in hopes of working through a plot hole; to my son, Evan, whose passion for skiing found its way into this novel; and to my daughter, Brenna, who kept my writerly brain fueled with her lovely baked goods.

Last, but far from least, to my readers: Thank you for traveling with me as I moved beyond the Everything series. I hope you enjoyed *Last Summer* and can't wait for you to read my next novel, *Side Trip*, coming summer 2020. I love connecting with readers. You can drop me a note on my website (www.kerrylonsdale.com). Be sure to tag me on Instagram (@kerrylonsdale) when you post pictures of my books—I love to regram. And if you want all my latest news and access to exclusive giveaways, sign up for my newsletter (www.kerrylonsdale.com/for-readers).

About the Author

Kerry Lonsdale is the *Wall Street Journal*, Amazon Charts, and #1 Amazon Kindle bestselling author of the Everything series—*Everything We Keep*, *Everything We Left Behind*, and *Everything We Give*—as well as other award-winning stand-alone novels. She resides in Northern California with her husband and two children. You can visit Kerry at www.kerrylonsdale.com.

Center Point Large Print
600 Brooks Road / PO Box 1
Thorndike, ME 04986-0001 USA

(207) 568-3717

US & Canada:
1 800 929-9108
www.centerpointlargeprint.com